DEAD EYES OPENED

DCI Greg Allison Crime Thriller Book 6

First Published in the UK 2022 by Mirador Publishing

First edition: 2022

Any reference to real names and places are purely fictional and are constructs of the author. Any offence the references produce is unintentional and in no way reflects the reality of any locations or people involved.

A copy of this work is available through the British Library.

DEAD EYES OPENED

DCI Greg Allison Crime Thriller Book 6

BY

ELIZABETH REVILL

Dedication:

For Marilyn Jobson-Scott

who is an avid reader of all my books and always supports me.

Acknowledgements

Firstly, I must thank my amazing commissioning editor Sarah Luddington who has been phenomenal in supporting and advising me and my terrific proof reader Jeff Jones who doesn't miss anything.

1

KATY VICARY SAT ON ONE of the seats on New Street station. She was a petite young woman about five-foot-three. She had long, tangled, curly blonde hair and wore a thick army greatcoat to hide her slim but curvaceous figure. She didn't want to attract the attention of the men in the squat. Better to wear some shapeless garment that disguised her body. Not that she'd been threatened but there was always an air of menace about two of them, in particular. One with very bad hygiene who dealt in drugs and his sidekick who, more often than not, was drunk and she didn't like the way he leered at her. Katy yawned and put her hand inside her coat and rubbed her bruised shoulder. She winced and suppressed an "ouch".

It was late, the weather wasn't great and she was too tired to return to the squalid house, besides she didn't have enough money to get back there. Her rucksack of Big Issue magazines was at her side. Some thug had taken her bag with all her day's takings, pushed her over and threatened her. She knew she would have to change her pitch. If it happened there once, it would happen again, of that she was sure. She would speak to her friend and colleague, Big Den, in the morning and change pitches with him or someone else. He could organise that. No one would dare attack Den. He was tall and thickset and looked as if he could handle himself. Katy was hoping to rent a flat in the same house as Den as he had managed to get a small place in Gillott Road, Edgbaston. He had told her she could come and stay there from tomorrow, if she wanted, until the studio flat on the top floor of the building became vacant. He knew the girl who currently lived there was moving to Sheffield and he had already spoken to the landlord. Katy hadn't wanted to put on Den but it was a much better option than the squat. She made up her mind to take him up on his offer especially after what had just happened.

Katy had seen the studio flat-come-bedsit and it looked smart, better than she could have expected. The place she was in, was rough but more problematical were the intimidating men that dropped in from time to time to buy drugs. There were too many of them. Katy didn't do drugs. She had seen what they had done to friends of hers. She enjoyed the odd drink when she could afford it and that was it. Now, it was late and the last bus had gone. She would need to get the more expensive night service, but she felt safer staying on the station concourse than trying to get back and risk the city's streets in the early hours of the morning.

At least it was dry at the station and warmer than outside. She couldn't face sleeping in doorways or subways again. She'd had enough of that when she first left home. Selling the Big Issue had given her a focus to her days and made her ambitious. She was going to do something with her life. What… she hadn't decided, but she knew she was worth more than selling herself to get a hot dog and a cup of tea like her friend Sara who had ended up turning tricks for some pimp called Mac and had become a junkie. Mac had made Sara dependent on heroin to control her. It wasn't going to happen to her. Oh, no.

The station was quiet tonight. Most of the staff had knocked off at eleven. Katy was fairly sure she'd be all right and if the police or security did come through on foot patrol she didn't think they would move her on. She knew she could have gone to the police about being mugged but she didn't fully trust them, besides the yob had disappeared now. Chances of finding him would be zilch. She just had to be more careful.

Katy's eyes scanned the surrounding area. She could sit in the photo booth; she would be hidden away from view there but doubted if she could sleep upright. There were seating areas inside the ticket barriers and further out in the open space hall. In the end, she decided to walk to the bottom end of the concourse near the Hill Street entrance close to the left luggage and public telephone. She was tucked out of the way there and could settle in the assisted travel lounge. Katy set off and found herself a spot away from anyone passing by and although the lights were brighter than she would have liked, she felt safe. She slipped down between the seats and using her rucksack as a pillow, pulled her army greatcoat around her and curled into a foetal ball to try and sleep as best she could, which was never easy in a public place. Katy snuggled down and did her best to snooze.

Sometime later, Katy was awoken by the voices of two men and from previous experiences she remained deathly still. She peeped out with one eye open and caught sight of two pairs of legs in blue denim slim-fit jeans and Doc Martens' boots. She risked lifting her eyes upward. One looked to be about six feet tall, with grey hair pulled back into a ponytail. He was dragging a rust-coloured suitcase towards the defunct left luggage office. He was a chunky muscular man and the person with him appeared younger and had an almost military style haircut. He kept his eyes focused on scanning the area as if acting as a lookout. Katy's interest continued to pique, but she remained motionless and tried to listen to their hushed whispers. But it was no good. She couldn't discern anything that was said.

The two men pushed the case right by the door of the Left Luggage Office and sauntered away, keeping their heads and faces averted from the cameras monitoring the station. Katy shuddered. Once she felt it was safe to move she crept out of hiding and stared at the case. There was something seeping from it, beetroot juice, honey or… blood. Katy decided then and there that it was no longer safe to remain where she was and she slipped out of the station. It looked like she'd be walking back to the squat after all.

DCI Allison stared out of the window at the building opposite Lloyd House, rapt in thought. He missed the sights of the Birmingham Children's Hospital, which was once the General Hospital where he would watch the activity from his old office window in Steelhouse Lane Police Station. It always seemed therapeutic and calmed him, especially after looking at the work that had piled up on his desk. But Steelhouse Lane had been forced to close with police funding cuts and the central police station was now in Colmore Circus,

Queensway. He could still see ambulances making their way to the hospital, which was now a few streets away. Allison knew that there was always someone worse off than him, and that thought always grounded him but now, it just wasn't quite the same. There was plenty of activity but not what he was used to. He glanced at his desk. He knew he would have to delegate and pass some of the files onto others in his department. He was hoping to take his wife, Mary out for a meal this week. Long suffering Mary, who never complained and looked after him better than most coppers' wives. He knew how difficult it was to keep a marriage together, so many ended in divorce. Some of his closest colleagues' relationships had gone that way, including that of his sergeant, Mark Stringer. He hoped it wouldn't happen to his daughter Cally who was due to be married in the spring.

He looked again at his overflowing in-tray. There were the usual petty crimes that could be dealt with by uniform. Mary, had always said he needed to relax and let others take off some of the load, but he found it hard to relinquish control, especially when a case seemed personal as it did with the house fire that had devastated the family of one of his own. Gurdip Singh, a bright and promising young copper, was in hospital and the arsonist and accomplices were wandering free. Suspicions had fallen on his sister's husband's family but chasing them down was another matter. When racial customs were involved, illegal or not, it made the task particularly hard. Allison was used to dealing with hate crimes but not honour killings, as by all accounts this appeared to be.

Allison felt the need for a Mars Bar.

Also, there was still the problem of tracking down Bannen Sadler who had wreaked indiscriminate revenge on any Asians that crossed his path after men of that race had abducted his daughter to sell as a sex slave. Bannen had changed his appearance dramatically and he had already brutally murdered many of the perpetrators in the sex trafficking ring. He was also wanted by the Turkish police for murdering an innocent young waiter who had dared to become attracted to his daughter for whom Bannen Sadler had harboured deeply unhealthy thoughts in this father and daughter relationship. He had forced her to submit to his will and this had led to a spree of vicious killings;

any Asian that crossed his path was lucky if he or she escaped Bannen's wrath.

Allison crossed to his desk avoiding the mountain of paperwork, wrenched open his desk drawer and pulled a chocolate treat from his stash. He ripped off the top of the paper to sink his teeth into the melting caramel chocolate delight, munched contentedly and returned to his spot by the window and gazed at the streams of raindrops, embracing and clasping each other like lovers and, as if in a suicide pact, watched them slide down the window together.

The phone rang, jolting him from his happy place of reverie, and he turned and grabbed the receiver. "Allison," he managed to choke out through a mouthful of chocolate, whisking his finger up to prevent the nougat strands from sticking to his chin, the movement almost toppling a pile of files onto the floor.

Detective Chief Inspector Greg Allison listened carefully, his face revealed concern and his bushy brows beetled together. His enjoyment of his chocolate indulgence ruined, he finally grunted, "On my way." Allison shovelled the last of the bar into his mouth and chewed vigorously as he replaced the receiver.

Allison lumbered to the door, he was a big man, in both height, bulk and presence. He had an intelligent face lined with years of experience but he still retained a merry twinkle in his eyes. He wrested his coat from the hook on the back of the door and seized his black felt fedora. He was not one for umbrellas, a hat would suit him fine, keep the rain off, and this one was waterproof.

Maddie, his loyal secretary for many years, looked up expectantly as Allison entered. "Anyone wants me, I'll be on my mobile." Allison felt in his pocket as he spoke to check it was there. He wasn't keen on using them and only wanted one for calls or texts, and nothing else. Cally always preferred texting to phoning. She said it saved time, 'just say what you want to say and no more'. Allison doubted that as he felt the tone of texts could be misinterpreted.

Allison emerged into the outer office and scoured the faces of those beavering away at their desks. There was no sign of Mark. He popped his head back around his office door, "Maddie, get Mark on the line and tell him to meet me at New Street station, left luggage."

Maddie nodded and the chief rolled out of the office and off down the stairs to make his way to the railway station.

The drizzling mist had engulfed the city streets as if to shroud the ones concealed in the shadows who were waiting to act against those whom they felt had dishonoured them. It was late morning and the sun had gone into hiding to escape the falling tears from the monochrome grey sky.

Siri's estranged husband, Pasha, was a handsome looking Sikh, who had a cruel twist to his lips and a menacing glint in his eyes. He stared up at the imposing hospital building, where Gurdip and his father were patients. He stood flanked by his two cousins, Ajeet and Kalbant. Ajeet was short and plump with eyes like currants, small and piercing. He wore the Western style dress of denim jeans and a check shirt with a leather bomber jacket and Cuban heeled boots. Kalbant was lean-faced, tall and slim wearing the traditional Sikh dress of a kurta with cotton trousers and a long hanging coat or choghah.

Pasha glowered at the building as if he could demolish it with a look. "We have to get inside and into ICU," he growled.

"Wouldn't it be easier to divorce Siri and take another bride?" said Kalbant.

Pasha spun on his heels and pulled Kalbant into him by his shirt. "I will not be dishonoured. There will be no divorce. Siri is my property and if she does not obey my wishes then she must die and her family with her. Then and only then might I take another bride."

Kalbant prised Pasha's fingers from his kurta. "That is not the way here. Our religion gives men and women equality." Pasha just snorted in derision. "We are not in a small village in India now," added Kalbant whose face showed extreme distaste. "You have already killed Siri's mother and little brother. Is that not enough?"

"It will never be enough. The whole family must be made to pay, especially Siri."

Kalbant turned away, “Then I want no part of this vendetta.”

Pasha removed his kirpan and grabbed hold of Kalbant’s arm. “Don’t make me use this against my own kin.”

Kalbant stared back defiantly, “You have brothers and others that will do your bidding. You do not need me.” He shook Pasha’s hand away and walked off into the enveloping fog.

“And you?” Pasha sneered looking at Ajeet. “Are you turning your back on my rights to mete out justice?”

Ajeet shifted uneasily from foot to foot before answering, “No, you know I will stand by you and your wishes. What do you want me to do?”

Allison hadn’t enjoyed his walk to the station. He felt damp, clammy and uncomfortable. The drizzling fine rain that seemed to soak into his coat, didn’t, however, have the same effect on his hat, where the water ran off but dribbled down the back of his neck. He soon reached the station concourse and searched around for the left luggage facility. He marched towards the platforms 10A and 11A, opposite the ticket barrier, and to his shock found the left luggage office closed, and according to the notice pinned up, the closure was to be permanent; such was the threat of terrorism in public places.

Greg wasn’t given to swearing but in this instance an expletive was muttered under his breath. He accosted a member of staff striding past, “Excuse me. Where do people go to leave their luggage?”

The worker shrugged and replied, “Try asking at the ticket office. They will be able to help you.” The man marched off.

Allison grumbled to himself again and made his way to the ticket barrier first, rather than walking back to the middle of the concourse. Allison flashed his warrant card at the fair- haired young man taking tickets from people who had oversized luggage and couldn’t use the machines that operated the automatic gates to enter the platform area. The man smiled brightly at the chief, “How can I help you, sir?”

“Left luggage. Where will I find it?” he demanded.

“Ours is closed permanently and not expected to reopen, I’m afraid.”

“I know. I’ve just discovered that. Where would someone go, then?”

The young man had a pleasant smile and chirpy manner, "Try eelway.com."

"What's that?"

"It's a booking site that finds a place for you to store your luggage close to the station. They work with local hotels and shops to find you the best deal."

"Where do you suggest I go?" grunted Allison, getting crosser and more impatient by the minute.

The lad indicated an exit ramp, "Try the Midlands Hotel in New Street next to the station, I'm sure they do it. There's no direct route now, I'm afraid. You have to walk all the way around."

Allison managed to thank him and was more than relieved to see Mark hurrying across to him. He acknowledged him with a curt nod of the head.

Mark signalled to Allison, "We have to go to the ticket office."

"Why?"

"Another call came through from the station, after you left." Allison raised an eyebrow. "About the suitcase. They neglected to tell you where the bag had been taken. Apparently, it was dumped outside the left luggage in the early hours. No one saw who had put it there. A station worker took it along to the ticket office and there it stayed, until curiosity got the better of them and they had the shock of their lives, when they opened it."

Allison snorted, "I bet they did."

They proceeded along the walkway to the ticket office and were admitted through the desk counter and into the back room. An old boy was sitting in a chair, keeping an eye on the offending article. A congealed mess of blood, looking like treacle, had seeped through the rust-coloured case and soaked into the canvas material covering the frame work.

Allison asked, "Has anyone touched it?"

The elderly man nodded, "Young Parker who brought it in here, and Geoffrey Clarke who opened it. No one else."

Allison took a pair of proffered surgical gloves from Mark and pulled them on, before slipping the case flat on its side and opening it up. It was heavy.

Mark gasped as he saw the contents, which held a male torso, dismembered arms and legs but no head, hands or feet. Allison grimaced and ordered Mark, "Get a team of SOCOs here. We'll need a cordon around this room and the left luggage area, not that I hold out much hope of anything. This Parker and Clarke will need to be fingerprinted to eliminate them." Allison sighed, "The areas are likely to be heavily contaminated, but we can try and see if anything useful remains although I doubt if anything of any relevance will be found. Contact Hurst. He'll need to get someone here to collect the body and take it to the morgue." Allison turned to the old boy, "I'll need to speak to the lad, Parker, who picked up the case, and to Geoffrey Clarke, who opened it and, of course, yourself. Can you get me their contact details? And, we will need to check any CCTV footage available from last night."

The old man grunted with exertion as he rose from his seat and shuffled towards a back office.

Gurdip Singh lay in his hospital bed staring out through the rain-streaked window into the boughs of a spreading horse-chestnut tree, which was as still as a tomb as not a movement or whisper of wind moved through the leafy branches. The mizzling rainfall echoed Gurdip's mood and thoughts as he tussled with the frightening problems that had beset his family. His mother and little brother were dead. They hadn't survived the house fire, which had turned into an inferno that he was convinced had been set by Pasha and his family. His little sister Ayesha and his married sister, Siri, were protected for the moment staying with someone who had taken them in, but he did not know who they were or where they lived. It was safer that way.

He lay back on his pillows and thought of his father still in CCU, Critical Care Unit, on life support and prayed that his father, Balbir, would live but he knew the burns that covered a large percentage of his father's body would leave him not only scarred but incapacitated should he survive. He realised that he would have to shoulder the responsibility of the family and he thought back to how he had insisted that there should be no relationship between his good friend, Ronnie, and his sister, Siri, before she married, and he was now questioning his judgement. He knew that Sikhs were allowed to marry outside of their religion in some circumstances but not in the traditional way unless the groom or bride converted to Sikhism. But now, all that seemed unimportant. All that mattered to Gurdip was that his family lived. He knew he could rely on Ronnie to look after and protect little Ayesha and Siri, and he sighed again as he argued with himself before reluctantly murmuring, "What will be, will be."

Ajeet was sweating even though the air outside was cold, but at least the rain had stopped, for the moment. He had filched a doctor's white coat and was strolling through the hospital towards the main wards and ICU. He had swiped a lanyard and adapted it for his own use using a new photo. He had adopted the identity of Dr Ranveer Patel.

Looking more confident than he felt, he attempted to keep his head down and his face averted from the probing gaze of the internal cameras, which monitored the comings and goings of visitors and staff around the hospital. He entered the Intensive Care Unit and studied the whiteboard at the nurses' station but couldn't see any mention of Balbir Singh. He walked out and studied the boards by the lifts and noted the Critical Care Unit and Burns department listed.

Ajeet hastily made his way across to the ward and followed on the heels of a nurse as he keyed in the admittance code and entered. The male nurse took no notice of Ajeet, and no one challenged Ajeet as he walked past the few bays on the wing, scrutinising the occupants of the beds. He noted the names on the single rooms finally stopping at Balbir's.

Ajeet was now sweating profusely. After carefully looking around, he stepped inside and studied the man in the bed on life support. He was heavily bandaged and sedated. For a moment Ajeet felt a twinge of regret, his heart was pounding, but now there was no going back. He knew his own life would be on the line.

Ajeet pretended to look at the chart at the foot of the bed before drawing the curtains around the patient. He picked up a pillow from a chair by the bed and, wearing gloves, he removed Balbir's oxygen mask and pressed the pillow down firmly on his face. There was not much of a struggle and eventually Balbir lay still and the machine supporting his breathing let out its alerting bleep as Balbir's vital functions ceased and his heart monitor flat lined.

Ajeet tossed down the pillow, drew back the curtains, and exited quickly. He shouted aloud, "Need some help in here!" And the staff came running to Balbir's room as Ajeet made his escape.

DCI Allison grunted as Maddie knocked and brought him in a cup of tea. This time, the pile of files on his desk toppled over and he thumped his desk in exasperation.

"Sir?"

"Sorry, Maddie. Bad night and bad day. The Chief Constable has chewed my ears off about not following protocol regarding Gurdip's little sister. Although, to give him his due he has understood our reasoning and has decided to let it go. But there are still far too many other issues outstanding. Not least the body in the suitcase murder. Ring Hurst and see if he's done anything about that. One of us should be present at the autopsy but we just don't have the manpower at the moment."

"Yes, sir."

Allison gestured to his growing heap of papers, and said almost to himself. "Why am I bothering you with all this?" He bent down with a struggle to pick up his scattered files.

"Let me help you, sir." Maddie crouched down and helped retrieve the wayward documents as Allison growled his thanks. "Oh, and Maddie."

"Yes, sir?"

"When Mark comes in, send him to see me."

"I think he's at his desk. I'll let him know," with that she left his office and walked out into the main workplace and spotted Mark. She waved him across as he was chucking a screwed up ball of paper at Bill Rennie, who ducked leaving the missile to strike young Josh Linton who wagged a finger at his sergeant.

"Mark! Chief wants you in his office, now," called Maddie before returning to her office.

There were a rumble of mutterings from Pooley, Taylor and the others as

Mark jumped up and straightened his clothes. He marched briskly to Allison's office, knocked and entered.

"You wanted to see me, sir?"

"Yes, come in and close the door."

Mark did as he was asked and shuffled forwards as Allison indicated a seat.

Allison pointed at his towering mass of papers, "All open unsolved cases and one of the worst is that of Bannen Sadler who is still on the loose."

"Sir."

"It's as if Sadler is wearing a cloak of invisibility. How he can disappear so easily without anyone knowing his whereabouts is astonishing."

"Sir."

"We need to allocate the right folders to those best suited for the job, while we work on the body in the case murder. Can you see to that?"

Mark felt himself flush with pleasure, "Of course."

"And then come back in here, we need to go back to the railway station."

"Sir." Mark picked up a bundle of paperwork and glanced through it before returning to the main office.

Mark play-acted staggering to his desk under the weight of the dossiers and spread them out on his desk. He selected Bannen Sadler's file and passed it to Josh Linton. "All yours, Josh. Pick anyone you like to work with you on this, you already have the necessary background."

Josh nodded, "Better than filing and dealing with petty crime."

"Which still needs to be solved," reprimanded Mark.

"Yes, Sergeant."

"But Bannen Sadler takes priority."

"Pooley, Taylor, you're on Gurdip's arson attack. Woodward – take your pick," Mark thrust three files at him. "Where's Soper?"

"Gone to see Gurdip," said Pooley.

"Right! Woodward, let him have a decko at these. I'll see him when he gets back."

Ronnie Soper was sitting at Gurdip's bedside. He was struggling with what to say. Gurdip looked at his friend. His voice was charged with emotion as he spoke in barely a whisper, "He's dead. My father is dead, Ronnie. Murdered."

Ronnie took his friend's hand, "I know. The nurse told me when I arrived. Even the chief doesn't know yet. There are no words. I cannot imagine how you must be feeling. Gurdip, I am so sorry."

Gurdip studied his friend, "You have no need to be sorry, you have always done right by me. Pasha and his family are the ones to pay and once I get out of here I will hunt them down no matter how long it takes."

"And I promise that I will help you."

2

ALLISON'S FACE WAS LIKE THUNDER as Ronnie imparted the news of Gurdip's father's death. "You better tell Pooley and Taylor that it's not only a case of arson, with two related deaths but premeditated murder now. They need to get to the hospital and learn what they can."

"Sir, I'd like to take this onboard. Gurdip is my friend."

"And for that reason, I have to say, no. You are too close to this."

"But, sir…"

"Sorry, Soper."

Ronnie's eyes reflected his disappointment together with a flash of annoyance. He knew the men they should be looking for and he wanted to keep his promise to Gurdip. However, he lowered his eyes and left Allison's office. His fists were clenched and his shoulders raised as he entered the squad room.

Allison sat and rubbed his emery chin thoughtfully. He completely understood Ronnie's feelings but he felt he couldn't have one rule for one and one for another. He needed consistency, even though last year, he had turned a blind eye to Mark's involvement in tracking down the missing hostess, Beth, from Kelly's Wine Bar, Bistro and Club, who was his girlfriend.

Allison sighed as he hauled himself out of his chair and strolled towards the window with a view of the street and route to the hospital that he so missed. His interest was caught by an ambulance with flashing lights pulling up opposite the police station. An anxious woman emerged from the building and beckoned the paramedic who jumped out of the ambulance and opened the back doors. He unloaded a stretcher and disappeared inside the building following the young woman. Minutes later they reappeared with the woman whom Allison assumed must be the mother of the small child now on the stretcher. She held the little one's hand as the kiddie was wheeled into the waiting ambulance and put inside followed by the mother and paramedic. With sirens wailing and lights blazing the ambulance moved off on its way to the children's hospital. It always saddened Allison to see a young child incapacitated by something or someone. He hoped the little one would be all right. He was just contemplating getting a Mars Bar when his phone rang and jangled insistently for his attention.

Clement Pugh had a mournful face. It was long, lean and he always looked as if he had the weight of the world on his shoulders. He was in the perfect trade for his looks as an undertaker. But Clement Pugh had been approached by two dark suited thugs. That's the only way he could describe them. He dared not report this threatening visit to the police as the heavies were prepared to expose his secret and that wouldn't do for business or his liberty. It wouldn't do at all.

Clement peered distastefully into the coffin due for cremation and shivered as he saw the head, hands and feet of a young man, placed in the coffin with the body of an elderly lady. He took his screwdriver and carefully tacked in the extra fixings and made sure they were twisted tightly. No one would be unsealing this coffin before it went into the furnace.

He leaned back against the rosewood casket. His heart was jumping like someone on a pogo stick. Where did those men come from? How did they know what he had done and how many more people might know about it? He had better not allow anyone else to suspect his wrongdoings.

Johnny Hurst, the pathologist had the torso and limbs on his slab. He had taken the necessary photographs and was examining the remains, inspecting each inch of skin almost microscopically. Whoever it was, he thought, must have had a record, either criminal or military, otherwise why go to such lengths to disguise his identity? There was a fresh cut on the inside of his right arm. The cut was too clean to be an accident. He estimated that the opening had been made with a size fifteen scalpel used for short and precise incisions and had been made pre-mortem. At least, that is what Hurst had concluded.

The man had also been circumcised, not that that was unusual. It was expected in certain religions and often used for other medical reasons such as phimosis and balanitis. The man had had an appendectomy that had left a neat scar, which Johnny surmised had been done as a child. There was no thickening of the scar tissue and the appearance of the scar had all but disappeared into a fine white line. Although, determining the age of wounds was important in cases of torture, it was impossible to be exact over the date of the surgery and resulting scar. But whoever had done it had done a very good job. Samples from the body had been taken for DNA testing, which would take a while, so if this person had a criminal record in this country, it would be on file and identification would be easy. Johnny continued with his monologue of his findings as he worked.

Unusually, there weren't any police officers present to observe this autopsy, a report would have to be written in the usual way as DCI Allison couldn't spare the manpower; they were overworked and under-staffed as usual, but Hurst knew someone would be along as soon as it was possible. *As long as it isn't Mark Stringer*, thought Johnny. He didn't fancy a mop and bucket job in the observation room. He was short staffed, too.

Johnny had thoroughly examined the outside skin of the torso and body parts. Rigor mortis had been and gone and the positions of lividity on the body had all been noted. There was a scar on the man's chest, which interested Johnny. He took his scalpel, very similar to the surgeon's tool, but was often longer to allow for deeper cuts while peeling away tissue and he began. The Y incision was the first cut to be made. The arms of the Y extended from the front of each shoulder to the bottom end of the breastbone, the tail of the Y extended from sternum to the pubic bone and typically deviated to avoid the navel.

Now came the exciting bit, at least to him, as he began pulling back the skin to reveal the chest cavity and inner organs and that is where Johnny was fascinated to see that a pacemaker or an ICD, implantable cardioverter defibrillator, was inside the man's chest just underneath the collar bone. He wasn't absolutely certain until he had excised it completely and could see its true size as ICDs were generally bigger than pacemakers although, ICDs had, with technological advancements, become much smaller than when they were first invented.

"Bingo!" he muttered as he interrupted his medical report on his voice activated Dictaphone. "A pacemaker." He took his forceps, plucked it out and dropped the item into a kidney dish for further examination. He called to his new assistant, Heather, a petite, serious-looking, pixie-featured woman with owl-like over-sized spectacles. She was dainty and neat and had a certain primness in her manner. She wore her long auburn hair up, so it wouldn't impede her study at the microscope, but behind her eyes was an irrepressible, mischievous sparkle.

Heather crossed the lab to Johnny's side. Johnny pointed at the kidney dish, "Take the pacemaker, clean it up and find the code, it's a set of numbers, unique to each device and get online to search out the manufacturer and who fitted it, then we should be lucky enough to learn this chap's identity. It will probably be quicker than waiting for the DNA results." Heather removed the dish and went to do as she was asked while Johnny continued with his examination. He resumed his report on age estimation by rib morphology analysis, the sternal end of the fourth rib yielding a better chance of accuracy without having a head, where the tooth enamel and cranial sutural closure were of prime importance in determining age. He knew he would also have to examine the bone structure most carefully.

His findings corroborated the results from the pubic symphysis and were often more accurate. Changes noted at the costochondral junction included the formation of a pit, its depth and shape, configuration of the walls and rim surrounding it, and the overall texture and quality of the bone. But Johnny was almost certain that the white male was aged between 39 and 45. Examination of the muscle, ligaments and tendons, which attach muscle to bone concurred with this. The man was past his fitness peak of thirty and

Johnny could see a slight decline in apparent muscle strength and size, but he stressed the age was only an approximation.

Trying to determine the cause of death was not so hard as the seemingly frenzied stab wounds were obvious and two had gone right through the heart. A thin blade had been used and the wounds to the heart had all but sealed up, which was usual, contrary to popular belief. However, there was massive internal bleeding. This killing had been up close and personal. He had been attacked from the front, fallen back and died quickly. Wherever he had been taken for dismemberment lividity had been set and was prevalent on the back of his body. Johnny approximated the time of death to have been between forty-eight to fifty-two hours previously. He also had yet to weigh and examine the internal organs and do a toxicology report. He hoped that missing persons, which he commonly called 'mispers' might come up with the identity of someone who had recently gone missing, but without a head or fingerprints this would be more than difficult.

Distinguishing marks were there, and were distinctive, a mole under his left breast in the shape of a brazil nut that was hairy, a small tattoo of a bluebird on the inside of his left arm just above the wrist area and apart from his appendix scar, another small scar in his right shoulder that resembled a healed gunshot wound. His body hair was fair and his skin freckled so the man could have been blonde or even ginger. That would help, too.

Heather alerted Johnny by her whoop of satisfaction, "Got it!"

"Well?" asked Johnny.

"Made by Medtronik an American-Irish company that operates primarily in the States. But it has headquarters in Minnesota and in Dublin."

Johnny prodded at some discoloured tissue, "Good job. I think they have a building in Galway, too."

"Yes, and Watford," called Heather. She flipped her glasses up onto her forehead. "So, our guy could be American?"

"Or Irish. We can't say for sure. We'll leave that to Allison."

Bannen Sadler was sweating. He'd hurried to his hotel room, a small chic boutique establishment. He had been travelling, and on the run, for many months after fleeing Nottingham for Cumbria. He had tried to like Cumbria and control his lethal urges but not knowing the area had made it dangerous. He finally decided that he would fare far better on home territory even if he was under the police's noses in Birmingham. Bannen's ego was such that he believed he could outsmart the plods, as he called them. And, he still could try to get to his daughter, Linda. His thoughts were at odds and he grimaced as he thought of her. He would find her and take her back and if he couldn't have her then no one else would. She had betrayed him. She needed to be punished. But then, he thought of what his daughter had already suffered and been through and was heavily conflicted. She was his daughter, after all.

His journey was uneventful although he did have a bit of a scare when a police car appeared to be following him for some miles. Bannen turned into a road leading to the railway station in Ravenglass. He paused there and waited a while. Should he risk leaving the car here and return by train? He discounted that idea. The plod's car hadn't followed him in. He was safe. He took out his map and planned his route back with a proposed couple of stop offs and he decided that he might have a little fun on the way. His eyes gleamed at the thought. But he would have to be careful. He didn't want to leave a trail of bodies from Cumbria leading all the way to Birmingham. Better let the authorities believe there was a killer on the loose in Cumbria wreaking havoc. And with that in mind he studied his atlas.

The coast road would be a more attractive run. He could meander down it and take his time using minor roads until he made his way to the M6, M5 and Birmingham. Yes. That would do nicely. There were many villages and towns to pass through and who knows what he might find or discover. Feeling very chipper that's what Bannen Sadler finally decided to do.

Clement Pugh sat in his office twiddling his thumbs. He was struggling to contain his excitement. The body of a thirty-year-old woman had arrived from the hospice. She had died from terminal bowel cancer and was due for embalming and preparation for burial. Clement had finished preparing the body for embalming. He looked at the petite fair skinned woman on the table and took out his pallet of makeup and body paint. She would serve him well enough for what he wanted to do but he felt the need to titivate her appearance. She had to look alluring and with some help she could look very desirable indeed. Clement let out a sigh of desire and stroked her perfectly shaped bald head. Clement had a supply of wigs for just such an occasion. He took one and with some spirit gum attached the hair to her head. He tousled it with his fingers before taking a brush and a pintail comb and began to style it into a flattering face framing style.

Clement clicked his tongue and murmured, "Missed my vocation. I could have been a hairdresser and make-up artist."

A voice behind him made him jump. "Am I interrupting?"

Clement turned to see two men, the same thugs as before, one tall thickset man with iron grey hair scraped back into a ponytail and the other wearing a hoodie that shaded his face. Clement dropped his brush and comb and stepped away from the coffin. The grey-haired man stepped closer, "Got a nice little thing going here, haven't you? You wouldn't want it to get out. We can have a good arrangement here. You will be paid well."

Clement stared in alarm at the two men. "What do you want?"

"You have keys to this place don't you?" Clement nodded. "Then it should be easy. We know you have your own cremation facility here, too. For use for those who don't want to use the official crematorium and funeral service."

"Yes, but…"

"Then it should be straightforward if we have any other items that need disposal…"

"But I don't have access to that part of the building. The smoke would be a giveaway. The boss only lives down the road."

"Then you will have to get keys, burn at night when no one is about and clear up afterwards. You will be well paid."

"But…"

"No buts. You will do as we tell you or your boss will know that you do more than embalming, so will everyone else… How will you live that down? We'll be in touch."

The men left and Clement stood there shaking. His sexual desires had vanished and he puzzled over how he would gain access to the private crematorium furnace adjacent to the funeral parlour. He slid to the floor sobbing.

Bannen had enjoyed his road trip, posing as a travelling salesman selling advertising space to businesses. He was taking his time. He was in no hurry. He had researched places to stay in Birmingham and had settled on the seedy area of Soho that was part of Handsworth. Bannen chatted affably to the owner of a small hotel on the phone, booked and paid a week's deposit for a room, transferring the cash to the landlord's account and assuring the man that he would be there that week, but was uncertain of the day. He convinced the man that he would let him know exactly when he would arrive and then he would pay in full for the week. He had travelled along the west coast and had now reached Morecambe Bay. He stopped off at a beach front café and perused others sitting drinking coffee. One person in particular caught his attention. He was a young Asian man, who appeared to have a succession of motley folk sitting at his table fleetingly.

Bannen narrowed his eyes and studied him as much as he dared. He noted small packets of something being passed under the table and money exchanged. The café owners appeared to take no notice or were oblivious to what was happening under their own roof. It was clear to Bannen that this man was dealing in drugs and therefore bringing misery to many. He didn't deserve to live. Bannen made up his mind. He would stick around and follow the guy.

He didn't have long to wait.

Bannen watched him drain his coffee mug and go to the till to settle up before accessing the toilet. Bannen hurriedly finished his own coffee and paid his bill enabling him to follow the man out of the café. Sea mist was engulfing the coastline and the low cloud and drizzle ensured that there were very few people out and about.

Bannen patted his jacket reassuringly and slipped his hand into his coat pocket to feel the comfort of a steel blade in his hand. He walked after the man who had set a brisk pace. His excitement was mounting, the anticipation of the hunt and the excitement of capture sent his heart thumping and filled him with adrenalin. He kept close to the man who was unaware of the danger that was approaching him.

The stranger paused as he took out his headphones and attached them to his phone, which he clipped onto his belt. He pulled up his hood and walked on. This was getting better and better. The man wouldn't hear him coming.

Bannen quickened his pace until he was almost on top of him. He removed the knife from his pocket and caught the man around the neck and sliced the blade across his throat. Severing the carotid artery. Blood pumped out and the man fell to the ground, his vital force mixing with the rain and forming puddles around him. A shout came from behind and Bannen snapped his head around as he saw a man running towards him. Bannen didn't wait. He took off at a gallop and raced away. He glanced back over his shoulder and saw the man bending down by his victim. The good Samaritan had taken out his phone and was clearly calling the emergency services, whilst trying to exert pressure on the wound to stop the flow of blood.

Bannen ran on, unnerved by the close encounter and crossed the road toward a parade of shops. He pulled his jacket sleeve down and closed his jacket to try and hide the blood spatter on his shirt. He headed towards the Arndale shopping centre and paused at St. John's Hospice charity shop and dived in. A cheery faced plump woman welcomed him in, "Good to get out of the rain, I would think."

Bannen flashed one of his brightest smiles and, standing side on to her he nodded, "Yes, but it's very wet out there. I could do with a good mackintosh."

The woman smiled and pointed to the men's section of the shop where the coats and raincoats were hanging. Bannen smiled again and pulled out a beige belted mac and tried it on. It fitted. It covered the blood stains perfectly. He picked up a trilby hat and a gentleman's umbrella from a stand of walking sticks and canes and took them to the counter. "I'll wear these, if you can remove the tags."

The woman smiled back and removed the price tags with a pair of scissors. Bannen put on the items and paid telling her to keep the change for the charity.

"That's very kind,' she gushed and followed him to the door. "It's turning into a filthy day. They will keep you dry."

"That's what I'm hoping," Bannen replied and gave her a wave as he left the store. He walked back the way he had come. Police cars were already at the site together with an ambulance. Bannen remained on the other side of the road and looked curiously at the scene. No one seemed to take any notice of him and he crossed to the car park and unlocked his vehicle with a chirrup from his fob. He sat in the driver's seat willing his heart to stop pounding so loudly. It was no good. He couldn't afford to stay longer. He had to get on the road right now and drive straight to Birmingham. No more stop offs. With a bit of luck, the cops might believe it was a drug deal gone wrong. Anyway, what the hell… it was one less villain in the world. Bannen allowed himself a secret smile as he started his car and moved away. He saw two policemen patrolling the car park that were taking down the details of each vehicle. That decided him, he needed to get away and ditch the car. The sooner the better. He could torch it, that way no forensic evidence would remain. But first, he had to get away.

Clement Pugh hovered by the reception desk next to the office. He had to get the keys to the private crematorium without being seen and get them copied. First, he would check the diary and remembrance book to see what had been scheduled. He needed to get the key when there were no privately booked cremations. He chatted brightly to the daughter of the funeral parlour's owner, Pam, who was manning the desk that day. She passed him the books for him to peruse while she answered the telephone using her most sympathetic and understanding tone as she dealt with a bereaved client.

Clement noted the name of a new apprentice that was being assigned to follow and observe him in his work. He clicked his tongue and Pam glanced at him questioningly. He smiled quickly and continued studying the diary.

Pam finished her call and looked at him, "Problem, Clement?"

He smiled nervously, "I've just noticed I've been assigned an assistant…?"

"Oh, yes. Sorry. I forgot to tell you. She is set to start next week."

"So, I see. Why me?"

"Come on, Clement you're the best at what you do. She needs to learn the skills from you. Why? It's not a problem, is it?"

"I hope not. I just prefer working alone."

"Well, you'll just have to get used to it, won't you?"

Clement grunted noncommittally knowing the problems this could bring. He closed the book with a bang. With Pam at the desk and someone else to deal with, he had no idea how he was going to get hold of the keys to the private crem.

Bannen's accommodation in the Soho area of Birmingham was perfect. There he could keep an eye on his own property and both Handsworth and Soho were a perfect hunting ground for him. He had ditched the car in Shropshire and left it blazing before making his way to Telford Station. There he caught a train to Birmingham.

Bannen Sadler's appearance had changed even more dramatically. He no longer had that distinctive very short, almost platinum coloured hair. It had grown much longer in the intervening months after he'd made his escape at the airport and was now shoulder length and teak brown. He'd dyed his eyelashes and eyebrows accordingly and had tinted his skin with a fake tan. He was no longer clean-shaven or sporting straggly facial hair but now, had a neat well-kept beard that was also darkened with henna.

He locked his door, stripped off his clothes and dashed into the shower, which he set at full force. He slipped in under the water while it was still cold. It invigorated him and as it warmed up, he luxuriated in the healing heat that soothed his taut muscles and cleansed his skin. The blood that had stained his body dissolved and ran down the drain. Bannen remained there until the water ran clear.

He turned off the jets and shook himself like a dog shaking its coat after a swim and his hair flicked across his face but didn't diminish his tan, which he knew was good for a couple of weeks before it would begin to fade away. He caught sight of himself in the mirror, which had misted in the steam and at first glance he looked like one of the race that he hunted. He smiled grimly, *That will do nicely*, he thought as he towelled himself dry.

He changed into fresh clothes and rolled up his bloodied shirt and stuffed it into his rucksack along with his chinos. Now he had to get rid of them safely and get to his date. He suppressed his urge to laugh. It had been so easy and he was quite looking forward to enjoying her before he ended her life. It would make up for losing the university student when he was marauding in Nottingham; and for his forced escape from Morecambe where he was unable to toy with his victim as he would have liked. Never mind, there would be more. He was sure of that.

Greg Allison and Mark Stringer were on their way down to see Hurst at the city's morgue. The day was somewhat brighter and although there were clouds, the sun managed to peep out occasionally putting a spring in the detectives' steps. As they approached the building Mark's pallor began to change. He hated going inside and he couldn't hide the fact that he was dreading it. The smell of the place always turned his stomach. Not that he was squeamish but memories of past cases with bloated bodies recovered from water filled his head as he recalled the smell, which triggered a rise of bile from his gut. He struggled to hide it as they reached the steps of the building.

Allison glanced across at his sergeant, "Suggest you stay here. You're not looking too swift."

Relieved, Mark nodded and gulped as his mobile rang, "What? Hold on." He put his hand over the phone. "Chief!" Allison stopped with his hand on the door and turned to Mark questioningly.

"There's another."

"What do you mean, another?"

"Another body. We think it's the same M.O. stuffed in a suitcase with blood that has seeped out from it. No one has opened it yet."

Allison frowned. "Where?"

"Same place. New Street."

"Get down there. I'll meet you there." He looked up at the sky, "At least it's not raining."

Relieved to avoid the morgue, Mark just nodded and marched off down the street and Allison proceeded to enter the building. He went down into the basement to find Johnny and pick up the report that he knew Hurst's secretary, Susan, would be busy typing up. He found Johnny in his office and on the phone.

Johnny waved the chief into a seat and Greg Allison pulled out the cushioned chair, which creaked under his bulk as he sat. Johnny continued with his conversation as Allison waited. "Thank you. You have been most helpful. Sorry, to have called so early." Allison glanced at his watch. It was hardly early, at 2:05 in the afternoon. He waited expectantly as Johnny put down the phone.

"Well?" grunted Allison as he waited for Johnny to speak.

"You're in luck. The guy in the case had a pacemaker. Heather, my new assistant traced the code on it made by Medtronik, an American company."

"Do we have a name?"

"We have the name of the surgeon that implanted it. He's American." Johnny looked at the notes scribbled on a pad. "A Doctor Gerry Marshall, who resides in New York. He performed the op at Mount Sinai Cardiology and Pacemaker Centre."

"But do we have a name for the victim?"

"I have the hospital number. They have records. He will know who received this model. They each have a unique number."

"So, our man could be American?"

"Looks like it. A call to Dr Marshall will either confirm it or not."

"Thanks, Johnny."

"Susan is typing up the PM report as we speak. If you want to wait, I can get you a coffee?"

"No, thanks. I'll hang on for the report but have to get to the railway station."

"Oh?"

"We've got another one."

Mark had arrived at New Street station. He noted that the left luggage area was still cordoned off as a crime scene. One of the CCTV cameras that was angled towards that area had been blacked out with paint. There was a man in overalls up a ladder, trying to remove it. He'd heard that the other camera that might have been useful kept flickering and produced only a fuzzy picture. It was obviously on the blink. This time the suitcase was still there and blood had pooled on the floor around it. After the last event, no one had touched the case or stepped in the area. The lad Parker had spotted it and wouldn't let anyone near.

Parker stood nervously outside the tape. "I rang the cops as soon as I saw it. Looks just like the other," he said with a sniff.

"Quick thinking. Well done," commended Mark. "You best be off now, and get about your work. We'll be in touch if we need anything more." The youngster nodded and marched off across the concourse. He didn't look back.

Mark got on the phone and rang Forensics for the scene of crime officers, or SOCOs as they were called, to organise a team to come out. Meanwhile, as he waited for Allison, he spotted Geoffrey Clarke from the previous visit and called him across with a whistle. The young man stopped and hurried across. "Yes, sir. Can I help?"

"I could murder a cup of coffee, 'scuse the pun," he said sheepishly. "I might have a long wait and can't leave the area unattended."

"Sure," said the young man. "What do you want?"

"A latte please with one sugar. Here," Mark fished in his pocket for some money and gave the man a fiver. "That should be enough and you can keep the change."

"Thanks!" Geoffrey scooted off towards one of the coffee carts. Mark looked about him and scoped the area. There was a seat a few yards along from the tape. He could sit there and wait, and hopefully enjoy his coffee before Allison or the SOCOs arrived. He crossed to it and sat, tapping his foot while he waited for Geoffrey to return.

The boy hurried back to Mark and passed him the Styrofoam cup and raced back to the ticket office. Mark removed the lid and let the steam from his coffee warm the tip of his nose before he took a sip. He suppressed a yelp, as it was scalding hot and burnt the roof of his mouth. He blew on it and cradled it in his hands waiting for it to cool down. It was unusual to have a bought latte as hot as this. Mark stared at the suitcase wondering what was inside. Maybe the head, hands and feet of the first victim were in there or maybe it was a different victim. Whatever was in there it wouldn't be pleasant.

After ten minutes, Mark's coffee had cooled considerably enabling him to drink it. He watched as the Forensic team arrived in their white suits with their bags and cameras and prepared to erect a tent around the area away from prying eyes and the press. Mark hoped Allison wouldn't be long. He took out his phone to ring his now fiancée, Beth. He had no sooner dialled the number when he saw the familiar sight of Allison striding across, so he hastily rang off without managing to speak to her.

"What have we got?" Allison growled.

"Don't know yet. The case hasn't been opened."

One of the team passed Allison and Stringer a pair of surgical gloves each and disposable PPE and shoe covers, which they wore over their clothes and footwear. Once suitably attired they stepped under the tape and into the tent where a freckle-faced young woman had photographed the case where it stood and the surrounding area. She was preparing to take more pictures once the case was opened. Another officer flicked the locks on the case and opened it up. Inside was another torso and dismembered limbs, this time of a woman. It was clear at first glance that surgery had been performed recently with a jagged scar on the abdomen and one higher up close to the sternum.

"Can't see us striking lucky again with a coded pacemaker. I expect this one is a mystery."

"Yes," agreed Mark. "A mystery we have to solve."

"Any joy with the CCTV?"

"The camera that would have been most useful was blocked out with black paint. A station official is searching the film of the cameras at the various entrances. One of the team is with them."

"Let me know as soon as they've got anything. See if you can bring in the relevant DVDs for the time frame for us to go over again. Things can get missed especially to the untrained eye."

Gurdip sat on his hospital bed. He was fully dressed. His shoulders were drooped in despair. Ronnie stood in the doorway and gazed sympathetically at his friend, "You can't go home. There's nothing there."

Gurdip stared stonily in front of him, "Then I'll join Ayesha and Siri."

"No, they may be watching. They could follow you and you would put them and our friends, who took them in, in danger."

Ronnie's words appeared to sink in and he lifted his eyes to Ronnie, "Then where? Tell me where I can go."

"You'll come home with me."

"But then I put you and your mother in danger."

"We'll be fine and we'll be careful. Meanwhile, we will look for somewhere to rent, somewhere they won't suspect. I've already spoken to Mum. She knows what's at stake. It will be safer."

Gurdip shifted off his bed, "I don't know. What about an hotel?"

"Can't afford that on a cop's salary. No, get used to it. You are coming home with me. I insist."

Gurdip looked as if he had no more fight left in him and he nodded slowly, "Very well. How do we do this? How can we ensure we won't be seen or followed?"

"We'll do the best we can do. Come on, my friend."

Ronnie picked up Gurdip's bag that was on the floor and waited for his chum to stand. "First, we will stop off at Lloyd House. I have an idea." Ronnie peeped out into the corridor. It appeared clear and he signalled to Gurdip to follow. Gurdip followed Ronnie, his confidence clearly rocked, he moved like an automaton and Ronnie nibbled his lip. It looked as if his friend had had all the stuffing knocked out of him. Ronnie knew it would be a long haul.

3

BANNEN SADLER TOUCHED UP HIS hair and beard to cover the regrowth and dressed casually. He checked himself out in the mirror and was sufficiently pleased with his appearance that he thought he would risk a visit to his house, just to observe, and see if his daughter, Linda, was still living there. What he would do then he wasn't certain. He couldn't make himself known but just needed to see. But first he had a meeting to attend with a man he'd met in Handsworth who could get him another car, no questions asked, and a gun.

Bannen smiled grimly, it was easy to get hold of anything if you knew the right people and Bannen knew more than enough of them. Money was not a problem and if you had money you could do almost anything. He was glad he had put plans in place before he had left for that Turkish holiday.

He stuffed his wallet into his inside pocket and pulled up his hood. It was soon time he left this accommodation and moved on, found a flat, a bedsit, anything where he could have a more permanent base. *In fact*, he thought, *why not go down the route of being a lodger?* If he could find the right place. That might be an even better bet. No bills to worry about, no council tax, just rent a room in a house. Yes, that could work. He would check the small ads section in the local paper and see what he could find.

Bannen stepped out into the corridor and locked his door. He ran down the small staircase and left his key at reception and went out into the streets of Soho. First things first, get this car then get home and appraise the situation.

With a jaunty stride he looked up at the sovereign gold of the sun and smiled. Things were looking good. A number of sparrows flew up from the sycamore tree with its leaves starting to change colour and Bannen marched off to Ed's used car lot in Handsworth.

Ronnie and Gurdip had arrived back at the police station. Their colleagues were pleased to see them both and commiserated with Gurdip. But the lively banter normally present was now muted out of respect and Ronnie was checking the area outside the offices thoroughly, before preparing to leave again. First, he peered through the window and then looked at the CCTV both in the car park and outside the station. All areas seemed to be clear. Satisfied, Ronnie walked across to Bill Rennie, "Bill I need your help and you, too, Pooley."

"You've got it," they chorused.

"Pooley, you're the same height and build as Gurdip. Can we dress you in his outside coat?"

"I can do that but won't I need a turban?"

"I've thought of that. The roller towel in the Gents' loo is broken. Cut off a length and Gurdip here will make an effort to tie it into the semblance of a turban. Pull the hood up on your coat and we may get away with it." Pooley nodded and hurried to the Gents' toilet. He soon returned with a length of the cotton towel.

"Where do I come into this?" asked Bill.

"I'm going to take Pooley here for a little ride. If anyone is watching the station they will follow us. As long as he keeps his head down that will be fine. Wait about fifteen minutes after we've left, and you, Bill, drive Gurdip to my house. Don't take the obvious route. My mother will be there and waiting. Drop him off then get back here."

"Okay. What if we're followed?"

"Then you'll have to get back here and we'll think of something else."

"Okay, Gurdip get your Blue Peter skills in order and bind up Pooley's head."

Mark and Allison had overseen the removal of the second body from the left luggage office and were now back in the cop shop. Allison buzzed his intercom, "Maddie, can you get us two teas please?"

Maddie acknowledged and Allison checked his watch, "What time do you think this Gerry Marshall will start work?"

Mark shrugged. "That's anyone's guess. Top surgeons usually start later than the rest of the hospital staff. Private health care in the States runs on different systems from ours."

"Good job, too," said Allison. "We're damn lucky here. Although, you wouldn't think so to hear how the press go on about the NHS."

"Do we have this surgeon's home number?"

"We can hope the hospital will give it to us."

"That's if data protection will allow it."

Allison snorted, "Data protection. What a load of..." he was interrupted by Maddie entering with two cups of tea and biscuits, which she set down before scuttling out. "A hospital doesn't close. Ring Mount Sinai now, they will be doing breakfast rounds I expect, see what you can learn. Here's the number." Allison passed a scribbled number on a pad to Mark. "See what you can learn. Use your charm, I'm all out of that at the moment." Mark took the proffered paper and rose. Allison stopped him, "Drink your tea first. Then get onto it."

Bannen had picked up a car and a gun, which he secreted in the side pocket of the driver's door and was driving steadily towards his house. As he turned into the top of the road he spotted a police car parked outside, obviously keeping watch on the premises. But, was Linda there or not? Should he flee or...? He gritted his teeth and made a decision.

Brazenly, he decided to cruise past. He glanced across at the car. Two uniformed coppers sat in there, drinking something or other. He peered up the drive to the house and couldn't see any more cars parked outside, which made him think that there wasn't anyone in residence or maybe because of the surveillance, Linda was feeling safe inside. He decided to drive around the block to the houses that backed onto his. Then he would feel safer, believing his decision was the right one.

Bannen coolly motored to the street behind the plush houses that stood behind his and parked carefully at the top of the road. He had slipped his firearm inside his jacket pocket and meandered slowly along the pavement until he reached one of the two houses directly behind his own. He studied the Tudor fronted building with its fancy latticed windows and glanced up and down the road. There was no one about and it didn't look as if the Baxters, who lived behind him, were home.

Bannen calmly strolled up the drive and opened the gate to their garden and slipped through. He dodged into the shrubbery and edged his way towards the adjoining fence and peeped over the top. He couldn't see any activity on the premises and decided to take a chance. He was just about to shin over the fence when he saw a dark man enter and move around his kitchen. Bannen bristled, had Linda shacked up with someone and worse still, someone of colour? He would soon put a stop to that. He waited until the man walked out of view and then he clambered over the fence. He crept through the bushes towards the garden shed and ducked down at the side before tiptoeing around and slipping inside his hut, which still held all the gardening equipment, lawnmower, his power tools and bags of potting compost. Bannen sat down on the spindly chair that was in there and waited. He determined that he would see this through, but he would wait until night had fallen.

Mark was at his desk on the phone to Mount Sinai Hospital in New York. He had finally got through to the surgeon's secretary but she wasn't very forthcoming. Somewhat protective of her boss she refused to give out any personal information. Mark was becoming increasingly frustrated, "All I need is the name of the patient who had the pacemaker fitted," he implored. "At the moment he's what you would call a John Doe and surely his family have a right to know what has happened to him and lay his body to rest? Imagine if it were your husband or son? The man's been murdered, for goodness sake, and in a most horrible way. The only identification we have is the pacemaker."

"I'm sorry, I am not authorised to give out that information."

"Then can you tell me when I can speak to Dr Marshall? Do you have a home number or private number for him?"

"You must understand I am not allowed to divulge confidential information. You could try Personnel. I can put you through, if you like?"

Mark rolled his eyes. The woman was being impossible and he asked again, "When do you expect Dr Marshall into the office?"

There was a pause, "You could try ringing here in thirty minutes. I can't guarantee he'll be in but I know he's rostered on and he sometimes comes in here first to check emails and so on."

"Thank you,"

"Look, I know how irritated you must be but it's more than my jobsworth. Let me put you through to Personnel and see if they can help. If not, you can still call back in thirty minutes."

"Yes, okay. Thank you."

"I'll just put you on hold."

Mark drummed his fingers on his desk as he was forced to listen to some classical music played down the line. He recognised the melody but couldn't put a name to it and had to suffer the same bars being played on a loop. Eventually, the secretary came back on the line, "Putting you through now."

"Personnel, Lexie Clarke speaking. How can I help?" she drawled.

Mark went through the whole explanation again, concluding, "So, you see, it's imperative we speak to Dr Gerry Marshall and discover the name of the patient he operated on. If you could let me have his private number…"

"I'm sorry. I do understand your problem. You will have to speak to Dr Marshall through normal channels. The most I can do is leave him a message in his pigeon hole and tell him why you need to know. I am unable to do more than that. Sorry."

Mark sighed, "I know. It's not your fault. I will call his secretary in …" he glanced at his watch, "twenty minutes. Hopefully, I'll catch him then. But in case I don't, can you give him my number?"

"I can do that."

Mark relayed his office and personal number, which Lexie seemed to note as she repeated it back to him.

"Okay, thanks for your help." Mark replaced the receiver.

Feeling frustrated, he got up, stretched his legs and yawned loudly. He glanced at his watch again. *Just time enough to ring Beth*, he thought. But once more he was thwarted from calling as his personal phone rang. "Hello?"

"Sergeant Stringer?" said a female American voice.

"Yes."

"Hold the line, I have a call for you."

Mark held on and heard the same loop of music he'd heard previously, so he knew it was Mount Sinai Hospital in New York.

A well-modulated voice interrupted the music, which finally ceased. "Dr Gerry Marshall, here. I understand you have a question about a patient of mine?"

Relief flooded Mark's voice, "Yes. Thank you for speaking with me." Mark launched into the reason for his call and waited.

"If the patient were still alive, I'm afraid I wouldn't be able to help you but under the circumstances I will tell you. I assume, if I refused you would have gone through police channels to get the information?"

"Of course."

"Then I don't see a problem. Saves us all a lot of paperwork and time. The identity of the man you want, is Jonas Rakowsky. He was forty-two years old and suffered from arrhythmia. We had tried all kinds of medication and decided a pacemaker was the best option."

"Do you know what he did or where he lived?"

"From what I understood, he was something to do with imports and exports. I'm not exactly sure but he was out of the country a lot and had many dealings in Europe."

"Do you have an address?"

"I'll need to check my records but I believe he had an apartment in New York and a place in the UK." Mark could hear someone else speaking in the background. "From what I understand from my secretary he had somewhere in France and Germany, too. I will see what I can find out and get my secretary to call you back."

"Thank you. That would be very helpful." Mark replaced the receiver thoughtfully. Now he had a name, he would input it into HOLMES 2, the updated version of the Home Office Large Major Enquiry System. He walked across to Allison's office, passed Maddie, knocked and poked his head around the door to inform Allison of the latest events.

"Good work!" praised Allison. "Let me know what you find."

"Sir." Mark nodded and crossed to his computer to access the data. He typed in Jonas Rakowsky and waited. He watched as a flood of red-flagged messages loaded on his screen and read them avidly. He gave a long low whistle at what he was reading, leaving it on screen before returning to Allison's office.

He knocked again, "Sir, you need to see this."

Allison scraped his chair back and moved out into the main office. He followed Mark to his computer, which still showed the list. "Well, well, well," murmured Allison. "This is interesting. So, our Jonas Rakowsky is involved in something more than ordinary imports and exports, if that's how he describes himself. Print off a picture. It's not very good but it will do until we get a better one."

"And it seems, he has a wife, Shirley, who reported him missing two weeks ago."

"See if you can track down any known associates and then we can pay Mrs Shirley Rakowsky a visit. See if she is a party to his shenanigans or innocent. She lives fairly locally."

"Sir."

"And in an upmarket part of Brum, if you can call it Brum. I'll get a car and meet you outside."

Allison stepped away and back to his office where he retrieved his hat and coat. Maddie rose to help him. He was a big man but could be surprisingly light on his feet when he wanted to be. There was a gleam in his eye that she recognised when he felt he was onto something to do with a case. It was good to see him engaged like this she thought, he had been looking somewhat tired of late. Maddie looked at her boss and questioned, "Car, sir?"

"Please; get someone to bring one around."

Maddie nodded and went to the phone as Allison lumbered out of his office to be met by Mark and they left together. It was just like old times, thought Maddie and she smiled.

Gurdip was settling into the spare room at Ronnie's house, he was full of polite thanks to Ronnie's mother, who smiled appreciatively. "It's no problem. You have helped Ronnie and I know how he values your friendship. I'm just sorry that you're here under such awful circumstances." Mrs Soper glanced about the room, "I'll leave you to finish unpacking. Then come down to the kitchen and I'll make us all a nice cup of tea."

Gurdip nodded his thanks and as she closed the door he sat on the end of the bed with a thud. His hands were shaking and he was uncertain if it was something physical or just everything that had happened catching up with him. His eyes filled with tears. How could things have changed so dramatically in such a short space of time? His whole family almost wiped out. He would never again see his mother and father nor his little brother. Gurdip gulped trying to choke back a sob. He remonstrated with himself, why had he been so hard on Ronnie? If he had been more liberal and more understanding, Siri would be safe and his family alive. His own prejudices had brought this about. Gurdip decided there and then that nothing else would harm his remaining family members and whatever happened he would have revenge on Pasha and his family who would not get away with these so-called honour killings.

He looked at the small bag he had brought with him. It was all he had left of his belongings. It wasn't much. He would need to go shopping. He sighed heavily and sat on the end of his bed uncertain what his future held for him now.

"Gurdip!" The shout came from downstairs. "Tea's ready." It was Ronnie's voice. Gurdip steadied himself. It was time to look forward to a new beginning and a new training regime. His and Ronnie's Karate skills would be honed to such a degree, no one would be able to jump them again.

Bannen had waited patiently although he was beginning to feel claustrophobic stuck inside the shed. He just prayed that no one would come out into the garden for anything. It was getting towards dusk now and fortunately, it wasn't raining. The weather had been iffy the last few days, with a series of low depressions whirling in from the west and circling the country. Today, however, was more settled.

Bannen eased himself out of his chair and moved slowly to the shed door. He peered through the dusty cracked window on his right and stared at the house. There were lights on upstairs in Linda's room and the bathroom. The curtains had all been drawn and there was a glow creeping through from the kitchen blinds so someone was at home, possibly Linda, he hoped. He hadn't seen any more of the man he had noticed earlier. Perhaps it was just a cop checking in on Linda. After all, there was a police car parked outside on the road.

Bannen stealthily crept out of the shed and closed the door quietly behind him. Next door neighbour's dog barked, a lonely sound in the darkening night. Bannen sneaked along the garden wall and tried to peer through the gap at the bottom of the kitchen blind, but he couldn't see anything.

Across the garden, Harry Williams, stared out at the night. He had switched his own lights off enabling him to see better. His dog never barked without reason and with the police patrolling the area he felt he was doing his bit by checking outside. A movement caught his eye and he noticed a hooded figure peering through the windows of the house that was adjacent to his and also backed onto the Baxters. Whoever it was, was clearly up to no good. Harry Williams took out his phone as he saw the miscreant trying the back door. He dialled, 999 and waited.

"Emergency, which service please?"

"Police," said Harry and proceeded to detail what he'd just seen. Reassured that someone was on their way, he pocketed his phone and continued to watch.

Bannen had come prepared. He fiddled with his keys until he located the back door key and slipped it into the lock but it refused to turn. "Bugger…" he swore under his breath. "Linda must have changed the locks." Well, that wouldn't stop him. He smiled grimly; he might have to teach his daughter a lesson after all.

Bannen crept to the dining room window at the back of the house and fiddled with the latch. It had always been faulty and now he was glad he had never had it fixed. He used his key as leverage and the wood around the catch splintered. He waited. Had anyone heard? Nothing seemed to have happened. He eased the window open and clambered up onto the sill. He pushed it open further and slipped inside.

A television was playing in the sitting room with some game show music heralding the end of 'Pointless'. Bannen scanned the dining room. Nothing seemed to have changed inside. He stepped out into the corridor and moved forwards, scarcely breathing, towards the stairs.

The police in the patrol car outside Bannen's house had been alerted to an intruder and the two uniformed coppers quietly exited their vehicle and tried to move as unobtrusively as was humanly possible down the gravel path.

Bannen peered into the sitting room as he passed and saw the back of a West Indian man's head. He had no idea who the hell he was and thought of killing the man there and then but he didn't want to alert Linda, not yet. He could come down and finish the job after he'd seen his daughter.

Josh Linton, the man in the lounge was fully aware that someone had entered. His muscles were tense and he prepared to move. He lay down on the sofa and disappeared from view before he peeped around the arm of the couch and just caught a glimpse of a leg and foot. He ducked back as Bannen began to mount the stairs. Josh rolled onto the floor and crawled towards the front door, slipped the catch and the two officers darted inside. They took out their tasers.

Bannen was no longer in view. One officer sidled up the staircase, while Josh waited with the other at the bottom of the stairs. The policeman had now reached the top and had sneaked across the landing towards the bathroom.

The others waited.

Time seemed to pass interminably slowly and there was a shot that reverberated around the house. Josh Linton's mouth dropped open. He signalled to the uniformed copper that he was backing off and he stepped back to use his phone and call for backup and an ambulance, stressing that there was an officer down. The second officer looked dumbfounded and raised his taser in readiness.

Bannen came blundering onto the landing and started down the stairs, too late he saw the copper poised at the bottom aiming his taser at him. In response, Bannen raised his gun just as the policeman fired. The taser hit Bannen with 50,000 volts shaking him up and he tumbled down the stairs dropping his gun, which fired twice. He collapsed forward from a sitting position at the bottom and was incapacitated.

The PC kept his finger on the taser until Bannen no longer seemed to be a threat. Josh came forward and pulled Bannen's arms behind him, and cuffed him, before running up the stairs to see to his uniformed colleague, who was slumped on the landing. He was bleeding from a wound above his stomach, below the ribcage. Josh grabbed a towel from the bathroom and stuffed it against the injury, applying as much pressure as he could to stem the flow of blood.

Downstairs, Bannen had started to move. The PC sent another pulse, which stopped Bannen in his tracks and he remained still. The young copper was relieved to hear sirens approaching.

4

PASHA STOOD ON THE STREET corner of City Road and Twyning Road. He would be glad when he could leave this Godforsaken hole with its inclement weather that threatened rain one minute and promised sunshine the next. Today, the weather was being kind but it did nothing to enhance Pasha's mood. The dust and noise of the traffic together with the fumes irritated him and affected his eyes, which smarted in the bright daylight.

The trees had started to drop their leaves of russet and gold leaving small birds unprotected from sight so sparrows huddled in the eaves of houses while others sought sanctuary in evergreen firs and holly. Their happy trill of birdsong was actually quite pleasant far better than the raucous squawks of parakeets. Pollution in India's cities had chased away many of the more beautiful songbirds to the countryside, where he lived. But Pasha wasn't bothered by birds. It was the thought of revenge that stoked the fire in his belly.

He was waiting for his cousin, who was late. Pasha scowled. His fine features twisted, his eyes retained that glimmer of cruelty and his mouth was turned down when he spotted Ajeet turning the corner. "You're late."

"Sorry, Pasha. I had to work."

"Thought you'd taken two weeks off?"

"I did, but they were short staffed. I had to go in. Never mind, I'm here now."

Pasha snapped. "Let's walk."

They proceeded onto the main road. Traffic flew past blowing the litter on the dusty streets. A sheet of crumpled newspaper whipped along the pavement and wrapped around Pasha's leg, which he removed distastefully. "My uncle has located some of Siri's relatives in India."

"Yes?"

"Let's say, no one will be visiting them any time soon."

"Oh?" Ajeet shivered.

"They are no longer a problem."

Ajeet looked sideways at Pasha, "What have you done?"

"What my family had to do. Now we have to deal with those left here."

"Hasn't your honour been satisfied?"

Pasha stopped abruptly and spun Ajeet to face him. "My honour will only be satisfied when the whole family has been wiped out. I need to know where the grandparents live."

"Parnani and Parnana?"

"And Pardadi and Pardada."

"Grandparents and great grandparents?"

"All."

"I believe it's only Siri's mother's parents that live over here. Bradford, I think."

"The others?'

"In the Punjab."

"Then my cousins will find them. I will need their names. Then, we must find Siri and her little sister."

"What about Gurdip?"

"I will take him last."

"That will be difficult. Him being a policeman."

"Then that will make the hunt that more interesting."

Ajeet fell silent and began to wonder what he had got himself into, but he was afraid of crossing Pasha. He had seen the results of what the man could do. But he knew he was now in over his head and he had already killed once for him. This he was regretting and he wished he had walked away like Kalbant.

"Why so quiet, brother?" Pasha asked.

"I was just thinking."

"And?"

"It will all take a lot of planning."

"And time is something we don't have much of. I must return to India in four weeks."

Allison and Mark turned into a cul-de-sac and drove up a road filled with impressive houses and parked at the kerb by a pair of fancy electric gates with gold leaf tipped arrow heads at the top that glinted in the sunshine. They gazed at an imposing white rendered frontage complete with balcony, with gold ivy-leaf trim, in front of a large set of bi-folding glass doors. There was a flagpole in the front garden with a Union Jack flag flying high. Mark and Allison exited their vehicle and walked to the gates with its code pad entrance and intercom and pressed the buzzer. A cool female voice answered, "Yes?"

"Police," said Allison assertively. "We'd like to talk to you."

"Concerning?"

"Your husband, Jonas Rakowsky."

The gates unlocked and opened slowly admitting Mark and Allison, who walked through them and up the path as the electric gates closed softly behind them and locked. They reached the ornate but stout wooden door with a peephole. A voice came from behind the door, "Show me your credentials."

Allison and Stringer took out their warrant cards and held them up to the spyhole. They heard bolts being drawn back, a key turning inside and a chain being removed. A willowy redhead with impossibly luxuriant hair opened the solid front door. She stepped back to allow them to walk in.

Allison cleared his throat, "Is there somewhere we can talk?"

Mrs Rakowsky led the way into the drawing room and gestured with her elegant hands that they should sit, her fingernails varnished with glittering silver gloss polish. "Can I get you a drink?"

"Thank you, yes," replied Allison recognising that they would all need something. He hated imparting news of this kind and tea was always a pleasant distraction. Mark and Allison sat together on a red Chesterfield settee and waited.

They both looked around the tastefully decorated room; the walls sported a number of paintings, one of which looked like an original Constable. The place was spotless and Allison suspected that Mrs Rakowsky must have had someone in to clean; judging by her hands she did little housework herself.

Mark whispered to Allison, "Smart place."

Allison nodded, "Needs money to keep a house like this."

"But it's not flashy."

"No."

"Have you noticed the paintings?"

"I have."

Mark gestured with his head, "Reckon that's genuine? Looks like a Constable."

"Could be."

They were interrupted by the arrival of Mrs Rakowsky carrying a tray, laid out with three fine porcelain cups and saucers, silver teapot, hot water receptacle, milk jug, sugar bowl, three spoons and a plate of luxury chocolate biscuits with three side plates and napkins.

"That was quick," remarked Allison wondering if he was going to get lukewarm tea, a thing he abhorred.

"It's the Quooker tap. It dispenses boiling hot water immediately, saves so much time and it does ice cold water and sparkling water, too. Very useful."

Allison acknowledged with a nod, all the while wondering what that sort of gadget would do to a household's energy bills.

"How do you like it?" she asked politely looking at the two men perched on the edge of the sofa.

"As it comes, please," said Mark. "Medium, no sugar but not too milky."

"The same," grunted Allison.

Once the pleasantries of tea had been administered, Mrs Rakowsky looked at them both. "You said this was about Jonas; you've found him, haven't you?"

Allison nodded, “It’s not good news, I’m afraid.” Mark took out his notebook and pen.

“What’s happened? Has he had an accident?”

“Not exactly.” Allison took a mouthful of tea.

“Then where is he?” Her face had paled and her gracefully refined hands were now trembling. She set down her cup and her hand flew to her throat.

“I am sorry to have to tell you that we have found his body.”

“How? Why? What are you not telling me?”

“I’m afraid he has been murdered.”

Shirley Rakowsky gasped. “No.” Her eyes filled with tears, “I knew he was in some sort of trouble, but I didn’t know what. When he didn’t come back from London and I hadn’t heard from him I waited a couple of days and then reported him missing. When he didn’t return I thought he had gone back to the States.”

“You say, you knew he was in trouble. What kind of trouble?”

Shirley shook her head, “I don’t know. He played his cards close to his chest. He wouldn’t talk about it.” She played with the pendant around her neck.

“What did he do for a living?”

“He was a businessman. I only knew some of the things he dealt in. He was into imports and exports, fine arts and so on.”

“Did he have a business name?”

Shirley nodded, “His company was West End Products Ltd.”

“Where would that be?”

“On the canal basin, a warehouse and shipping office, close to The Opposite Lock.”

“You say, you thought he was in trouble? Why would you think that?”

“He’d become very secretive the last couple of months, staying out late at meetings, so he said, and was very nervy and jumpy whenever the phone rang or the buzzer went for the gates. I tried talking to him but he just kept saying it was nothing to worry about. That things would soon be back to normal.” Tears began to spill down her cheek. “I’m never going to see him again, am I? I can’t believe it. Do I have to come and identify the body? I’ve never seen a dead body.” She began to weep afresh.

"I don't think that's a good idea," said Allison.

"Why? It would give me some closure, a chance to say goodbye."

"Mrs Rakowsky…"

"Shirley, please."

"Shirley… you wouldn't be able to identify him."

"Why ever not? Oh my God. Was he in a fire? Is he horribly disfigured?"

"No."

"Then why?"

Allison paused, "We identified him through his pacemaker."

"I don't understand…"

"There's no easy way of saying this. All we had to identify him was his torso and limbs. There were no hands or feet and… no head."

Shirley's face was more than shocked and she put her hand to her mouth with her napkin as bile rose up into her throat. "Excuse me…" she dashed from the room.

Mark and Allison politely drank their tea and ate a couple of the biscuits while they waited for her to return, which she did a few minutes later.

"I'm sorry. I wasn't expecting that," she murmured wiping her mouth. "How horrible. It was that body in the suitcase, wasn't it? The one that was all over the local news?"

"I'm afraid so. I am sorry we had to be so harsh in telling you but there was nothing else we could say."

"But it was the truth," Shirley said quietly.

Mrs Rakowsky… Shirley, I know this is a very difficult time for you and these questions must seem unimportant but we need to get a feel of Jonas, the man, and if there is anything, anything at all you can tell us, any small detail that you might not even feel is important, we would like to hear it. Do you have a recent photograph of Jonas that we can take away?"

Shirley nodded and slipped away to another room. She returned moments later with two framed photographs. "Will either of these do?" One showed Jonas on a fancy yacht standing at the helm, smiling with a captain's cap on. The life-saving ring had the words, 'Maid of Honour' imprinted on it. The other, was one of him on a rock looking at a view and pointing ahead.

"Can we take both?" Shirley nodded and began to remove them from the frames.

"Much of a sailor, was he?"

"He loved the water, tried to get away whenever he could. We both did. We often used to take a canal ride to Worcester or take a trip to the Birmingham local canals and eat at one of the bars. I don't suppose I shall be doing that again."

"The other?"

"He enjoyed rock climbing. Not something I liked. Too much hard going for me. He used to go with a friend."

"Does this friend have a name?"

"Madhav, Madhav Sharma." Allison and Mark exchanged a glance.

"Do you have an address?"

Shirley shook her head, "No, sorry. He was one of his sporting associates, I think. I'm afraid he kept his address book at work." Her hands were trembling and she was struggling to keep from crying. Her eyes were glistening with unshed tears.

Allison nodded. "Do you have an envelope I could put these in?" He indicated the two photos. Again, Shirley nodded and went to the bureau drawer and removed an A4 envelope, "Will this do?" Allison grunted his thanks and popped the pictures inside it.

"Is it possible to see his study? I presume you do have one?"

Shirley nodded, "Yes, he would catch up on his work there. I don't use it." She rose and gestured to them, "Follow me." Alison noticed her wiping away tears that had spilled from her large eyes. She was doing her best to retain her composure and Allison felt sorry for her. It couldn't be easy hearing that your husband had died in such horrific circumstances.

They walked from the room along a corridor to the study that was larger than many peoples' bedrooms. It had a huge hand carved wooden desk in what looked like mahogany, on which was an Apple desktop computer, cordless phone, silver letter opener, blotter and writing pad. Pens and pencils sat in a silver container and a smart gold pen lay on the blotter. An in-tray contained some paperwork. There was a filing cabinet and some family photographs, a book shelf showing an eclectic mix of books from biographies to the latest Jeffrey Archer and James Patterson novels, a printer and copier.

"Is there anything missing from here?"

Shirley glanced about her, "His laptop and briefcase. Otherwise it all looks much the same."

"Do you mind if we look around?"

Shirley shook her head, as she dabbed at her eyes with a lace hankie, "I'll be in the drawing room."

Allison nodded cursorily, "Thank you. We will try to be careful." Shirley attempted a smile and walked away. Allison looked at Mark, "I'll take the desk. You the filing cabinet."

"What about the computer?"

"We will have to take it away. Check the contents of the waste paper basket, too."

"Where have we heard the name Madhav Sharma?"

"Bit of a local celebrity. Does rock climbing to raise money for good causes."

"Nothing nefarious, then?"

"I don't think so. We'll get someone to just check him out. But I'm sure he'll be fine. He did something recently for the children's hospice."

"Now I remember. Won some sort of award didn't he?"

"I believe he did."

The two detectives systematically began their search. Mark began with the top drawer of the filing cabinet, which appeared to hold invoices from various companies, a bills paid folder and several catalogues. He moved onto the second drawer, with company information, VAT and tax return files, phone records and bank statements, which Mark began to sift through. He removed the bank statements and itemised phone bills and noted that they covered two different numbers.

Allison rooted through the desk drawers, which held his desk diary that he removed and a mobile telephone, which he pocketed. He examined the paperwork on the desk, which all seemed innocuous. The bottom drawer held an assortment of keys, spare car keys all labelled including ones to business premises and a new passport together with some old ones.

Mark tried the third and bottom drawer of the cabinet but it was locked. “Do you have a filing cabinet key amongst that lot?” asked Mark jerking his head towards the bunch Allison was sorting through.

Allison poked through them and shook his head. “I can’t see one. Wait a minute.” He rifled through the pen container and at the bottom found two keys. He tossed them to Mark, “Try one of these.”

Mark fitted one into the lock and the drawer opened. It appeared to be filled with new stationery, headed notepaper, envelopes and copy paper. “Why would anyone lock a stationery drawer?” He lifted up the papers to reveal a cash box. He opened the cash box with the other key and it contained two thick rolls of fifty-pound notes. “There’s a lot of money in here and a cash book.”

“How much?”

“Each roll must be about three grand. Must be why that drawer was locked. That’s a lot of petty cash.”

Allison’s eyes gleamed, “Maybe. But if the cashbox was locked there wouldn’t be the need to secure it. Take everything out.”

Mark lifted out all the stationery and placed it on the floor. Allison studied the depth of the drawer. “The base of that doesn’t appear to fit with the size of the compartment.”

Mark looked at it, “You’re right.” He tapped the floor of the drawer inside and fiddled with it, pushing it down at one end where it sounded hollow. Something popped metallically and with a bit of manoeuvring he was able to push up the false piece of metal and remove it. He gasped. There wrapped in a cloth was a firearm, a Glock 17 and ammunition. “Now, why does Mr Rakowsky need this?”

“We will have to ask his wife that.” They continued to examine other items before moving onto the bookshelves. Mark removed each book one by one and shook them. A couple of bookmarks fell out and a piece of paper with a list of numbers fluttered to the floor. Allison picked it up and put it with the diary. He checked the cordless phone for the last numbers dialled and received, and made a note of them. "We'll take these away with us and get back to Shirley." Allison picked up the letter opener and pen and put them into a bag and sealed it. "These will be useful, if we bring Holly in at any point." Mark assented with a nod. Holly was the police psychic who had been instrumental in helping to catch serial killer, Tony Clifton and had aided them in a number of other cases like recovering the precious jewels known as the Tears of Solomon together with helping solve the disappearance of girls from a Birmingham nightclub.

They gathered up the items and made their way back to the drawing room where they could see Mrs Rakowsky had been crying. She dabbed at her eyes with a fine linen and lace handkerchief.

"With your permission we'd like to take these away with us." Shirley Rakowsky nodded. "Mrs Rakowsky… Shirley, have you any idea why your husband would need this?" said Mark who unwrapped the gun still holding it with the cloth.

Shirley stared at it in shock, "No… I've never seen it before. I didn't know he had one."

"He also had about six thousand pounds in cash in his cash box."

Shirley shook her head, her luxuriant hair shimmered as she did so and she gasped, "No. Jonas always had about two thousand that he would keep in case of emergencies." Allison wondered why someone would need two thousand pounds for an emergency. Shirley continued, "But not that amount."

Allison grunted, "We will have to take it with us to check the serial numbers and so on but it will be returned to you as long as the money has not been involved in anything suspicious."

"Suspicious?"

"It's just routine, protocol. We have to check all manner of things when it comes to murder."

Shirley sniffed. Her nose and eyes were now looking red. "Of course."

"Do you have anyone that could come and stay with you today? A friend or family member?"

"Um," Shirley sniffed again, "I have a good friend, Leeanne Parkes. I could try her."

"Call her now, we'll wait."

Shirley went to the phone on the bureau and dialled a number. She waited a moment until it was answered, "Leeanne? Are you busy?... Could you come around?... Yes, today. Something terrible has happened…"

Allison gestured to Shirley and took the phone from her, "Ms Parkes? This is Detective Chief Inspector Allison. Mrs Rakowsky has had an unpleasant shock and she shouldn't be left alone. Is it possible for you to come over and stay with her for a while, perhaps a day or two?... Yes… That's great, thank you." Allison ended the call and passed the phone back to her. "She said she will come around immediately. We will leave you now and let you do whatever you need to."

Allison and Mark walked to the door carrying the items removed from Jonas' study. "We will be in touch, someone will need to take a statement and if you recall anything else, please do not hesitate to contact me. Here's my card. Ring day or night." Allison passed Shirley his card. Shirley nodded dumbly and took the proffered card and studied it. "We'll see ourselves out. Please accept our sincerest condolences."

Shirley stifled a sob and sank into a chair, her hair flowed around her face like a bird of prey shielding its catch from other predators Allison and Mark left. They heard her pitiful wail as they reached the front door.

Bannen Sadler was in custody in Interview Room 4, after spending the night in a cell. Recording had been set up announcing the names of all present and that he, Josh Linton would be conducting the interview. After Bannen had asked for his lawyer he remained stubbornly silent to all questions only replying, "No comment," to each one asked.

Josh Linton was becoming increasingly frustrated. He looked at the other officer sitting with him, "This is getting us nowhere." He turned to Bannen, "You may believe you can escape justice by not answering our questions, but you should know that we have irrefutable evidence that you have committed murder. Eye witness statements, DNA and more. You are also wanted in Turkey on another count of murder. We can easily extradite you. They are anxious to prosecute you and you do know in Turkey that although they have abolished capital punishment in 2004 it's been replaced by aggravated life imprisonment, which means you will be incarcerated in a single cell in a high security prison and only allowed out for one hour for exercise each day? I don't fancy your chances over there, especially as many politicians are agitating to reinstate the death penalty. I've a good mind to send you back right now and see what happens." Bannen looked up sharply. "Oh, have I alarmed you?" Josh smiled humourlessly. "When, and if we pull you back here we will try you for the murders of Ashok Kumar, Malek Akhtar, Kaseem Abidi, Raiden Dhanial." Josh stopped, "And the attempted murder of a police officer. That will do for starters as I know there are others to take into account." Josh rose, and gestured to the constable standing at the door, "Get him out of here. Interview terminated at …" he checked his watch, giving the correct time.

The officer stepped forward and took Bannen's arm, which he shook off glowering furiously but still remained silent. Josh watched as the constable led him away.

Allison and Mark sat outside the Rakowsky house. "So, Madhav Sharma. Fancy that," said Mark.

"Who'd have thought it? Wonder how he got mixed up with Rakowsky? Yes, a man of many talents, running, kayaking."

"And rock climbing."

"Even if he is a good guy, we still have to check him out."

"You never know it may be a cover, which would make him look Teflon coated... So, he's an associate?. We'll check records and see if there's any other enquiry into the man. Someone can interview him."

"Always looked clean cut, if I remember."

"We think," grunted Allison in agreement and fell silent.

Mark started the car, "Where to now, sir?"

"Think we need to get to Gas Street, don't you?" Mark started the engine and moved away from the select neighbourhood. "So, what did you think? About Mrs Rakowsky"

"I think she knows more than she's saying," said Mark. "But I don't believe she's complicit in his business dealings, whatever they are. In fact, I'm not sure of anything right now."

"Hmm," said Allison and his stomach rumbled. "If we hurry, we can park at Brindley Place, and grab a bite at one of the bars by the canal."

"Yes, and waive the twenty quid parking fee."

"Being in a cop car does have some perks," agreed Allison.

"Canalside is good, and if it's busy, there are plenty more to choose from along that stretch of water," said Mark. "From there we can find our way to Gas Street canal basin and the warehouse."

Allison frowned, he didn't like walking too far unless the weather was good, which fortunately today, it was. He patted his rumbling tum as if to shut it up. They made their way back into the town along the Hagley Road and turned off Broad Street and into Brindley Place Q parking, which was fairly empty. They parked in a vacant slot and left, crossing the paved way with its bollards preventing people from driving into this pedestrian zone. The clouds were few and the sky a stunning azure blue. It was a fresh morning but the sun still felt warm and by the time they had reached the water, Allison was feeling quite hot. They moved down the steps and walked along the quay towards 'Canalside', a pub and eatery on the canal. A clean looking recently repainted white fronted building decorated with hanging baskets that were a profusion of colour was before them. There was an outside seating area with bright umbrellas, where people could sit and watch the barges go by. But they weren't there for the view. They entered and found a table close to the bar. Lunch was ready to be served so they ordered pizza and Allison and Mark both ordered non-alcoholic beers although Allison was tempted by the real ales on offer, as he wasn't driving, but decided against it. He needed a clear head.

The barmaid, Queenie, looked at them curiously. She had a cheerful face with a mass of chestnut curls reminiscent of the permed style Barbra Streisand sported many years ago, in films from way back in 1976, Allison thought. Her voice was bubbly as if she was always on the verge of laughter.

She had seen Mark before with a very attractive blonde but this hulk of a man who towered over him was new to her. "And what brings you two gents this way?" she said perkily.

"Food," said Allison. "Got a rumbling tum," and he patted his stomach.

"Well, it won't be rumbling for long after your feast." She turned to Mark, "I'm sure I've seen you in here before?" She finished pouring their drinks and passed them across.

"Quite possibly. I've been here a couple of times with my fiancée and with my kids when we did a canal boat ride in the summer."

"I thought so. I never forget a face."

Allison opened the envelope and placed the two photos of Jonas Rakowsky on the bar. "If you never forget a face, have you ever seen this man before?"

Queenie studied the pictures and nodded, "Yes, many times. Often used to come in here with an Asian fellow and sometimes with his wife, at least, I think it was his wife, she wore a wedding ring." She studied them both again, "You from the police?"

"How did you guess?" said Allison wryly.

"Hard to miss, when you're showing photos and such. Why, what's he done?"

"Nothing as far as we know. He's dead," said Allison as he replaced the pictures.

"Oh my," Queenie coloured up. "I'm sorry, I didn't know. It wasn't suicide was it? … Was it an accident?"

"Why would you think it was suicide?"

"Dunno really. Except the last time he was in here, I overheard him saying to someone that he was done for. That he needed to clear out or top himself. Said he wasn't going to be cut to pieces."

Allison's eyes narrowed, "Did he by George? Who did he say that to?"

Queenie furrowed her brow, "Some ginger haired bloke… freckled, must have been about fifty, fifty-five."

"A regular?"

"Never seen him before. Name's Queenie by the way… better than Bess hence the nickname Queenie… Good Queen Bess," she said with a laugh.

"Since we're doing introductions…" He pointed to himself, "DCI Greg Allison," and gestured to Mark, "DS Mark Stringer. Now what else can you tell me about this conversation?"

Just then, the pizzas arrived and Allison and Mark were forced to retreat to their table to eat. He turned to Queenie, "We'll pick this up again, later." Queenie nodded cheerfully and turned to another customer as Mark and Allison crossed to their table. Allison squeezed onto the bench seat and faced the rest of the bar.

He sawed through his pizza and picked up a slice and munched. A dribble of melted cheese clung to his chin, which he wiped away with his fingers that he cleaned in his mouth. Nothing was said for a while as they ate. As soon as they put down their knives and forks Queenie came across to remove their plates.

"I've been racking my brains about that day and I've just remembered something."

Allison looked up with interest. "It was the last time I saw him in here. When he left with the other bloke, the ginger man looked back at an Eastern European fella sitting in the corner. No one I've seen before. Nothing was said but it was as if they knew each other like some sort of signal between them. The foreigner got up and left his pint hardly touched and his meal. I thought it was odd at the time but dismissed it and now you've come in here asking about him and him being dead and all, I thought I should mention it."

"Thanks, Queenie. That's very useful. Do you think you'd remember this man again if you saw him?"

Queenie frowned, as she thought, "Yes, I expect so."

"Would you be prepared to come down to the station and have a go with our police artist?"

Queenie pondered a moment, "Yes, okay… but when? I'm here most week days from eleven to three. I could come after I knock off. Saturdays I work from ten in the morning to chucking out time."

Allison took out a card and passed it to her. "That's my direct line and mobile number. Have you got somewhere I can contact you?"

Queenie picked up a pub card with the number on and scrawled on the back, "That's my mobile. I don't have a landline. Can't afford it."

Allison nodded. "Understood. I'll be in touch. And if you remember anything else, call me."

Queenie nodded and pocketed his card. She whisked away the plates and Allison made his way out into the now dazzling sunshine followed by Mark.

Allison grunted, “Well, that was unexpected.”

“Unexpected but useful.”

“Right, let’s find this warehouse, West End Products, wasn’t it?”

5

GURDIP WAS SLOWLY BEGINNING TO sort out his emotions and his feelings about his future and life in general. He was staying with Ronnie but was afraid of attracting Pasha's murderous intentions to his friend's house. He knew how good Ronnie had been to him and he treated and regarded him as a brother.

It wasn't an ideal situation. Mrs Soper was kind and accommodating but it wasn't like being in his own home. His home had gone, burned down. He still had the headache of sorting out the insurance. He had never had to do anything official with death or insurance and was uncertain about what was required.

He picked up Misty, a large fluffy grey tabby cat, the Sopers' family pet. Misty nestled into him and began to purr. She rubbed her face into Gurdip's shoulder and put her nose up to his face. He obliged and they almost rubbed noses. She was a gentle beautiful cat and Gurdip found her comforting. The stress he was feeling as he waited for Ronnie to come home from work seemed to evaporate as he stroked and cuddled her.

Gurdip was keen to talk to Ronnie about his plan. He was unaware that Pasha was watching Lloyd House Police Station from one of the buildings opposite, waiting to catch sight of Ronnie and to follow him. Pasha was certain that Ronnie would lead him to Gurdip and if Gurdip had known he would have warned his friend.

Katy was standing on her usual pitch outside New Street station on the street calling out, "Big Issue… Get your Big Issue here." She was wearing fingerless black knitted mittens and had ditched her greatcoat for a duvet style puffer jacket that was well insulated, after a visit to a charity shop. The manager there was good to Katy and let her have the jacket at a bargain price, even for a charity shop. The weather was bright but cold and a stiff wind had sprung up making Katy glad of her jacket. But Katy was still incredibly nervous after her experience at the hands of the mugger. She glanced up at the three faced clock of Slaters' Menswear at the junction of New Street and Corporation Street, wondering how long she had left of her shift.

She had been feeling more upbeat after her chat with Den. He had arranged for her to swap pitches with another seller who was only too eager to change from the Bull Ring to the railway station but they weren't able to do this until the following Monday, so Katy remained on edge. Then again, everything seemed to be happening on Monday. That was when she was moving in properly with Den, while she waited for the studio flat to become available.

That thought cheered her up. Big Den was a good guy and she was glad not to have to stay any longer than necessary at the squat. Katy was lost in her train of thought, perfunctorily calling out to folks passing, even those who didn't give her a second look she would call out, "God bless you, ma'am or God bless you, sir." But, she suddenly froze in her usual sales repertoire as she spotted the man with the grey ponytail from the other night. This time he was alone and he rounded the corner of New Street and strode up Corporation Street and paused outside Urban Outfitters 5-7, Corporation Street. He studied the shoppers passing him by and then stepped inside the shop. Katy gasped. That was the man. That was one of the chaps who had deposited the rust-coloured suitcase outside the left luggage office. Of that she was absolutely certain.

A plump blonde lady approached Katy holding out a fiver. She waited a minute or two and then announced in a shirty manner, "Well, if you don't want the business."

Katy apologised profusely and passed her a copy. She fumbled with the two pound change, but the woman waved it away. "No, you keep it. It's a good read. Well worth it."

Katy was even more effusive in her thanks but her hands were shaking and she almost dropped the five-pound-note as she stared up the road.

Allison and Stringer had finally reached the canal basin at Gas Street and soon spotted the warehouse named, 'West End Products Ltd'. They walked to what appeared to be the entrance and tried the door, which opened. Inside there was a hulk of a man, sitting at a reception hatch. At first glance he reminded Allison of a gross toad or Jabba the Hutt from Star Wars.

The man looked up as they entered and spoke with a thick Brummy accent. "Yes? Can I help you?"

"DCI Allison and DS Stringer."

The man's expression changed, "Police? What do you want?"

"We'd like to talk to the manager, if possible."

"I don't know if he's available…"

"He will be. Tell him it's about his boss or partner, Mr Rakowsky."

The man studied them both, "Can I see your identification?" They both showed their warrant cards. The man sniffed and picked up the phone and dialled. He waited until someone answered. "Police here to see you, sir." There was some sort of expletive, which travelled down the line. "Yes, sir." He looked up distastefully at them. "He says to go on up."

The man indicated a staircase with a jerk of his head across the warehouse floor, which was surrounded by shelving filled with all manner of boxes and other items from rugs to large painted ceramic pots resembling those big vases with ancient Chinese designs that were popular. There were also racks of women's clothes that looked as if they belonged in a costumier's or a fancy-dress shop with numerous types of outfits from Salome's eastern style of dress to that of a French maid.

Allison nodded curtly and made his way to the foot of the stairs where he waited for Mark to catch up whose attention had been caught by a large ostrich feather fan amongst the trappings and rails of female clothes. Allison cleared his throat and Mark hurried across and they mounted the wooden stairs. There were no handrails on either side and Allison put his hand on the inside wall to steady himself. He muttered, "Health and safety would have a field day with this lot. Looking at all those clothes it might not hurt to get fire prevention involved, if we need to." They reached the top of the stairs and Allison scanned the storage area. There were several doors leading off from the main warehouse floor and this mezzanine floor projected out over half of the warehouse space. The stairs continued to an upper floor but were more well-structured with handrails on both sides and led up to another large space. Off the landing on the right were a couple of offices. A door opened from one and a fit looking man, with bulging biceps and sandy coloured hair in a tight T-shirt emerged. He excused himself as he moved past them and ran lightly down the stairs. He was followed by several more in the typical brown coats of warehouse workers who were of various nationalities, Mark thought. These men also returned to the ground floor and spilled across the area. A forklift started up and a dark-haired driver began removing boxes and stacking them by a large roller door. Allison finished perusing the activity and stared into the first office window where a woman looked to be typing up invoices or similar. He moved onto the next and was just about to peer in through the glass when the door opened. A svelte tawny haired beauty in a figure-hugging jumpsuit gestured them across. "Please come in, Mr Kelland will see you now." Her accent sounded Eastern European from Bulgaria, Romania or Russia; Allison wasn't sure. But she was a very striking woman. Allison put his hand under Mark's chin and closed his mouth. They entered the office.

The workplace was well laid out and thickly carpeted as it was springy underfoot, a good underlay, Allison thought. They needed new carpets at home. He was sure Mary, his wife, would approve of something like this. But his mind's wandering was cut short as a man rose from behind his desk and walked to greet Allison. He stretched out his hand, "Martyn Kelland, I'm Jonas's partner. How can I help?"

Allison took the offered hand and shook it. It was a firm grip. "DCI Allison." He indicated Mark, "My sergeant, DS Stringer." Mark shook hands with him and they were both invited to sit.

"Thank you, Mr Kelland. When did you last see or speak to Mr Rakowsky?"

"That would be last week. We had just secured a good deal with Pier Imports in the USA. We went for a celebratory drink and Jonas said he was going to take some personal days as he had some family matters to attend to, his elderly mother is in a care home."

"When was this exactly?"

"Er…" Martyn Kelland opened his desk diary and flicked back through the pages, "That was Tuesday last week. Why are you asking?" He looked curiously at the two detectives.

"I will be coming onto that. Did you have any other contact with Mr Rakowsky?"

"No, none at all."

"Was it unusual for him to take time off in this way?"

"Not really, but, we're very flexible. We help each other out. Look what is all this about?"

"Did you know his wife had reported him missing?"

Martyn Kelland looked astounded. "No. I have been away myself. Oh my God. This is awful. What's happened? Have you found him? Has he had an accident?"

"No, sir. It's more serious than that."

Martyn looked from one to the other and watched as Mark scribbled in his notebook. "What do you mean?"

Allison looked the man keenly in the eye, "I'm sorry to have to tell you that Mr Jonas Rakowsky is dead."

"What? How?"

"His body was discovered two days ago."

"Poor Shirley. I must call her." He studied Allison's face with his unblinking eyes. "I'm sorry, I don't understand what all this has to do with me? Do you want me to identify the body or something?"

"That won't be necessary. Can you tell me where you were Tuesday night?"

"At home. Why? Surely you don't think…?"

"I don't think anything. This is merely routine and will help eliminate you from our enquiries."

"Eliminate me?" Martyn Kelland blustered. "I take exception to your insinuations, Chief Inspector."

"I am not insinuating anything. You must understand that this is a murder enquiry. We need to find out who did it."

"Murder? No one mentioned murder." Martyn Kelland cleared his throat and answered, "Tuesday, I was at home."

"Can anyone vouch for that?"

"My wife."

"What did you do?"

"After dinner we had a couple of glasses of wine and watched TV."

"What was on?"

He thought for a moment…"Er…We watched a Sky channel. Alibi, I think. Louise likes 'Hudson and Rex'. She's mad about dogs." He scratched his chin as he spoke and hurriedly removed his hand when he saw Mark note something down in his pad.

"Hudson and Rex?" Allison raised an eyebrow.

"A cop show with a detective and his dog as partners who solve crimes."

"And then?"

"Uh… the Sy-Fy channel to watch a rerun of 'Quantum Leap'. I like that. After that we watched an episode of 'The Stranger' on Netflix but we had to pause it as one of our neighbours popped around to see Louise. I left them to it and went up for a bath. I needed to unwind."

"Why was that? Difficult day? Trouble at work? Had you fallen out with Jonas?"

"No. Stop putting words in my mouth. Nothing like that happened. We were friends."

Allison grunted his acknowledgement and continued, "I will need your home address and your neighbour's address to verify what you have told us. If you could give me those now, please." Allison waited while Martyn Kelland wrote something on a sheet of copy paper and passed it to him. "Thank you. We will be in touch again and be prepared for us to call you to come down to the station to make a statement. That will be all for now."

Mark put away his pen and pad as Allison rose and he followed his boss out from the office. As they moved down the stairs they noticed another tall man talking to the hulk in reception. Mark looked sideways at him whereas Allison was bolder and made a point of speaking and noting the other man. "Thank you. We'll see ourselves out but we'll be back."

The man tossed his head and Allison noticed his hair was tied back into a long grey ponytail.

Ronnie finished looking around the flat that Gurdip had found in the classified ads in the Birmingham Post and Mail. It wasn't too far to walk and catch the number six bus, which had a good service into town and more importantly the flat looked okay. It was in Poplar Avenue and the area was notorious for student bedsits and house shares. It was clean and well equipped. And it had the added benefit of a third bedroom, which meant there was room for Siri and Ayesha to stay if she wanted to visit. It appeared perfect for the two of them and he couldn't wait to get back to speak to Gurdip and tell him that his friend had spotted a winner. He assured the estate agent he would ring him as soon as he'd conferred with his pal. The rent was £650 per calendar month, which was £325 each. They could afford that. Ronnie had the figures for council tax and estimated bills to help them work out their finances. It was looking very promising.

He shook hands with the estate agent on the doorstep of the property. The agent was a slim well-dressed Irish man, in his forties, with a gentle lilting accent and twinkling eyes. Ever wary, Ronnie looked around and was shocked to see Pasha on the other side of the road. He was unwrapping a piece of chewing gum. He popped it in his mouth and began to chew. As he caught Ronnie's eye, he gave him a two-fingered salute and grinned at him.

Ronnie shuddered. He spoke to the agent and said something. The man looked across the road at Pasha and frowned. More words were exchanged. They shook hands again and this time walked together to the agent's car. Ronnie got into the passenger seat and they took off towards Bearwood.

Pasha stamped his foot as he watched them drive away. He hurried to his hired car that was facing in the wrong direction. He started his motor and turned hastily in the road. He attempted to follow the agent's vehicle, but not being acquainted with the area he did not know where they had gone. He slammed his hand on the driving wheel in frustration.

The estate agent had first driven to his office in Bearwood High Street and given Ronnie some more advertising material of other properties he had to let that were of a similar standard on his books. He then drove Ronnie back into Birmingham and dropped him off within easy reach of the police station.

Ronnie whistled as he ran into the building and once in the office was faced with shocked glum faces. "What is it? What's happened?"

Bill Rennie was the first to speak. "Where have you been? We've been trying to get hold of you for two hours."

Ronnie slipped his hand in his pocket and took out his mobile, "Battery's flat. Died on me. Why?" He studied the faces of those around him trying to discern what was wrong. There was an uneasiness, a feeling of tension in the room. Eventually Bill spoke up, "I'm sorry Ronnie. There's no easy way of saying this…"

"What is it?"

"You better sit down, mate."

Ronnie had paled. He sat down slowly and stared up at Bill, "What's happened? Tell me."

Allison came out of his office and nodded at Bill who continued, "Someone has attacked your house."

"What do you mean attacked?"

"Someone tried to torch it."

"What? In broad daylight? But, my mum?"

"Safe. She has been taken to her sister in Wolverhampton and before you ask, no she wasn't followed."

"How do you know?"

Bill raised his eyebrow, "Come on, Ronnie… we know."

"When did it happen?"

"This morning, around eleven."

"Gurdip?"

"He's fine."

"Where is he?"

"Being checked over in hospital."

"What?"

"Ronnie, Gurdip got your mum out. He saved her life. He went back inside to rescue the cat and suffered from some smoke inhalation. But he wasn't burnt."

"And Misty?"

"Safe."

"But where is she?"

"With your mum. In the cat box."

"And the house?"

"You can't go back there, I'm afraid. It's not safe."

Ronnie put his head in his hands. "Then where do I go?"

Allison stepped forward and put his huge hand on Ronnie's shoulder. "You're coming home with me. You and Gurdip."

Mark was checking through the footage he had finally acquired from New Street station. He was examining the arrivals at the different entrances and exits, studying the passengers and shoppers who were leaving. Foot traffic reduced considerably after 10:30 at night.

Mark yawned as he watched people come and go and saw the concourse empty of staff and commuters. His attention was taken by someone coming through the entrance from Smallbrook Queensway. It was a woman; she was carrying a hessian bag with the Big Issue poking out from it. He lost her on the next camera and changed discs and found her sitting on the station concourse floor close to the ticket barriers. She looked tired and wary and kept looking around. He watched carefully and saw her rise and walk towards the Hill Street exit. He swapped discs again and forwarded to the same time and picked her up passing the photo booth and left luggage office expecting her to leave by the Hill Street egress but instead saw her turn into the assisted travel lounge. She didn't come out. He continued to watch and saw on the periphery of the camera footage two men; one was pulling a rust-coloured suitcase. He froze the frame and studied the men. He couldn't see their faces. They had kept them away from the probing camera lens and were wearing hats that were worn low on their heads. He caught a glimpse of grey hair. But nothing else. He continued to watch. There was no more activity. He called, Allison, "Chief! Think I've got something."

Allison lumbered across and asked, "What am I looking at?"

"Here." Mark froze the frame showing the young female Big Issue seller. "There. She came in but she didn't leave."

"You've checked all the exits?"

"Yes. I believe she went into the assisted travel lounge, possibly to sleep."

"So?"

"Look at this." Mark highlighted the two men with the suitcase, who were just in vision.

"Any more on these two?"

Mark shook his head, "Nothing."

"We need to find that young woman. Start with the Big Issue. Try their collection and distribution point."

Something gnawed at Allison, an elusive caterpillar of thought that wriggled away from his mind. Never mind, it would come. But first he needed a Mars Bar.

6

CLEMENT PUGH STARED AT THE body on the embalming table. She was young and nubile, at least she would have been if she was alive. She couldn't have been more than twenty-two or twenty-three. She had thick shoulder length wavy, ash blonde hair with golden highlights that framed her heart shaped face. Her body was perfect, she had fine pert breasts with pink nipples. Her pubic area had been shaved or waxed. Clement was fascinated by her naked Mound of Venus and he felt himself growing hard.

Clement licked his lips. He knew he was alone in the building and would be until the morning but still, he minced to the windows, drew the blinds and locked the double doors. There was no Y cut on this body making her all the more appealing. She was perfect having died in hospital from a viral infection so no need for a post mortem. Clement gently stroked the young woman's face. His fingertips touched her full, soft lips that seemed yielding and he thought she might smile at him at any minute.

He sighed deeply, his breath coming in stuttering gasps and he slowly began to undo his shirt, he had an urgent need to feel her skin against him. He didn't mind that she was cold he would soon warm her up.

Clement took a key from his pocket and went to a cabinet and opened a locked drawer. He removed a tube of intimate gel, hidden under some soft cloths and a make-up tray used for making corpses seem alive and merely sleeping. It was an art and Clement had used his talent to make her even more beautiful and to simulate her looking as if she was merely resting. He squeezed some of the tube's gel contents onto his fingers and crossed back to the table. He carefully moisturised between her legs and sighed again as he unzipped his trousers and stepped out of them. He removed his boxer shorts and stood there using some more of the lubricant on himself. He couldn't wait any longer he was beginning to leak. He clambered onto the table with her and drifted into his imagination where he talked to her, whispering sweet nothings and played with her body without fear of rejection or any type of refusal. There was no disgust, no belittling. She was his utterly and completely.

Mary glowed with pleasure. She had fussed around Ronnie and Gurdip as if she was their mother. She beamed at her husband as he followed her into the kitchen, "This is such a good idea, Greg. It's like having the girls home."

"You just like someone to take care of," said Allison with a wry grin. "You need to remember, Gurdip is being hunted. He must stay out of sight. He cannot return to work until he's healed and we have caught the villains. Ronnie must be very careful, too."

"I know," said Mary with a smile. "It's just so lovely to have them both here."

"I thought I'd get Holly and Paul across. She may be able to shed some light on this vendetta against Gurdip's family. We will do it off the record, nothing official."

"Good idea. It's some time since I've seen Holly or Paul. I wonder what he's up to now? Still funding his paintings with his architectural jobs, I'm sure. Do you think she's agreed to marry him yet?"

"No doubt we'll find out."

"We can have a proper get-together. A lovely meal and some good wine."

"Yes, why not?"

"As long as there aren't any more bodies… I've not known anything like it since those Tony Clifton murders back in the nineties."

"I think Bannen Sadler has come pretty close," said Greg. "He is a fiend."

"But he's in custody now, isn't he? And you said there was enough evidence to put him away for a long time."

"The legal battle will begin for his extradition to Turkey. It will be what the courts decide. In some ways, I hope he goes there, less expensive for the taxpayer and I doubt if he'd get out to stand trial here. You never know that country may even reintroduce the death penalty."

"And that's a good thing?"

"In his case, yes. He doesn't deserve to live but I expect he'll play the Human Rights' card and appeal. It could take forever. I haven't seen such evil in a long time."

Katy Vicary lay in her sleeping bag on Den's floor. She was awake now but was so warm and cosy she didn't want to get up and face the day. Den stumbled through into the sitting room, his hair sticking up like a lavatory brush. "Morning, Katy. Want a cuppa?"

"Ooh, yes please."

Den stumbled through to the small compact kitchen, filled and switched on the electric kettle. That was Katy's signal to get up. She slipped out of her cocoon and pulled on her jeans, grabbed her shirt and put it on over her bra and camisole. She rolled up her bed and brushed her hair vigorously. It needed a good wash. She would ask Den when she could use the bathroom. She knew it didn't have a lock on the door, but Den was a gentleman and was good about letting her use it.

Katy was tussling with her conscience. The local papers and news were full of the story about two bodies found in suitcases. It had even made the national news and major newspapers. Katy knew she had valuable information about the case that was dumped at the station but like many in her situation she was terrified of getting involved. She tried to reason with herself and argue that it was for the best that she said nothing. But it still niggled at her conscience. It had made her jumpy and nervous of her own shadow.

She eventually decided that she could always make an anonymous call and tell them what she knew and then just fade away into the background as always. But no, they could trace the call and that would lead them to her, to her patch unless she called from the town centre or the railway station itself. There would be nothing to link her then... then of course, there were CCTV cameras everywhere. One of them could pick her up. No, that was no good she would just sit tight. She hadn't mentioned it to anyone, and didn't dare to talk about it with anyone. There wasn't anyone she trusted.

The problem was it was making her lose sleep. Katy had always tried to do the right thing. There were those who had said she did the wrong thing by running away but she couldn't stay at home, not since her father had died and her mother had become involved with Don. At first she had thought he was okay. He was funny and made her laugh. He seemed to treat her and her mother really well but that was in the early days. It was as if he was a split personality like the two-faced Roman God, Janus that she'd learned about in school or more like Jekyll and Hyde, one side of him good and then the other… Katy shuddered she didn't want to think about him. He was fine until he had too much to drink and then it was as if someone had flicked a switch and he turned into someone else. No, there was no going back now and anyway, she had better make a move. She wanted to get to the collection point and pick up her magazines. She needed to make up the money she'd lost to that yob from the other day.

Den strolled in carrying two mugs of tea and passed her one. Katy accepted it gratefully. He asked her, "Do you want to use the bathroom first?"

"After my cuppa, please."

"No problem, why don't you take it in with you? I need to iron a clean shirt."

"If you're sure?"

"Go on. I'll put some cereal out and you can help yourself or have a slice of toast."

"Thanks, Den. I won't be long." Katy hopped up and carried her tea, through to the bathroom while Den got out the ironing board.

Katy often wondered what had happened to Den. He was a big man but quite private and very gentle. He never talked about his past. But, then again, neither did she. She had heard he had been in the military and suffered PTSD afterwards and had just looked inward. How true it was, she didn't know. It was all supposition. One day she might find the courage to ask him. But for now, now she would luxuriate in getting herself clean and wash the grime of the city from her hair.

Mark had arrived at the Big Issue collection point for sellers. There was quite a bit of activity as transactions were made and sellers collected their stock. The detective felt somewhat out of place amongst the ethnic mix of people. They were dressed for the street in a variety of styles ranging from what Allison would have termed beatniks and hippies, to Rastas and military types. Mark drew some suspicious looks dressed as he was in a suit and tie. Mark was a good-looking man, clean cut with piercing blue searching eyes that set many women's heart a flutter and fear into the rogues and criminals he'd interrogated. He walked up to the distributor and showed his warrant card.

The distributor looked uneasy and left his assistant to continue dishing out the papers. He was a portly man of medium height with a pleasant cherubic face. His voice was warm and engaging and Mark could see how he was perfect for this job as his manner was kind and amenable. "Sorry to hold you up," said Mark apologetically. "You have a seller, a female seller, who wears an army greatcoat." The man's eyes, immediately flicked to a petite young woman, with tangled blonde hair that was a cluster of curls. Mark turned around to see who he was looking at and saw Katy. "I don't want to alarm her."

"Why? What's she done?"

"Nothing that we know of."

"Then why do you want her?" persisted the man.

"And you are?"

"Derek, Derek Jimson."

"She's not in any trouble. But we think she may have some information that would be helpful to us."

"Is it about the mugging?"

"Mugging?"

"Yes, she was mugged and all her day's takings stolen by some thug. Folks try to get back on their feet and then…" he trailed off.

"I didn't know. Has it been reported?"

"I don't know."

Mark looked around again but the girl had gone. "Where's her pitch?"

"She's not in any trouble?" he questioned again.

"No, no. Really. We just want to talk to her. She's done nothing wrong."

"Have a word with Big Den, he's over there. He will know her." Derek Jimson pointed at a man who was just exchanging a few words with a pretty, young, mixed-race girl with beaded, braided hair. He was reminded of Patti Boulaye who he remembered watching on TV when he was a very small child. His mother had been a huge fan. Mark began to walk towards them. People moved aside as he asked politely, "Excuse me..." He eventually reached Big Den who was at least six foot six and Mark thought he'd get a crick in his neck just looking up at him. He had short cropped hair and there was something of the military about him.

"Excuse me," Mark showed him his warrant card.

"Yes, what is it?" Den snapped.

"I'm hoping you can help me find one of the sellers. A young lady who wears an army greatcoat."

"Why do you want her?"

"Do you know her?"

"Maybe."

"Look, she's not in any trouble but she may have some information that will help us in our enquiries."

"And what might that be?"

"That's something I'll discuss with her."

"Sorry, I can't help you."

"Can't or won't?" said Mark in exasperation.

Den shrugged and picked up his bag of papers and strode out of the door. A young Indian girl watched him go and she tugged on Mark's sleeve. "I know who you want."

Mark sighed in relief. "Thank you."

"What's in it for me?"

Mark reached in his pocket for his wallet and took out a twenty-pound note to pass to her.

"Not so obvious. Not here," she said looking around anxiously.

"Sorry. Then where?"

"Outside. There's a coffee shop opposite. I'll see you in there." The girl left hurriedly and Mark waited a few moments trying to see if he could spot a female in a greatcoat or the blonde girl from earlier. He couldn't, and so he went on to find the coffee shop. He saw the almond-eyed youngster standing in the doorway of the café. He hurried across to her.

"I must be quick. I don't want to be seen talking to you," she muttered with her eyes scanning the road.

"I'll wait until you're inside."

She looked furtively around her again and went inside the café. Mark waited a moment before he followed her in. She moved to a vacant table away from the window at the back of the store. "This will have to be quick. I need to get to work."

A waitress came up and Mark ordered two coffees. "Do you want anything else?"

"No, thanks. I said this needed to be quick."

Mark took out the twenty quid note again and she grasped it with her long slender fingers spoiled by badly bitten nails. She stuffed the money into an inside pocket on an over-sized man's jacket she was wearing as the waitress returned with their drinks. The girl waited until the waitress had gone back to the counter.

"I think her name is Kate or Katy."

"Surname?"

"That I don't know. Her pitch was on the corner of New Street and Corporation Street but I have heard that from Monday she's changed to the Bull Ring area. Seems something has spooked her. Shame cos near the station is one of the best pitches in town."

"Anything else?"

The girl shook her head, "Sorry… I do know she was living in a squat in Bearwood somewhere, but she's kipping on Big Den's floor until a flat becomes available in the same house."

"Are she and Big Den an item?"

"No. No way. He just looks out for her."

"Can I have your name?"

She shook her head again, "I'm Lydia and that's all you need to know." She stood up.

"Wait. Aren't you going to drink your coffee?" The girl shook her head again although it looked more like a shudder. "What if I need to speak to you again, where is your pitch?"

She hesitated then said, "It's not a secret. You'll find me if you look hard enough." She rolled her dark brown eyes, "Top of Corporation Street outside Rackhams."

"House of Fraser?" She nodded and left swiftly.

Mark drank his coffee thoughtfully. What was she so scared of? Why so frightened? Was there something else going on?

Allison was trawling through the files Mark had printed off regarding Jonas Rakowsky. It was making interesting reading. It seemed Jonas Rakowsky had at one time been suspected of importing stolen antiques and other valuable relics and artefacts for sale to private sellers but there had been no concrete proof of Jonas' involvement and all the evidence was circumstantial. He and his partner, Martyn Kelland, had been flagged up by both Interpol and Europol.

Investigations so far had revealed that Jonas was somewhat oblivious to how his company was being used. It now appeared that it was his business partner that had used the company to branch out into other more questionable operations, of which Jonas was unaware that is, until he was approached by an undercover officer who had granted Jonas immunity for any previous crimes if he co-operated in uncovering the extent of the more unsavoury activities of his business partner.

Jonas had vehemently denied any wrongdoings and had been spooked by surveillance on his house and family. It seemed he was always looking over his shoulder. Even more so, when he stumbled on something he shouldn't, it was then that he began to see how his company was being used.

It was after he met with agent AW that he went missing.

Allison took out a Mars Bar and ripped off the paper. He took a savage bite of the mouth-watering velvet chocolate and gooey caramel toffee that stretched in luscious strands.

Who the heck was this agent AW? How could Allison find him and get him to talk about what he knew? And what secret service or force was this AW attached to?

Clement Pugh had had another visit. This time the two heavies had brought him a head and hands of a woman who, if it wasn't so gruesome had clearly been quite a looker when she was alive. He wondered what she was guilty of to provoke such an horrific end.

He was shaking as he sealed the coffin of a young man badly battered from a motorcycle accident. The young lad, because that's all he was, had just turned eighteen. He was barely recognisable.

The two thugs that had assaulted him in the Chapel of Rest had been particularly threatening demanding that the body parts be dealt with immediately. He had tried to explain that it wasn't always easy. Often coffins lay open in the Chapel of Rest for relatives to pay their last respects. It was only sometimes that they were left sealed in such cases as it would be too distressing to view them in their condition or for those who would find it too upsetting to see their relatives one last time.

Clement was a master at his art. He would make those who had passed appear as if they were merely in repose and he was proud of his talents to do his best with the bodies in his care to make them appear presentable.

He was relieved that the penchant of the Victorians for taking photographs of dead people with their families had long since passed. He remembered only too well that past customs had at one time allowed this and he found it a very macabre practice. But now he had a dilemma. The parents of the teenager had changed their mind about cremation and had purchased a family plot at the cemetery and returned to Clement wanting the coffin unsealed so that they could put some of the lad's favourite items in the coffin with him. He had tried to dissuade them explaining that the casket had been closed and to undo it might cause damage and splinter the wood. He had argued that they could place the items on top of the coffin when it was lowered into the grave, but they had insisted they wanted these objects placed in the coffin with him. Nothing he could say would deter them. He had managed to persuade them that in order to do this it would take some time and they should return in the morning. Fortunately, the couple had accepted this and left.

Now he had to open the box up and remove the woman's head and hands. He would wait until the business was closed, but where on earth was he going to hide the dismembered parts? It wasn't as if bodies were piling up giving him plenty of choice. He glanced up at the clock on the wall, not long now and he could begin.

Mary was adding the finishing touches to the dinner table. She was singing while she did it, feeling very happy. She had a surprisingly good voice, Ronnie thought. He wondered if he could ever persuade her to go to a Karaoke night out with the chief but somehow didn't expect his DCI would want to do that but said so, anyway.

"You know, Mrs A, you've got a really good voice. Ever thought of joining us on a Karaoke night out?"

"Oh, I don't know. I used to sing a lot, choirs at school, even at one time with a band."

"Really?"

"Yes, with a couple of girlfriends. We called ourselves the Trixettes and sang with a band called The Impacts. We did small time gigs at weddings and local dances. I even sang in the middle of a Bingo Session at the Aston Hippodrome once." Mary laughed. It was a full warm and throaty sound. "In fact, and I shouldn't really be telling you this… it's how Greg and I met."

"Oh, do tell," pleaded Ronnie. "Why did you stop?"

"Well, the other two girls moved away and started work. That just left me. I missed them. I wasn't as confident on my own even though I won a talent contest at Bingley Hall, as it was known then."

"That's a shame. You could have gone on and been a star."

"Maybe. All water under the bridge now. I met Greg and he was none too keen on trailing around after me. We got married and then had kids. C'est la vie." She smiled brightly, "I'm happy. I don't think my marriage would have lasted if I'd stayed on with the band, working till all hours."

"Then maybe we'll just have to get a Karaoke machine as a gift for you and you can entertain us at parties." Mary laughed again. "So, tell me, how did you meet the chief?"

"At a dance. Greg was there with his mates and I was on stage singing. He stood near the front and watched. When we had our break, he came across and asked if he could buy me a drink. The rest as they say is history."

Ronnie grinned gleefully. He could hardly imagine the chief at a dance let alone falling for the singer with the band. He stored that information away for another time and Mary continued to sing along with the golden oldy songs on the compilation CD that was playing in the background.

"Anything I can do, Mrs A?"

She looked at the table, "Um... yes... Light the candles and change the CD. Put some soft music on to help the ambience. No one wants to hear me warbling away. I'll be in the kitchen and if the doorbell rings, answer it. Holly and Paul could arrive at any time. And get Gurdip down here."

"Gotcha!" He was just about to shout up the stairs, when the doorbell rang.

Katy sat shivering in a doorway afraid to move. She had tried to make herself look as small as possible. Tears streamed down her face. She didn't even know if it was safe to come out from hiding. She had just moved away from her new pitch and was walking back towards the town centre. The underpass had been closed to traffic in both directions because of a small fire. The road looked pretty deserted except for one vehicle a BMW X5.

Katy was just about to enter the pedestrian subway. There were few people about. It was then she saw him. The beefy man with the long grey ponytail and another man wearing a hoodie, were following a pretty young mixed-race girl with beaded, braided hair that they appeared to accost. She was another Big Issue seller. Katy had seen her around. She wasn't sure of her name but had seen her at the distribution centre.

The hooded man caught hold of her and she appeared to slump in his arms. The other man grabbed hold of her on the other side and they marched her away. She didn't resist and she wasn't walking but seemed to be dragged as if she'd been incapacitated in some way. Katy quickly glanced around. She was more than aware that she was on her own and the increasing darkness was oppressive as evening progressed to night. Her heart began to thump wildly.

Uncertain what to do she tried to see where they were going and tried to memorise the registration number before she attempted to shadow them as unobtrusively as possible. She followed at a discreet distance and saw them manoeuvre the girl into the black BMW X5. The man with the ponytail turned around and caught a glimpse of Katy whose heart was pounding out of control. He yelled and started back towards where he had seen Katy who had now fled. She darted down behind some overflowing rubbish bins and remained as still and quiet as she could and waited. She heard heavy footsteps thunder past and held her breath.

She waited for what seemed like an eternity and then made a dash for the street diving into a shop doorway that led to a small arcade, which she thought would keep her hidden from view. Katy removed her scarf and tied it around her head to hide her hair, believing she should try and change her appearance even if only slightly. She crouched down shaking like the leaves on a tree in a gale. In spite of this, she removed her coat and stuffed it into her bag with her papers. Fortunately, she was wearing an oversized jumper and she crept out from the doorway to the arcade and stepped out into the street and almost bumped shoulders with the man with the grey ponytail who perfunctorily mumbled an apology and pressed on into the arcade.

Katy's heart was still racing like a runaway train but she forced herself to walk on calmly towards Colmore Row and the buses. The sooner she was out of town the better as far as she was concerned.

Ronnie started for the door but for some reason he felt uneasy, call it a copper's instinct, intuition or what you will, but he stopped suddenly and darted for the front room and surreptitiously peered through the net curtains. An Asian man stood there wearing traditional Sikh dress. The Asian stepped back on the path and looked up at the bedroom windows. Ronnie was sure he had seen him before. He hesitated. The man didn't appear to be carrying any kind of weapon except for his kirpan, which was part of a Sikh's uniform. Ronnie was about to return to the hall and open the door to challenge the man just as Holly and Paul started up the path. The man turned and muttered something about it being the wrong house and he shouldn't have come, then hurried back down the path and brushed past Paul and Holly. Holly shivered; she stopped and looked after him as he disappeared into the road. Ronnie raced to the front door and before they had time to ring the bell, Ronnie opened it and did an exaggerated bow and waved them inside.

Paul was tall, broad shouldered with short cropped blonde hair and a muscular body. He would have looked good with a helmet sporting horns, carrying a spear and shield like a Viking. Holly was diminutive with huge dark eyes. They greeted each other like old friends, which they were. Ronnie closed the door firmly behind them. Holly trembled as she hugged Ronnie. She swallowed hard.

"What? What is it?" asked Ronnie fully aware of Holly's gift.

"I'm not sure… not yet. Give me time." She turned to Paul to retrieve the flowers he had been holding together with a bottle of wine.

Mary came out into the hall to welcome her guests and ushered them into the living room, where Holly passed her the flowers. "These are for you."

"How lovely, thank you. There was no need but as you know I do love flowers. I'll just put them in water."

"And pop this in the fridge," said Paul. "I know the chief always has ample red and that you like a good Pinot Grigio. It is chilled, best to keep it that way."

Mary smiled graciously and reached up to give Paul a peck on the cheek. He had to bend his knees and chuckled. Mary turned to Ronnie, "Ronnie, perhaps you would like to get our guests a drink and call Gurdip down."

"Sure thing," said Ronnie chirpily and he dashed into the hall and shouted up the stairs, "Gurdip! Guests are here. Come on down." Ronnie returned to Holly and Paul. "Right! What can I get you?"

"I'll have a glass of whatever's open," said Paul in his throaty voice tempered by years of smoking and rolling his own from Old Holborn tobacco.

Although, he'd given up smoking now, the timbre of his voice remained the same.

Ronnie rubbed his hands and gave one of his engaging grins. "Right! I won't be long, drinks are coming up. Make yourselves comfortable."

"Something smells good," said Paul sniffing the aromas coming from the kitchen. They looked around at the Allisons' tastefully decorated living room and sat on the leather settee together. Paul touched Holly's arm, "What is it? You sensed something, didn't you?"

"Hard to miss," said Holly. "Better wait for the chief. I don't want to repeat myself." She slapped her tummy as it rumbled loudly. "Didn't realise how hungry I was," she said as a form of apology.

They heard someone coming in through the front entrance and into the hallway from outside. Greg Allison popped his head around the door, "Won't be long," he assured them. "Just going to change." They heard him go back to the hall and run up the stairs as Ronnie came in carrying a tray with three large glasses of chilled dry white wine and a glass of orange juice.

"Who's the orange juice for? Not the chief, surely?" said Paul.

"No, it's for Gurdip. He doesn't drink," he explained. "It's against his religion."

"What's against my religion?" asked Gurdip as he walked in and smiled.

"Drinking. Not allowed."

"Only allowed if you're unbaptised, but I have chosen not to drink alcohol. However, I can easily get high on orange juice. It's the sugar rush. Cheers!" he said raising his glass.

Mary entered with the flowers now in a vase and placed them on the sideboard. "They're lovely. Thank you. I'll just get my wine; Greg won't be long and dinner will soon be ready."

The dinner party was going well, fuelled by good food, wine and company. They had all enjoyed their lamb shanks, which had provoked discussion about what Sikhs could or could not eat. Gurdip explained that while baptised Sikhs, Amritdharis and those that follow the Sikh Rehat Maryada are vehemently against the consumption of meat and eggs that it was generally accepted that

Sikhs are free to choose whether or not to eat meat as long as it was Jhatka meat.

"What's that?" asked Holly.

"When an animal is killed instantaneously, with one blow. We do not believe in causing the slow deaths of animals for Halal or Kosher. All life is precious."

"That sounds far more humane," said Mary and the rest of the table agreed.

"I know that if I had to hunt and kill my own meat I would be a vegetarian," said Holly. "Hypocritical I know but I have reduced my meat consumption and eat far more vegetable-based dishes than I ever used to."

"We are the same," said Gurdip. "We eat many vegetarian meals but we eat meat, too, as long as it is killed in the proper way."

Mary rose, "Well, I've learned something today. Thank you, Gurdip. I'll just clear these plates away and I will bring in some coffee. I'm sure we could all do with some."

There was an agreed nodding of heads and Allison turned to Holly. "Lovely as it is to see you and Paul, I did invite you away from the office for some help." He turned his attention to Ronnie and Gurdip.

Holly glanced up interested. "Would that be to do with the attack on Gurdip's family?"

Allison looked up sharply, "How did you know? You haven't been told about this, have you?"

"It wasn't hard, especially after meeting that young Asian man who came to your door and then afterwards hugging Ronnie when we came in."

"What young Asian man?" questioned Allison.

"He was dressed traditionally, like a Sikh," she said, looking at Gurdip whose face flooded with horror.

"No. He has found us. Haramzada!" exclaimed Gurdip and then flushed almost turning purple. "Sorry, I am not normally given to swearing."

"Don't be alarmed,' said Holly. "He was here to help, and you can swear as much as you like because we don't understand your language. Is it Indian?"

"Punjabi. But… this man…" Gurdip looked confused. "What? Who is he? How did he find me? What did he say?"

"I saw him," said Ronnie. "I recognised him from the wedding."

"Tell me, Holly. What did he want?"

Holly focused and closed her eyes. "Give me your hand." Gurdip stretched out his hand across the table to her while the others watched in fascination.

"He is unhappy with his family, with the one who married your sister."

"Pasha?"

"Pasha, that's right. He came to warn you about Parnani …"

"Parnani and Parnana?"

"Yes. And Par…." Holly struggled with the unfamiliar words.

"Pardadi and Pardada?"

"Yes. Who are they?"

"My grandparents… and great grandparents," Gurdip put his head in his hands. "No, no … They have done no wrong. None of my family have."

"This Asian man, who is he?" asked Allison.

"I'm not sure. He is a relative of the bridegroom."

"Pasha has many relatives. Can you be more specific?" asked Gurdip.

Holly tried to fix on the young man's energy again and shook her head. "It was too brief. But I am getting the initial K."

Gurdip thought hard, "Kamapal? Kamaldeep?" Holly shook her head.

"Kal… Kal… Sorry, I can't get his name."

"Kalbant?" said Gurdip suddenly.

"Kalbant…" Holly mulled over the name and exclaimed, "Yes! Yes, Kalbant."

"Pasha's cousin. He seemed a good man, with a good heart."

"Yes, he is. I feel it. He wanted to warn you."

"Do you know where to find this Kalbant?" asked Allison.

"No. But Siri would know," said Gurdip.

The table fell silent. Finally, Allison spoke, "Then we will have to telephone her. No one must visit. If this cousin has found you here then, others will, too."

"So, what do we do?" asked Ronnie.

They looked from one to another. No one had any answers.

7

KATY SAT ON THE FLOOR of Big Den's flat hugging her knees. She was nervous and really spooked. Den was trying to reason with her, "What do you want to do?"

"I don't know. I've seen two things now that I shouldn't have. I don't want that poor girl ending up in a suitcase."

"You said you recognised her?"

"She's one of the sellers, I am sure I have seen her at the distribution centre. She's not very old and she is a pretty girl. I am afraid for her."

"What else can you tell me about her?"

"She's West Indian, I think, or mixed race with braided, beaded hair. But I don't know her name. She must only be in her teens."

"We have a few that fit that description. Let me think…"

"She wears a long scarf and often ties it around her head."

"Sounds like Lydia. I'll check her pitch."

"But she won't be there now."

"No, it will have to wait until tomorrow."

"By then it may be too late," said Katy with a frown as she tussled with her conscience.

"What do you want to do?"

"Make a phone call."

"Are you sure?"

Katy nodded, "It's the best I can do but it will have to be anonymous. Where is there a public phone?"

"They're popping up all over the city centre. Trojan phones the Birmingham Mail calls them. Brings in the revenue to the council from their advertising."

"Are there any near us?"

"Can't think of one."

"Then it will have to be town." Katy stood up and grabbed her puffer jacket.

"You're going now?"

Katy turned her soulful eyes on Den, "If I leave it till tomorrow it may be too late."

"Then I'm coming with you."

The dinner party continued with coffee and chatter and when Allison pushed the plate of petit fours to Holly, they brushed hands. Holly felt a flicker of something and shuddered. Allison stopped, "What? What is it?"

"I'm not sure. I just had a flash of something… about a suitcase. And bodies… It doesn't make sense."

"Oh, but it does," said Allison. "It makes perfect sense."

"But it's body parts…" Holly trailed off. "Horrible."

"What? What about them?"

"I don't know. It's confused and other things are impinging on it. If I hadn't had so much wine…"

"Never mind. Don't push it. Can you come into the station tomorrow?"

Holly looked at Paul, who nodded and said, "I'll drive you in. I have to go for some art supplies anyway."

"Thought you bought everything online?" said Holly.

"Not everything. Some things you have to buy personally, get the feel for the canvas, the paints and colour. You just can't do that online."

"Okay, then. Yes. What time?"

"To suit you."

"I'll have her there by ten," said Paul.

"Great. And I'll have something for you to work with. Now, who's for a liqueur with another coffee?"

Siri and Ayesha sat at the dinner table with Hilda and Jessica who served a vegetable casserole with lashings of mashed potato. Siri looked soulfully at Hilda, "Thank you so much for looking after us. We do appreciate it. But we don't want to be a burden."

Hilda nodded, "We will do what we can. I know what it's like to be hunted like a criminal and to lose my parents. Both Jessica and I know how it feels to be in grave danger."

Siri lowered her eyes that were welling with tears, "How long do we have to stay here? When can I see my brother?"

Hilda lowered her knife and fork and looked at Siri until she lifted her eyes, "I don't know."

"Why were we placed here?" asked Siri.

"The police were good and kind to me. They helped me find myself, when I had lost my memory, and they reunited me with my friend from a Nazi concentration camp, as well as helped to save Jessica who was being held hostage. So, when they asked for our help we didn't hesitate." Hilda paused and sighed, "Siri, you have no home to go to. The house has been destroyed. Your family have been murdered and only you two and your brother, Gurdip remain alive. I had heard that your relatives in the Punjab have also been killed. The police are watching your grandparents' house in Bradford trying to protect them." Siri stifled a sob. "You and Ayesha can stay for as long as you need. Your brother will be able to visit soon, when it's safe but until then…"

"Until then, we are prisoners, too."

"Not prisoners… we hope to keep you safe from harm."

Siri nodded, "I know. I know. It is just so hard… Do you think the police will catch him?"

"Who? Your husband?" Siri nodded. "I don't know. They need to find him and get evidence against him. It will be tough. That's why you need to stay here. No one will find you here. You are safe."

"But we can't stay here forever."

"No. We just have to wait." Hilda smiled sympathetically at Siri, and Jessica patted her hand. "Now eat up. If there is anything you don't like or can't eat, just let us know."

"But we aren't contributing to the bills, the food or anything."

"Don't you worry about that. I have more than enough to accommodate you and Ayesha. It is our pleasure."

Siri picked up her knife and fork and began to eat as Hilda and Jessica exchanged a look.

The telephone rang.

Katy and Big Den had reached the city centre, where it was easy to find a public phone. Big Den looked about him as Katy picked up the phone. "What do I dial? 999?" she said looking at him.

"Isn't there a local number? It's not an emergency," advised Big Den.

"What? Like 101?"

Big Den nodded, "Try it."

Katy's hands were shaking as she punched the buttons. She waited while she listened to a range of options, 'report a crime or incident, report a hate crime or hate incident, or to speak with an officer'. Katy selected to report an incident.

Once she started talking the words tumbled from her, she explained about the men with the suitcase and seeing the same man in New Street and then of him following a young girl with another man and seeing the girl, who was a Big Issue seller, being abducted.

The female on the end of the line urged, "You really need to speak to a police officer."

"No, you can pass the message on."

"Can I have your name, please?"

Katy hung up. "Come on let's go."

Big Den tucked Katy's arm in his and they stepped out towards Colmore Row. He turned and looked behind him. He didn't see the man in a doorway watching them who pulled his hood up and stepped out after them into the street.

The light was starting to fade and street lamps shone their amber glow on the pavements and neon lights in shop windows helped to light up the roads. They walked past Rackhams and cut through the churchyard to Colmore Row and the buses.

The day appeared dismal at first glance with smoke grey clouds clumping together and shrouding the sun. The early morning fog had cleared leaving behind a drab ceiling of leaden skies. The pavements glistened with a damp sheen from the night's rain, but the sun was fighting to push through the dull lumpy sky and was accompanied now by a brisk wind, which was finally succeeding in sending the graphite veils of grey on their journey northwards. A beam of sunlight broke through and pooled on Allison's desk. He stopped what he was doing and looked at his watch. It was 9:45, Holly and Paul would be here soon. That thought cheered him up. It had been a good night last night and he had enjoyed the evening as had Mary.

Allison rose and gazed out of the window at the street below alive with traffic. He had kept up to date with the investigations and was pleased to learn that Bannen Sadler was being held on remand at Winson Green Prison, to await trial. With any luck he would be waiting a long time. Josh Linton was the chief witness, alongside Linda Sadler, Bannen's daughter, who had received immunity for her testimony. The injured cop was recovering in hospital and appeared to be improving, while his partner had to face interviews with professional standards over his use of the taser. Allison believed this was a formality and much as they disliked PSD, Professional Standards Department, and Internal Affairs who were always unduly suspicious of all police actions brought to their attention, it was necessary to root out rogue or bent coppers on the force. This use of the taser, however, Allison believed, was without question, an appropriate action taken to subdue a dangerous man who had killed many times and had attempted to kill one of their own. He hoped Bannen Sadler would never get out. He deserved to die inside.

There was a knock on the door and Maddie popped her head around. "Holly is on her way up shall I get you both some tea?"

"Thanks, Maddie. That would be perfect." Maddie nodded and closed the door. Allison returned to his seat and waited.

The phone rang.

"Allison," he listened… "When was this?" His expression changed, "Why wasn't I informed of this when it happened? ... I don't care, if I had gone home… You know you can get hold of me day and night… It's never stopped you before." There was a tap on the door, which opened and Holly came in. Allison gestured her to sit opposite him as he continued to remonstrate with whoever was on the phone.

Holly gazed about his office and then fixed her eyes on the chief, who hung up the call in exasperation. She engaged him with her soulful eyes and asked, "Problems?"

Allison snorted, "Important information failed to reach me when it should have done. Now I have to try and find the witness who left the message." Allison ran his fingers through his hair, "Sorry, Holly, I know it's not your problem but I'm hoping you will be able to help me. Bear with me a moment. Maddie should be in with some tea in a minute."

Almost as if Maddie had been listening at the door, she tapped lightly and entered with a tray of tea things and a plate of chocolate biscuits. She set them down on Allison's desk and exited quietly.

Holly looked at Allison expectantly, "Well, what have you got to tell me?"

"More like, what have you got to tell me?" said Allison with a laugh.

Holly studied Allison's face, noting his intelligent eyes with his bushy hammock eyebrows. "Where do we start?"

"We will have our cup of tea and then make our way down to Interview Room 4 where things will be laid out for you and we'll go from there."

"Fair enough," said Holly reaching for a biscuit. "Let's enjoy these pleasantries while we can," and she bit into the chocolate covered digestive and munched happily.

Mark had called the Bradford police force, with whom he had a reasonable relationship since preventing a terrorist bombing disaster in a large shopping mall, the previous year. He had checked the records and information he'd received on Madhav Sharma who was the fund-raising athlete supposed to have enjoyed rock climbing with Jonas Rakowsky, and saw he'd been out of the country for the last three months preparing to climb Mount Kilimanjaro. He was then flying from Africa to Nepal to attempt to scale Everest on another major charity event. He made a note of this and decided he would request permission for someone from Lloyd House to interview him on his return regarding his connection to Jonas. It didn't appear that the man was involved in anyway and deserved his celebrity status as a record-breaking charity philanthropist.

Mark looked at his watch. Queenie from Canalside had called ahead already, as requested, and Allison had asked Mark to fix her up with an accomplished sketch artist who could produce a likeness of the men she had seen in the pub. Mark had met with Stacey Cooper, the artist, at the front desk and taken her up to the squad room where a photo-fit book was also available. He settled her in a quiet corner, where she laid out her utensils, pencils, colours, drawing pad and putty rubbers.

He checked his watch again. It was time. Mark rose from his seat to go down to the foyer to collect Queenie, ensuring Stacey had been given some refreshment while she waited..

Stacey was a talented painter in her own right and Allison had often found her sketches were much more likely to resemble the perpetrator than the mix and match facial pieces from the photo-fit collection.

Mark soon returned with Queenie, who had been on time and introduced them. He sat with them and listened while Queenie described first, in detail, the ginger haired fellow seen with Jonas Rakowsky. He may have had sandy gingery hair and freckles but he also looked as if he could handle himself. She said she couldn't be sure of his eye colour but Stacey had taken his colouring into account and given him pale watery blue irises that had a coldness about them with a ruthless cruel glint. His eyes were so realistic they made Queenie shiver.

Mark observed as Stacey worked, adjusting the chin to be more chiselled. And the neck thicker. She managed to inject personality into her drawings and as Mark watched the portrait evolve, he was sure he had seen him somewhere before, but he struggled to remember where. Once satisfied with the image produced, Queenie started work on the Eastern European she had seen and Mark disappeared to make a number of copies of the first sketch.

By the time he returned Stacey was well ahead in setting down the likeness of the other man. Mark watched fascinated as the portrait grew into what appeared to be an easily recognisable face. There was something slightly familiar about this person in the sketch, too. Mark knew he needed to wrack his brains to remember.

Gurdip was helping Mary in the kitchen to make a medium curry. He had gathered a range of spices together, turmeric, ginger, garlic, cardamom seeds, cumin, chili powder, garum masala and coriander in different proportions. "Far better to make our own curry mix rather than the bought stuff as you will see."

Mary continued chopping onions and murmured, "I am more than willing to learn and I will be fascinated to discover how to make parathas. I just hope I have everything you need."

"We need plain yoghurt; do you have any? If not, I can use milk…"

"I have both, depends how much you want?"

"And we need yoghurt, mint and cucumber for the raita."

In truth, Gurdip was actually enjoying himself and it was the most relaxed he had been in a long while. Mary smiled, "Now, what do I do next?"

She didn't have the chance to find out as the phone rang. Mary wiped her hands down her pinny and went to the hall telephone, "Hello?... Yes, of course. Hold on… Gurdip? It's for you."

Gurdip came out from the kitchen wiping his hands on a tea towel and took the phone from Mary who returned to the kitchen. "Hello?" His tone flooded with relief as he heard his sister's voice, "Siri, is that really you? It's wonderful to hear your voice."

"I'm sorry I couldn't talk last night; I am doing my best to protect Ayesha. I couldn't let her hear what we were saying."

"Where is Ayesha now?"

"In the kitchen helping to make pancakes."

"Seems we are both in the kitchen," said Gurdip with a laugh. "I am helping to make curry."

"You said it was urgent. What is it?"

"I need Parnani and Parnana's address."

"Why?"

"They are in danger. Pasha wants to wipe out our whole family. The police will keep watch on their property. The Chands have already murdered so many in Punjab, too."

"Pardadi and Pardada?"

"Gone. Oh, Siri I am so sorry. I am sorry I forbade you and Ronnie to see each other. I regret it with every fibre of my being."

"That doesn't matter now. We were all fooled by Pasha. But, Gurdip, I need to be divorced to be free of the brute."

"I know and when it is safe I will see to it that I talk to the Gurdwara Committee. They will be made to understand that there can be no reconciliation or mediation because of Pasha's extreme cruelty and the murder of our family members. Even so, it will not be easy."

"I'm not going back to him or going with him to India. He wants to kill me."

"I know, I know. I will do my best for you, you know that."

"I know," said Siri softly.

"And now, I need that address, Siri."

Interview Room 4 was laid out with photographs, Jonas Rakowsky's letter opener and pen. There was also the cloth the gun had been wrapped in, together with some paperwork. Holly entered before Allison and Mark who was carrying the completed sketches by Stacey and she shivered.

"Is something wrong?"

"There is a bad energy in here."

"From these?" asked Allison gesturing to the items.

"No… something else. Residue of a presence, a strong presence of a very bad man."

Allison turned to Mark, "Who was the last person interviewed in here?"

"I'm not sure."

“A man who has killed many times and enjoyed it,” said Holly looking from one to the other.

“Must be Bannen Sadler,” said Allison.

“Bannen Sadler…” said Holly slowly. “Yes… yes... that’s him. An evil man.”

“Is this going to interfere with what we need to do?”

Holly nodded, “Possibly. His energy is so powerful…”

Allison gestured to Mark, “See if one of the other interview rooms is free. I’ll gather these up.”

Mark left and Holly waited for Allison to pick up everything. Holly put her hand on his arm, “Wait! This man, Bannen.”

“Yes?”

“Is he on suicide watch?”

“No, I don’t think so.”

“Then he should be. I don’t see him living for much longer.”

“Suicide?”

“Maybe…”

“I’ll get onto it as soon as we’re finished.”

Holly pursed her lips and followed Allison out of the room into the corridor and saw Mark standing outside Interview Room 2. He gestured them across.

As soon as they got inside, Allison spread everything out on the table. Holly heaved a sigh of relief once she was seated, “This is much better. Thank you. Although the last person in here, a woman, was falsely accused but I think you know that…”

Mark grinned, “God, you’re good! She was … It was a case of mistaken identity, which was all cleared up.”

They sat around the table and Holly picked up and studied the photographs. She held the letter opener and pen and closed her eyes. “This man is troubled. He wants to do the right thing but…” she suddenly jolted forward. “It’s not what you think… he’s discovered something…something bad. He wants to put it right but he’s been stopped… Oh, my God, he’s dead. This is the man in the suitcase isn’t it?”

Allison nodded. "Yes. Can you tell us anymore? Why did he die?"

"He knew too much. They had to kill him."

"Do you know what he knew?"

Holly shook her head, "Sorry… I can't tell you that." She frowned, "I know he was innocent of wrongdoing, someone was using him and there are others involved… I can tell you that there were two men involved in his murder on orders from someone else." She opened her eyes and looked at Allison, "I'm sorry I can't tell you anymore… it's very hazy. I'm not being very helpful am I?"

"On the contrary, you have given us a great starting point. If Jonas Rakowsky was trying to put something right, and stopped, we know to look further into his business partner and his associates. Can you feel anything else?"

Holly closed her eyes again, "I'm getting a similar feeling that I did from Beth's disappearance last year."

"Similar? In what way?"

"I don't know… involving young women and an outside agency?"

Allison exchanged a look with Mark, "Are they connected?"

"No, but…"

"But?"

"Someone Mark knows, working for…" she screwed her face up as she tried to think. "Sorry, it's gone. It was so fleeting."

"Not to worry…Would it help if you took something of his away with you?"

"It might. Although, if you knew where it happened I might get something more. Sorry, Greg."

"One more thing," said Mark. "Do you get anything from either of these sketches?" Mark passed her the two sketches that Stacey had done with Queenie.

Holly studied them. She pointed to the sketch of the sandy haired man and almost choked.

Allison looked concerned, "What is it?"

"That's one of them. One of the men who killed Jonas Rakowsky. I can feel it."

Allison and Mark exchanged a look.

"But…"

"But?"

"The eyes, one is right but the other…."

"What?"

"I'm not sure let me think on it."

"What about the other?" pressed Mark.

"Hmm. He's involved but not in the murders. He is something to do with the girls. Sorry, I can't tell you anymore. At least not yet."

"That's fine. It's a starting point. Mark, take Holly to the railway station, see if she can pick up anything there." Allison passed Holly the letter opener in its bag, "Here, take this. Keep it as long as you need."

Holly put it into her bag and followed Mark to the door while Allison cleared away the rest of the items. When they walked along the corridor Holly stopped.

"Are you okay?" asked Mark.

"Sorry, my head seems to be swimming. I've got a really uneasy jittery feeling."

Mark ushered her into the main office and sat her down. He went to get her a glass of water from the dispenser.

Holly gripped the desk as waves of fear rippled through her. Drowning Pool's Nu Metal song, 'Bodies' appeared to infiltrate her mind; the harsh sound of screaming and counting echoed in her head. She disliked the song for its extreme anger and violence but somehow it resonated with the many deaths that had already occurred and she feared there were more to come and said so.

8

KATY WAS EXCITED. SHE WAS due to be moving in to her studio flat the very next day. No more sleeping on Big Den's settee in a sleeping bag. She would have her very own place. She could hardly believe it. Tomorrow couldn't come quickly enough. Selling the Big Issue had been her lifeline when she was at her lowest ebb. It was Big Den that had encouraged her. He persuaded her that she could do it, when she was at rock bottom. She had so much to thank him for.

Katy stretched and yawned loudly, one more sleep and she would have her own place. She wriggled out of her sleeping bag and walked to the window that overlooked the street and partially pulled back the curtain. The people opposite from across the road were getting up. Katy watched as they opened their curtains fully. Folks were leaving their houses and going to their cars. She watched as a smartly dressed man opened the door to his Volkswagen Golf, pulled out from the kerb and drove away. It was then she noticed a black BMW X5 approaching. It pulled into the space vacated by the Volkswagen but no one alighted.

Katy frowned. No one was getting out of the car. She couldn't see inside the vehicle because of its tinted windows but a shiver passed through her body. It looked identical to the one that she had witnessed spiriting away the young Big Issue seller. Katy let the curtain fall back. Uncertain what to do she dressed hurriedly and went into the bathroom. She scrubbed her teeth and splashed cold water on her face. She could hear sounds of Big Den moving around. She grabbed her brush and dragged it through her tangled curls and stared at herself in the mirror.

It was no good, her hair was too distinctive, if someone was looking for her, she could easily be spotted by her hair. Katy went into the sitting room and hunted in her bag of clothes until she found what she was looking for. She scrunched her hair into a bun and pushed it all under a baseball cap. Content that it changed her appearance sufficiently she rummaged through her garments and swapped her jeans for a bohemian type of skirt with an Indian design and tassels, which she teamed with a loose cheesecloth embroidered top and a black velvet waistcoat. She studied herself in the mirror on the wall and was satisfied that she looked sufficiently different from how she usually appeared.

Big Den wandered in yawning loudly, "Cup of tea?"

"Please."

He rubbed his eyes and stared at her, "Blimey! You've undergone a change… I'd hardly recognise you. What's all this about?"

Katy explained about the vehicle parked opposite the flat. Big Den opened the curtains with a flourish and peered out. He saw the offending car. "Do you think it's them?"

She shrugged, "I don't know. I haven't seen anyone get out."

"Have you been watching all the time?"

"Well, no. Not all the time. I went to get changed and do my teeth and so on."

"Let's not get paranoid or ahead of ourselves. It could be perfectly innocent. I'll make that tea. You keep a low profile."

"Low profile?"

"Stay away from the window."

Katy moved back and sat on the settee. She couldn't shake the feeling that they were being watched, both her and Big Den.

Gurdip was healing well. He was managing at the chief's house and enjoyed sharing knowledge of his Indian cuisine with Mary. He was turning out to be a real help in the kitchen. Ronnie had bought home some more literature on flats and houses to rent but Allison had advised that Gurdip and Ronnie should stay put until Pasha was found to which they had both agreed. Mary had gone shopping leaving Gurdip alone and he took a moment to ring his sister Siri at Hilda and Jessica's.

Hilda answered and Gurdip replied with the prearranged code word as proof of identity before asking to speak to his sister. It was a necessary safeguard. The word was only known to the few of them involved. As it was made up it was not on record, and no other police knew of it nor where Siri and Ayesha had been taken.

Gurdip was keen to tell Siri what he was going to do, "As soon as it's safe I will go to the temple and speak to the Gurdwara Committee, I will explain all that has happened. They must allow your divorce. You have photographs?"

"I took pictures of each injury and Ronnie took them of my face the night I fled to his house. Hilda and Jessica have made a video diary with me of all that has happened. It's a record of all my beatings and how I have been treated by Pasha."

"That is good. Very good. I will need that."

"Have they caught Pasha yet? Do they know where he is?"

"The police are working on it but I have no news yet."

"I am wondering how long I must stay here. Oh, it's very pleasant and they are very kind but it is not the same as being home."

"Except we have no home now. There is nothing left."

"Then what will we do?"

"Ronnie and I are going to find a flat for us to share. We will extend our wish list so that you and Ayesha can come with us. As soon as Pasha is found."

"Ayesha should be starting school soon. She will need her education and I will need a job to provide for us."

"Can't you continue your studies?"

"I don't know. Pasha insisted I stay at home. I know now that was to control me. He doesn't believe in equality as our family does and as our religion dictates. I don't know if the education committee at the university will let me carry on with my training. I am supposed to have dropped out of the course."

"I'm sure that with the right input from the correct people they will let you resume. After all, it was your passion to become a nurse."

Siri sighed, "I know. But what of Parnani and Parnana?"

"I have heard that the police in Bradford are keeping a close watch on them. They should be safe, for now. As long as the surveillance continues."

"They cannot do that forever."

"No," Gurdip paused. "We will deal with that when and if it happens."

Katy had eaten her breakfast and grabbed her mug of tea and crossed to the window, where she peeped out trying not to be seen. The car was still there. Big Den came up beside her and looked out. "It may be nothing, Katy. Don't worry."

"But I do worry. I worry about what I saw and what these men want. I know they saw me when that girl was taken. They know I'm a witness. What they don't know is what else I have seen." Katy shuddered and Big Den put his arm around her.

"Don't. I'll be looking out for you, I promise."

"But you can't be with me all the time. Maybe I should move onto another town, start again. Get away from here."

"But you've got your own place from tomorrow and you have a good pitch. You have friends here. You'll be able to do anything you want. Besides…" he indicated the car, "it might not even be them. You don't know for sure."

"But it is the same car. Have you ever seen it parked here before? It's a bit up market for this road, don't you think?"

"There's only one way to find out."

"Den, no! Please. Don't get involved."

"But I am involved. Look we can't stay here all day. We have to get to work. We will leave together as usual and get into town. We will see what they do. Come on, grab your coat. Let's go."

Katy drank down the rest of her tea and put on her puffer jacket and her

Ugg boots that she had bought in the charity shop. They were warm and flat and if she needed to run in them she could. Reluctantly she followed Den out from the flat and down the stairs.

Mary was loading the boot of her car in the supermarket car park and was unaware that she was under the scrutiny of an Asian man wearing traditional Sikh clothes. She managed to get everything in and closed the trunk firmly. She foraged in her coat pocket for her car keys and unlocked the driver's door of her Ford Focus and eased herself into the seat. She was shocked when the passenger door opened and a strange Sikh man got in and sat beside her. She was about to scream when he spoke, "Please, do not be alarmed. I mean you no harm."

"Then what are you doing in my car?"

"I just want to speak to you. I know you are the wife of an important police officer. Do you think I would risk being arrested? This is about Gurdip Singh. He is staying with you, is he not?"

"Why would you think that?" said Mary aghast and still in shock.

"I have been following Gurdip's friend, Detective Constable Soper. He has been very careful but if I have found out where Gurdip is staying then so will Pasha. The man is relentless."

"Who are you?"

"Kalbant, Kalbant Singh. Now, would I tell you my name if I were any kind of threat?"

"But you have a knife?"

"That is a kirpan. It is part of my religious dress, a symbol like your cross that you wear around your neck."

"What do you want?"

"Pasha is cruel and out of control, using outdated ideology that bears no resemblance to the way we live in this country or that of our ancestors. His beliefs are akin to the Sharia Law of Muslims. We are not Muslims. We believe in love. His bloodlust has not been satisfied; he wants to destroy the whole family."

"Why are you telling me this?"

"Because…" Kalbant sighed. "It is wrong, many people have suffered already. He must be stopped but he has family friends who will join him and do his bidding. Gurdip's family is good. Pasha's bride, Siri, did not deserve the beatings she suffered at his hands. I can help."

"How can you help?"

"I have information. I know what Pasha has done. I will testify as a witness. I will speak to your husband."

"How do I know that this isn't a trick? To gain my trust and then…"

"In the name of our sacred Guru Nanak. I assure you I am telling you the truth. I can give you another name. My cousin, Ajeet. He has had a hand in these arson attacks and murders as has Pasha's immediate family, who have since returned to the Punjab. It is Pasha alone now, with Ajeet who are pursuing this vendetta."

"What do you expect me to do?"

"Tell your husband. Follow Ajeet. I understand Pasha is currently in Bradford hunting Siri's grandparents. He must be stopped."

"Where will he find Ajeet?"

"He lives in Twyning Road. Siri will know the number."

"And you? How will he find you?"

"I am in City Road. On the opposite side to the convenience store and off licence, which used to be Darleston's, next door to the medical centre." Mary went to speak again but Kalbant put up his hand, "No… tell your husband what I have said. The killing must stop."

Kalbant got out of Mary's car and walked away across the car park. Mary's hand was still shaking as she put her hand in her bag to get out her mobile phone and she dialled Greg's direct line.

Greg hurriedly moved to his desk from the window where he had been standing scrutinising the view opposite and was in the process of finishing off his Mars Bar thinking over what he'd just learned from Interpol regarding Jonas Rakowsky. He was deciding how to proceed when the phone jangled for attention. He grabbed the receiver and growled, "Allison." Then he heard Mary's voice and listened as he bumped heavily into his seat, his face creased in worry. He picked up a pen and scrawled on a notepad the names and addresses that Mary gave him. "Are you all right to drive home? I can send someone to take you and a car will follow you back. Thinking about it that may be a good idea anyway."

"Don't be silly, Greg. I'm perfectly capable of driving back."

"No. Stay put. Where are you?"

"Sainsbury's in Brindley Place, Five Ways."

"Wait there."

"But, Greg…"

"Do as I say. You never know if it's some sort of ruse. Pasha may not be in Bradford at all. He may be watching you, now. Stay there."

"But I've got frozen goods. They'll melt," protested Mary.

"I don't care. Please do as I ask."

Mary grumbled some more but Greg didn't allow her to come up with any further arguments. He put down the phone and marched out into the squad room in the outer office. He scanned the room. Soper was in, as was Josh Linton, Mark, Bill Rennie, Woodward, Taylor and Pooley.

"Taylor and Pooley. We have a lead on the arson attack and murders." Allison quickly explained what had transpired.

Ronnie looked concerned, "Is Mary, Mrs Allison all right, Chief?"

"For the moment. Pooley and Taylor get yourselves to Brindley Place. One of you drive Mrs Allison home, the other follow them and wait outside. Keep an eye on my house and keep a look out for anyone shadowing you. Go on, get going, now!" Pooley and Taylor scrambled up from their desks and hurried out. "Soper!"

"Yes, Chief?"

"Now, I know I said I didn't want you anywhere near this one, but I want you to go with Bill and check out these addresses. See what you can learn from Kalbant Singh and Ajeet Singh. You know what they both look like and be careful."

"Yes, Chief," they chorused. Ronnie jumped up hardly able to suppress the grin from manifesting on his face. Bill grabbed his jacket and the two went out after Pooley and Taylor.

"What about me?" asked Mark.

"You'll be with me. Something else has come up regarding the bodies' murders. Linton?"

"Yes, Chief?"

"Now that Bannen Sadler's dealt with, you hold the fort until we get back?"

"Yes, sir."

"Oh, and Linton?"

"Sir?"

"Phone Winson Green. Just check that they have put protocols in place to keep tabs on Bannen Sadler. I spoke to the governor's secretary after Holly came in but I have heard nothing back. It needs to be chased up."

"Yes, Chief." Josh picked up his phone as he watched Allison and Mark hurry out of the office.

Bill turned to Ronnie as they signed out a car and went into the car park. "Do you know where these bozos live?"

"More or less."

"Isn't Darlaston's where we sent in a specialist group to sort out a racial harassment case? BNP bullies or something…"

"Think that was before my time. But the newsagent has changed its name, now. It's KP News or something like that?"

"Sure? I thought KP was a brand of peanut."

"That, too. It's a convenience store and off licence. Do you know the way?"

"You can direct me. What's the parking like?"

"Terrible. But the pavement's wide enough to park a car. Shouldn't be a problem. Deliveries and so on always park outside. There's a money transfer place next door, odd name, 'I'm stitches' and a beauty parlour next to that."

"That is a funny name… 'I'm stitches'. What's that got to do with transferring money?"

"I have no idea."

"Okay, where to first?"

"Let's see if Mr Kalbant Singh's at home first."

"Righty, oh. Is there a back way in or do we have to go up the Hagley Road?"

"We can get on the A4040 that's City Road, by going through the jewellery quarter. We don't need to go the long way around. We need the higher end, at the junction of Dudley Road"

"Just shout directions, we'll get there."

Bill negotiated the ring roads and they were soon on their way. They turned into the top end of City Road from the junction with Dudley Road and Bill parked on the expanse of pavement outside the convenience store. They alighted, locked up and crossed the busy road in search of Kalbant Singh's house.

They passed the medical centre and walked up the path to number 7. Ronnie rapped on the door boldly and waited. The front of the house was ordinary with a big bay window. The wood surrounds needed painting and could have done with some fresh putty on the glazing.

Bill and Ronnie could hear a soft footfall as someone approached the door, which opened with a squeak. Kalbant Singh stood inside the threshold and looked at the two men on the doorstep. "Yes?" He studied Ronnie's face, "You are Gurdip's friend. I'm sorry I don't know your name. Please come in."

"DC Ronnie Soper."

"And DC Bill Rennie." They both flashed their warrant cards.

They stepped inside and he closed the door after them. They followed Kalbant down a pretty Victorian tiled passageway that looked spotlessly clean and freshly scrubbed. They entered a cosy kitchen diner where he invited them to sit.

Ronnie perched on the edge of the couch whereas Bill sat back and sank into it.

Kalbant stood, "Some refreshment, gentlemen?"

Ronnie nodded, "A cup of tea would be good. Thank you."

Bill agreed, "Tea would be great, please. Milk no sugar."

"Same for me," added Ronnie.

Kalbant inclined his head graciously and disappeared into the kitchen. The kettle could be heard boiling as Bill tried to move himself forward in his seat. He grunted as he tried to lift himself out of the sunken dip in the sofa and finally managed to sit on the firm edge of the settee as Ronnie had done. "Very comfortable, if you can stretch out and watch the tele but not so good for sitting upright."

Ronnie laughed. "One too many pies, Bill I think."

Bill grinned, "Cheeky monkey. Just you wait till you get older."

Kalbant returned with a tray and set it on the table. He passed out the mugs. "You are lucky you caught me in. I have to be in work this afternoon."

"What is it you do?" asked Ronnie taking a swig of his beverage as Bill took out his notebook and pen.

"I'm an accountant."

"Where do you work?"

"Handsworth. First Choice Accountants. It's my morning off."

Ronnie nodded agreeably, "You said you had some information for us."

Kalbant nodded. "It is a sorry state of affairs. We are not violent people. We believe we should live a creative and practical life of truthfulness, fidelity, self-control and purity. Spirituality and morality are at its core. We strive to be at one with God. What Pasha is doing goes against everything I have been brought up to believe."

"What is it that Pasha's doing?"

Kalbant's face creased in disgust, "He is breaking all the fundamental rules of marriage. Men and women are created equal and once wed are one soul in two bodies. Domestic violence such as he perpetrated against Siri is abhorrent and wrong. She has every right to walk away. There is no divorce in Sikhism except in very few circumstances, domestic violence and cruelty are one. Pasha has a twisted view of marriage. He thinks she is his property to do with as he wants. He feels humiliated that she has left. This so-called honour killing where he feels Siri should die is bad enough but to annihilate the whole family!" Kalbant was becoming quite emotional.

"You clearly feel very strongly about this," said Ronnie at a loss for what to say and feeling his own anger rising regarding Siri's treatment.

"It is not our way. It is murder."

"You said you had information?" pressed Ronnie.

"Pasha and his brothers set fire to the family home when he could not find Siri."

"How do you know this?"

"I was there when the discussion took place. I stated my dissension then. His brothers have since returned to India. It was then he tried to involve me and his other cousins like Ajeet."

"Why didn't you report it, then?"

"I couldn't believe he was serious. I honestly thought it was all hot air, spoken in anger, but then I heard what had happened to Gurdip's house and family and regretted not making a bigger stand and yes, I am sorry I didn't speak up." Kalbant put his head in his hands. "My wife warned me about him."

"Your wife?"

"She's a doctor in Dudley Road Hospital."

"What did she say?"

"She had heard rumours from Pasha's sister. His sister told her that she hoped Pasha would be different this time."

"What did she mean by that?"

"Apparently, there was a girl in the Punjab. Pasha pursued her but she was unwilling to become his bride. That girl died."

Ronnie and Bill exchanged a look. Ronnie continued, "Tell me about Ajeet."

"Ah, Ajeet. He is a weak man, easily led. Pasha asked us both to join him in his vendetta. I refused. Ajeet didn't. I understand he was behind the death of Gurdip's father and both of them responsible for the arson attack on another property." Ronnie bristled as he thought of his own home. "I am now being more careful about my own safety and home. Pasha is a cold-blooded murderer. His way is not ours. He is relentless. I know he is even going after Siri's grandparents in Bradford. The family in the Punjab have already been dealt with by Pasha's brothers. It must be stopped. I will speak out; anything you need, to bring him to justice."

"You are prepared to testify?"

"I am."

"Even against Ajeet?"

"You will need more than my word to prosecute him, but yes. If necessary."

"We will be visiting his house when we have left here."

"Is there anything else you can tell us?"

Kalbant shook his head, "I don't think so. But if I do, I will call you. I am not afraid to speak up."

Ronnie drained his mug, took out a card and signalled to Bill to rise who hurriedly drank down the rest of his tea. "Thank you. If you hear or think of something else, no matter how small or unimportant you think it is, please call this number." He passed the card to Kalbant who acknowledged with a nod and followed them to the front door.

"I am in the process of ordering a security camera to monitor the activity around my house, just in case. I know we have to be careful."

"I think that's an excellent idea," said Ronnie. "Goodbye and thank you."

Bill chuntered his thanks and the two left.

9

BANNEN SADLER SAT IN HIS cell in Winson Green. He wasn't used to being cooped up. He needed his freedom. Waiting on remand gave him time to plan. He had an opportunity to converse with a lawyer that had been provided for him and he was none too happy with the choice. First off she was a woman, second off she was of Asian extraction. But she was beautiful. He believed it was someone's perverse sense of humour that had meant his case had been assigned to her. He had no idea who else was on this wing but what he did know was that most of them were from an ethnic minority of Anglo-Indians or of West Indian Caribbean or African heritage. Here, Bannen was in the minority.

They were allowed out of their cells for one hour of exercise outside per day, weather permitting, but Bannen was reluctant to do this. He didn't want to mix with them anymore than he wanted to share a cell with one. Rumours spread through the wing and it was soon common knowledge that Bannen was accused of a string of murders involving British Asians. How they knew was uncertain, whether a guard had let it slip or it was something else, his photo in the local press or on television, but they knew. Bannen was feeling very unsafe and had demanded to be moved to another prison. That request had been denied.

Reluctantly he got up from his bunk as the guard opened his cell door and ordered him out. The guard prodded him in the back to make him move more quickly until he reached the exercise area and then he stood back as Bannen joined others on remand preparing to jog or walk around the yard.

Bannen Sadler squinted up at the sky where bubbling leaden clouds were gathering, sometimes impinging on the warmth and light of the sun. He took a deep breath and began to jog lightly around the space. Others walked and some ran. The guard yelled at them to move in the same direction before he retreated to the wall to chat with a fellow prison officer. Two Asians came running up and slowed to Bannen's pace and deliberately jarred his arms and shoulders before sprinting past. This happened several times much to Bannen's annoyance but he managed to stop himself from bursting out with a load of expletives. He heard more footsteps running behind him and deliberately stopped with his elbows jutting out and felt a burning pain in his lower back and another higher up, which made him double over as a group of men ran past. Bannen dropped to the ground and a few stray feet kicked him as they ran or walked by.

A few minutes passed before the guards seemed to notice and ran to Bannen's aid. It was too late; Bannen Sadler was dead.

Allison and Mark were studying their board of photographs of victims and notes in the squad room and collating what they knew so far. Allison grumbled, "We haven't got very much. We need to bring Mrs Rakowsky in, and interview her again. I'm sure she knows more than she's saying."

Mark chipped in, "I feel the Big Issue vendors are a promising link. We know that one of them is a potential witness to the first suitcase murder or at least its disposal. Then there was that anonymous phone call."

"Lots of little pieces of the puzzle but nothing we can run with. We know Jonas Rakowsky was involved in something either unknowingly or with the help of some undercover agent but which agency and who? All we have are the initials AW…"

"I think we should pay another visit to Martyn Kelland and West End Products."

"Agreed. What about the female victim? What have we got?"

"Next to nothing. What did the PM reveal?"

Allison picked up a report from the desk, "Johnny estimated her age between nineteen and twenty-one. It looked as if she had been physically and sexually abused; there were vaginal and anal tears and bruising and dried blood between her legs."

"Raped?"

"Most certainly. There was no other explanation."

"DNA?"

"Semen was found in every orifice; we will know more when the results come through."

"So, what's next?"

"We bring in Shirley Rakowsky see if there is anything else she remembers."

"And Martyn Kelland?"

"We'll pay him another call."

Clement Pugh was panicking. It was hard to hide a dismembered head, hands and feet. He had managed to find a heavy duty holdall to hide the plastic wrapped body parts and had put them in refrigerated storage but he lived in fear of it being discovered. He knew the parts would slowly decompose even in these circumstances and only last for three to four weeks. He needed to freeze them or get rid of them. Time would soon be running out.

Clement had been unable to dispose of the pieces as other workers in the funeral home always seemed to be around whenever he had an opportunity to move them to a suitable casket for cremation. He had been assigned a young apprentice to learn the embalming process and she was more than enthusiastic, staying on late and following Clement around trying to learn as much as possible. Clement was finding it hard to shake her off.

There was nothing for it, he would have to return later that night and get rid of the bag somehow. There were two cremations scheduled for the next morning. Clement would try and place the body parts in one of the caskets. He locked up as usual and said good night to Gilly Sanders who waited for him and walked with him to the bus stop, chattering and asking questions and he was forced to get onto the bus with her. Maybe next time he would drive, he thought to himself. But then, he might be expected to give her a lift. No that wouldn't work.

He would be back later.

Kelly's Nightclub and Bar was getting busy. The hostesses were all in and sitting at their usual tables. Lionel the resident singer was crooning "If you go away." Two of the hostesses were dancing with customers, the others were waiting for company.

Martyn Kelland and his two henchmen, Marcus Paulson and Bernie Carter, came into the front bar, strode to the dance floor and surveyed the girls at their tables. They conferred together and walked back to the bar to get drinks before sitting in the Bistro part of the club.

Connie the petite Chinese waitress sashayed across in her cute uniform, of black satin shorts, waistcoat, stiffly starched Lloyd George collar, bow tie and cuffs, fishnets and a little bowler hat. She carried the menus. "You like drink first?" she asked with a smile as she passed a copy to each of them.

Martyn asked for the wine list and watched her as she wiggled back to the bar and picked one up. She passed it to him and he caught her hand. Connie stopped and frowned. "Say… are you for hire?"

Connie shook his hand off, "I am *not* a hostess."

"Pity. What time do you get off? We could have our own party."

"That's not my job. You want wine or not?"

"Wine not!" said Martyn with a laugh enjoying her discomfort. He glanced at the red wine section. "A bottle of Primitivo, please. What do you have that's non-alcoholic?"

Connie shrugged, "You mean wine or beer?"

"Anything?"

Connie pointed to a part of the menu, displaying soft and non-alcoholic drinks. "You look and choose, I get wine." She took the opportunity to make her escape as Martyn went to pat her bottom. He eyed her lasciviously as she made her way back to the bar.

"She would be a great acquisition," said Kelland watching her work at the bar. He sighed, "But, most likely to be missed. The hostesses though… they may be worth a shot."

"I think that maybe a step too far," said Bernie Carter. "Remember this place was in the news not long ago with missing girls and hostesses. It would attract too much attention."

"Shame. There are some choice women here. Tell me, when is the next consignment arriving?"

"I heard from Bogdan, earlier. He is en route with twenty girls. Three sixteen-year-olds, newly released from care in Bulgaria, who are looking forward to working in the UK." He laughed cruelly.

"And the others?" asked Marcus.

"Mail order brides. Or at least that's what they believe," chortled Kelland.

Connie returned with the drinks and set them on the table and sashayed back to the bar where Josh Linton waited. He had come in for a drink especially to see Connie.

Across the dance floor Alex Wallace formerly known as The Chameleon but now, special agent with MRF, Military Reaction Force, sat with his commander, Roy Chapman. They were covertly watching Kelland and his men. Suddenly, Alex ducked his head down and moved rapidly, turning his seat away from the bar.

"What? What is it?" asked Roy.

"Mark Stringer has walked in."

"Stringer? Who's he?"

"You remember? The detective sergeant? He was instrumental in the case of getting your granddaughter back. His girlfriend is Beth. She was the one who helped with Cathy's escape. Now do you remember?"

"Right. What are you worried about?"

"He knows me… and it could be dangerous."

Clement Pugh had returned to the undertakers under cover of darkness and let himself in. He secured the door and ensured the blinds were down so that no light would escape. Working only with a torch he went into the refrigerated room and retrieved the bag. The cremations planned for the next morning were in the centre of the chapel. He examined them carefully and found that they had been fully sealed. It could only mean enthusiastic Gilly had done this, thinking she was helping him.

Clement dithered, he didn't have time to unseal them and daren't risk causing any damage. There was nowhere he could hide the body parts. He swore softly. He needed to get rid of the bag somehow… but where?

Clement was in a blind panic. He had been unable to get the key to the private crematorium yet… but he would… His face was covered in a slick film of sweat and he was turning redder by the minute as he weighed up his options. He could hang on until another suitable death came in and he would do what he had before, hide them in the coffin before cremation or burial if the casket was to be sealed. But then he didn't know when that would be and already the parts were degrading even though kept refrigerated. He could take them home and put them in his freezer, but he didn't fancy that idea or he could get rid of them somewhere else. But where? Perhaps he could weigh the bag down and dump it in the water somewhere.

Clement wasn't thinking straight. He could try Edgbaston reservoir but that would be tricky. There was a boating club there and it was a popular place, what if it came back to the surface? No. That was too close to home.

Clement quickly exited the Chapel of Rest and locked up. He slung the bag in the boot of his car and drove off. He needed to do some research. His heart was racing like an adolescent girl on a scary, adventure park thrill ride. Clement was getting himself in more and more of a state. He made a decision and headed for home. His deep freeze would have to do until he had a better idea. Clement quickly made his way to his house in Stanmore Road.

A police car pulled in behind him as he drove along the Bristol Road. Clement kept looking in his rear-view mirror. Now, was not the time to go over the speed limit or attract attention to himself.

The car appeared to keep pace with him and Clement was becoming more and more anxious especially as the car followed him up Lee Bank to Five Ways. Fortunately, when he reached the roundabout the police car swerved off to the left towards Moseley and Clement breathed a huge sigh of relief. He cruised up the busy Hagley Road and turned off before the parade of shops, where the Hagley Road divided from Sandon Road. He turned into Stanmore Road and parked in his driveway. He opened up his garage before wrestling with the large bag in his boot and took it into his garage, which housed his deep freeze. Clement shoved it inside and covered the bag with frozen items and cuts of meat. Satisfied it could not be seen, he locked up the garage and his car and went indoors.

Clement drew the curtains in the front room. It was cold so he lit the gas fire, which hissed and spat in the grate with its register plate and flue travelling up the chimney. It was getting late but Clement settled in front of his computer screen and booted it up, pulling up a Google search for stretches of water in the West Midlands. He found seven but dismissed them all as they were places of attraction for visitors and just too close to home; so, he looked further afield and came upon Dosthill Quarry near Tamworth.

Clement pulled up a map and directions. That settled it. He would go tonight, when it was quieter as long as he could get in. He thought he had better eat something first. It was going to be a long night and he didn't see himself getting much sleep.

Kelly's Nightclub, Bistro and Bar was getting busier as more and more customers arrived. The hostess tables were all occupied. Lionel, the resident singer, was singing a Jack Jones number from his easy listening repertoire. The small dance floor was crowded with couples smooching to the honeyed tones of the singer.

Josh and Mark were standing in the crowded front bar waiting for a table to become available while Connie and another waitress were working feverishly to complete orders. Josh had taken a shine to Connie and had been frequenting the club for the past six months ever since the case of the disappearing girls from the club. He was going to attempt to ask Connie out having discovered that there was no one special in her life and after being egged on by Mark, Josh was feeling bolder about getting a date.

"So, are you hanging on till chuck out time?" asked Mark.

"That's the only time I'll be able to speak to her alone," Josh replied.

"I remember those days," said Mark with a grin. "Hope you don't expect me to hang around till the bitter end? I have a home to go to and a fiancée. Besides it's getting somewhat crowded in …" He stopped as he gestured around the club and caught sight of Martyn Kelland. His eyes narrowed as he studied Kelland's companions. There was something familiar about the two men with him. His curiosity piqued he wondered what they were doing here when he realised they were connected to West End Products. *Of course*, he reasoned in his head, *it could mean nothing but on the other hand…* Mark caught Connie's eye, "Say, Connie, have those blokes been in here before?" He gestured with his head, "Over there. At that table?"

Connie shook her head, "Not seen them before, no. They cheeky men."

"Cheeky?" asked Josh.

"Yes, him on this side. Wanted me to party with him." Josh bristled. "He treat me like hostess. I told him, I not one."

"Thanks," said Mark who turned to Josh, "maybe I will stick around a little longer."

Josh looked puzzled, "Why?"

Mark began to explain and Josh nodded in understanding. "Connie? When you serve them again, listen in to what they're saying, will you?"

Josh put his hand on Mark's arm, "Hang on a minute. You don't want to get Connie involved in something that might be dangerous."

"No, of course not. Just to report back anything she might hear."

Connie interrupted, "It no problem. I do."

Josh looked at her, "You just be careful."

"I be careful. I got two strong men here."

"Who are they, then?" said Mark cheekily and Connie laughed.

"I'll do, Mr Mark. I'll do."

Clement Pugh had driven the ten miles from Birmingham to Dosthill Quarry and began to have serious misgivings. It also looked like some sort of tourist attraction offering all sorts of activities, from cliff jumping and walks to cold water swimming and diving. Clement wasn't sure that it was the best place to dump the parts. He began to sweat, this wouldn't do. It wouldn't do at all. A diver could easily become curious about a weighted bag, maybe even bring it to the surface and open it. Then what? No, he had to find some other way and he didn't have long to work out a plan.

Clement hopped back in his car and drove back to his home in Stanmore Road. Once again the bag was unloaded and returned to his deep freeze. This time he wasn't so careful about hiding it amongst his frozen produce. Clement needed to do much more research. Dosthill Quarry was much too risky. And he knew another thing he needed to do. He had to put some kind of lock on his deep freeze. He couldn't risk anyone peeping in there. Now, how could he do that? It was another problem he would have to solve.

In Kelly's, the customers were beginning to thin out. Mark was trying to be careful not to be spotted by Kelland. He whispered in Josh's ear that he was moving to the back bar to be out of view. Josh remained where he was keeping a safe eye on Connie.

Mark crossed the dance floor that was now almost empty. The DJ had put on some soft easy listening music while the band packed up. He passed Alex Wallace who had his back to him and Roy Chapman still sitting at their table but initially he didn't take any notice of either of the men who were chatting with one of the hostesses, Zelda.

Mark walked up to the back bar and ordered an alcohol-free Estrella as it made a change from Kaliber. He leaned on the bar and studied those left in the club. There was something familiar about the man burying his face in his drink and who seemed to be trying to be as unobtrusive as possible. So, Mark's suspicions were aroused. He attempted to watch the man without being obvious as his brain went into overdrive trying to remember who he was. He almost snapped his fingers, of course he knew him. He recalled how the man had been an important part of defeating the Islamist bombers in Bradford and the fact that he had met him at his ex-wife's wedding in Ironbridge. He was almost tempted to go across and join him when his sixth sense warned him that maybe there was a reason for the guy to avoid him. What the heck was he called? Inexplicably, the name Alex popped into his head. The brain was a wonderful thing. Yes, it was Alex and they were on the same side… he thought.

Mark took one of his cards from his pocket and scrawled on the back, "Call me." He wrote his private number on the back. Mark carried his drink back across the dance floor towards Josh at the front bar He paused at the table and smoothly placed his card in front of Alex who feigned surprise but engaged in eye contact and in recognition he nodded. Mark walked on by and re-joined Josh at the bar.

Connie was at Kelland's table clearing glasses and bottles. She accepted a generous tip from the man with a smile and exchanged some words. Kelland resisted patting her on her bottom and Connie swung away with her famous wiggle.

Connie arrived at the bar and began sorting the wine glasses and tumblers to load in the glass washer and left the other waitress to wipe down the bar surface and deal with last orders. She then strolled to the bistro tables to wipe them down and all the while she kept an ear out for any conversation she could discern from Kelland's table.

Mark turned to Josh and asked, "Well? Has she said yes? I got out of your way to let you ask her."

Josh beamed. He was grinning from ear to ear. "Yes, Monday is her night off and I am taking her out for a meal."

"Let's hope you don't have to work," said Mark with pursed lips and raised eyebrows.

"Don't say that. I am booking Monday night off. Someone else can take their turn."

"Fair enough. And congratulations, she's a lovely lady."

"I know," said Josh beaming like a Cheshire cat. "I feel like I've won the lottery."

The bar had completely thinned out. Kelland and his men got up to leave. Kelland glanced across to the bar to raise his hand in goodbye to Connie when he spotted Mark and frowned.

Mark caught his eye and acted surprised lifting his hand in acknowledgement. The men gathered themselves and left without a backward glance. Just then Connie returned and put more used champagne flutes into the glass washer. She popped her head above the counter, "Have men gone?" Mark assented and Connie continued, "I have bad feeling about men. They no good."

"Why? What did you hear?"

"Not hear much. Something about Bogdan and girls from Bulgaria and Russia. Think that's what one said. They talk about girls gone missing from Kelly's."

"Sounds suspicious."

"I not like go home. That man said, he wanted me to party. Feel afraid."

"No need, Connie," said Josh. "I will take you home. You'll be safe with me."

"Thank you." Connie smiled and looked around the nearly empty club. "Men go onto Rainbow. Wanted me to follow. They know I gamble sometimes."

"Well, tonight you're not."

"No. I stick close to you, Josh."

Josh beamed again. "Right, get your coat. Let the others finish up. I'm taking you back, right now."

Mark looked across at the dance floor and tables and saw Alex and his companion disappearing out of the back bar, which led to the dressing rooms, Gents' and back door to the car park.

"What is it?" asked Josh.

"I'm not sure," said Mark. "I hope nothing."

10

CLEMENT PUGH HAD HIS BACK against the wall in the embalming room at the Chapel of Rest. The thugs had returned and were threatening him again.

"Be prepared," said the man with the long grey ponytail. "We will be delivering another package at the end of the week."

Clement Pugh's eyes rolled wildly. He protested nervously, "I can't do this anymore. It's not as easy as you think. You will have to find someone else."

"And you better think hard. If you don't want your dirty little secret to come out then you had better think again."

"I can't," whined Clement. "I haven't been able to deal with the last one yet. It's only a matter of time before I'm discovered. I am trying, honestly. Please… find someone else."

"There isn't anyone else. Only you. Remember I can ruin you, just like that," and he snapped his fingers in front of Clement's face making him flinch.

Clement could feel his heartbeat rising rapidly as if he was running a marathon. He gasped aloud before making one final plea, "Please. No. I'm begging you."

The man with the ponytail removed a knife and held it at Clement's throat, drawing a pin prick of blood "You don't get a choice, Mr Pugh. We'll be back on Friday with a new delivery."

The other man who had been keeping a look out growled, "Hurry up. There's someone coming."

The ponytailed man, Marcus Paulson, shoved Clement roughly against the wall and hurriedly secreted his knife. The two men walked out from the embalming room passing a grieving family who were gathered around an open coffin with young Gilly Sanders who was murmuring something sympathetic to them. The family took no notice of the men and Gilly only caught a back view of them. She apologised politely to the family and went to find Clement in the embalming room who had slid down the wall and was clasping his chest. Spittle drooled on his lips and his breathing was ragged.

Gilly ran to him, "Mr Pugh? Mr Pugh are you all right?"

His face was turning grey and his lips blue. He was wheezing and a phlegm rattle could be heard in his throat. Gilly took out her mobile phone and dialled nine, nine, nine. "Ambulance please. It's urgent I think my boss is having a heart attack." She gave the address and looked around her finally removing her cardigan to use as a pillow for his head as she attempted to make Clement comfortable. The undertaker looked as if he needed a defibrillator. There wasn't one at the funeral home. Dead people didn't need resuscitating and even if there was Gilly didn't know how to use one. She had seen demonstrations of how to do CPR but didn't feel confident enough to try and she was afraid of doing any more damage and as for the kiss of life, well for Gilly that wasn't an option.

Sirens could be heard approaching. Gilly left Clement momentarily and exited the room and went outside to wave the ambulance down, but it was too late. Clement Pugh was already dead.

Allison and Mark were sitting in Interview Room 3 with Mrs Shirley Rakowsky who had a steaming cup of coffee in front of her. Allison identified himself and Mark, and the name of the uniformed copper standing at the door.

Shirley dabbed at her nose with a fine lawn linen hankie, "I don't know why I am here. I've told you everything I know."

"It's just routine Mrs Rakowsky."

"I've told you it's Shirley. Do I need a lawyer?"

"Do you think you need a lawyer?"

"I don't know. Do I?"

Mrs Rakowsky… Shirley… you are not under arrest. We merely need to go through a few more questions. Sometimes people remember things they haven't said before. It is, I assure you, as I said, just routine."

"Well, I don't know what more I can tell you, really."

"You said that Jonas had not been himself. That you felt something was troubling him."

"Yes. He was out a lot at meetings and very nervy whenever the phone rang."

"Do you know why?"

"No. As I said before he was always very secretive. He didn't like me to press him."

"But, weren't you curious? Just a little bit?" Shirley blushed and looked down. "What is it?"

"I don't know why but…" she bit her lip. "I thought he might be having an affair."

"Why would you think that?"

"The hours he kept. The fact he had two phones. He said one was for work and one was personal. He wanted to keep them separate." "Surely, if you thought Jonas was having an affair, you would have been suspicious of all his phone calls and might I suggest you may have even tried to listen in on occasion?"

Shirley coloured up again and took a sip of her coffee, "I'm not proud of it, but yes. I did."

"And what did you overhear?" Shirley hesitated. "Please, it might be important. And you do want us to find Jonas' killer, don't you?"

Shirley sighed heavily, "He would get calls late at night on the landline from someone he called, Al. It was as if he was reporting to him. Giving him information. He had discovered his business was being used for something else."

"Go on."

"One night I picked up the phone in the hallway to listen." Allison and

Mark exchanged a glance. "Some guy was briefing him on what he had to do."

"What do you mean?" quizzed Allison.

"He was talking about breaking a ring."

"A ring?"

"He wanted more evidence to prosecute Martyn Kelland. That's all I can tell you."

"Did you ask him about it?"

"I didn't dare or he'd know I had been listening in. I was just relieved it wasn't another woman. Jonas' business partner was doing something very wrong and using the company as a front and Jonas was going to put a stop to it. It was after that phone call he went missing."

"Is there anything else?"

Shirley shook her head, "I don't think so…" She thought for a moment and added, "Jonas mentioned something about a man called Bogdan?"

"Bogdan?" said Mark quickly and raised his eyebrows. Allison looked at Mark sharply.

"Yes. Some Bulgarian that was bringing a special consignment across. But I don't know what. I'm afraid that's all I can remember."

"Thank you, Shirley. If you remember anything else, anything at all, please call me," said Allison and he rose to let her out. The constable accompanied her to the station entrance.

Mark and Allison stepped into the corridor and watched her go.

"Do you believe her?" asked Mark.

"I do. That's what she must have been holding back when we saw her at the house. Now tell me, how do you know the name Bogdan?"

"Not much to tell you, really. Just an overheard conversation."

At that moment they were interrupted by Maddie who said, "Sir, there's a young woman on the line who wants to talk to about some type of threat. She will only speak to you."

Allison turned to Mark, "We'll pick this up later."

Gilly Sanders was answering the questions the uniformed policeman was putting to her as the paramedics removed Clement Pugh's body. "What can you tell me about Mr Pugh?"

"Not much. I've only just started working here. He's not one for communicating much. Says what he has to and no more."

"Do you have an address for him?"

"It will be with the secretary in the personnel files. She's in the main building in Reception. This is all very sad."

"Why is that?"

"Mr Pugh was starting to teach me all his techniques. He was very good at his job." The policeman looked questioningly. "He does all the embalming and lays the bodies out. He was great at making them look as if they had just fallen asleep. I was learning from him."

"Does Mr Pugh have anyone at home?"

"I don't know. I think he might have been a widower. I haven't heard him talk about a wife or family."

"That'll be easy to check. Who else was here at the time?"

"Um… a family, the Andersons, came to view their son's body in the Chapel of Rest. He had died very suddenly, a brain aneurysm. So sad." Gilly shook her head as the copper began to put his notebook away. "Oh, yes. Two men were leaving. I don't know who they were. This was just before Mr Pugh … er… collapsed."

"Can you describe them?"

"I didn't see their faces. But one was very tall, thickset. He had a long grey ponytail down his back."

"And the other?"

Gilly shook her head, "Not as tall but looked as if he worked out, pumped iron or whatever you call it and he was wearing a hoodie. I think he had gingery hair but I'm not a hundred percent."

"Thank you, Miss…?"

"Sanders. Gilly Sanders."

"Where can we contact you if we need to speak to you again?" Gilly gave him her phone number and the policeman nodded and bade her goodbye.

Gilly slumped down to the floor. The shock was just beginning to set in.

Allison and Mark stood in the squad room studying the board of photographs and post it notes with links regarding the suitcase murders. Allison started to quiz Mark. "What did you think about Shirley Rakowsky?"

"I thought she was telling the truth."

"Been a damn sight easier if she'd told us from the beginning," grumbled Allison. "So, what is it with this Bogdan? Bulgarian name, isn't it?"

"Mark rubbed his chin, "It is and as I said, I have heard it before."

"Tell me everything."

Mark began to explain about his evening at Kelly's Wine Bar and what Connie had overheard.

"So, Kelland was talking about this Bogdan with his men?"

"He was."

"I believe we need to keep our eyes on Kelland and his enterprise. I've a funny feeling about this."

"Sir?"

"Yes, Mark?"

"What did the girl on the phone want?"

"I don't know. She'd hung up before I answered… She'll ring again."

"Can't you ring her back."

"Tried that! Did the old 1471 and discovered it was a phone in the city centre not a private number."

Allison snorted and shook his head so his jowls slapped together. Mark tried not to laugh. "What?"

"Nothing."

Allison patted his stomach, "Cost me a lot of money that has. But… needs must."

"Sir?"

"I'm going on a diet. The waistband on my trousers is getting too tight." Allison stared at his sergeant, "Not got anything to say?"

"No, sir," said Mark wondering where this was all leading.

"Just as well. I don't pretend it will be easy but Cally is getting married in the spring and I don't intend to walk her down the aisle like this. It's about time I trimmed up. And before you say anything I don't want it spread around and I am not forsaking my Mars Bars. I'll just limit them."

"How are you going to do it?"

"I've already got the books from Slimming World and given them to Mary. She'll monitor everything for me. No need for meetings and all that rubbish. And no cracks from you either. I'll count the Mars Bars as my daily syns or whatever they call them"

"Yes, sir," said Mark uncertain as what to say.

"Anyway, enough of that claptrap. Think we'll pay another visit to West End Products and speak to Mr Kelland again. Then, back to the Big Issue distribution centre. See if we can find that girl."

The phone interrupted them and Allison's expression changed, "Where? We'll be there in fifteen minutes." He turned to Mark as he grabbed his coat off the hook. "Get your coat. We're leaving now."

"Sir?"

"Stanmore Road. Some bloke who's pegged it has got the head, hands and feet of a young woman in his deep freeze."

"Ours?"

"More than likely. Let's go."

Allison and Mark left Lloyd House and made their way through the traffic up to Five Ways and the Hagley Road. Although busy, vehicles on the thoroughfare were moving quickly. They sped on past The Ivy Bush with its group of stores and then, the Quality Inn on the corner of Saint Augustine's Road and towards the small parade of shops and turned off to Stanmore Road.

They saw the house immediately with police cars outside, lights flashing and the arrival of the Forensic team in their whites and parked behind them. Allison hopped out fairly nimbly for a man of his size and approached the youngster in uniform who was keeping nosy passers-by away.

Allison flashed his warrant card but the youngster, Luke Chappell, knew who he was and waved them both through. Allison put on gloves and foot covers as he moved towards the garage where the attention seemed to be centred. A plastic sheet was on the floor with a holdall resting on it with the zipper undone. Allison peered inside and saw the bagged head of a young woman with filmed over eyes staring out and dismembered hands and feet, also encased in clear plastic He tried to suppress the acid rising to his throat. He noted where someone else had spewed up by the hedgerow. "Need to get this to Hurst as soon as possible. See if it's a match for our girl. Has anyone checked the house yet?"

"SOCOs are in there now," said a female police officer, Cherry Keith.

Allison nodded to Mark, "We'll get inside now. Have a look see what we can find." They entered Clement Pugh's house wondering what they would discover. Was he a murderer or was it something else, Allison wondered? He barked an order at Mark. "Get onto the station. Get Pooley or Taylor to look up everything they can find out about Clement Pugh, his place of work, any record. Oh, and check his financials."

Ronnie and Bill Rennie were in Twyning Road watching the house of Ajeet Singh. They had tried calling on him before but he never seemed to be at home so now they had decided to sit outside, close to his house in an unmarked car and wait. After all he had to come home at some point or so they thought.

"You know what this man looks like, don't you?" said Bill.

"Yes. I think so. He's a bit on the plump side, with a doughy face."

"Tells me a lot."

"Not too tall, around five foot six or seven. Small eyes."

"What we gonna do when we see him?"

"Watch him. See if he goes anywhere and follow him."

"And if he doesn't?"

"Then we'll go knocking again and pull him in. We have Kalbant's statement. That will be enough for questioning. We need to get a handle on Pasha. He's the one responsible for it all."

"And with a bit of luck this Ajeet might sing like a bird. And with even more luck this may be our bird waddling along now."

Ronnie peered to see where Bill was pointing and nodded, "That's him."

"What do you want to do?"

"Let's wait a while and watch."

They settled back in their seats and kept an eye on Ajeet's house and waited.

Ten minutes passed and Bill yawned, "If we sit here much longer I'll have trouble getting up." He leaned back and closed his eyes.

"Hold that thought," said Ronnie. "Our man's on the move."

Ajeet emerged swinging a bunch of keys. He walked to a Volkswagen Yaris parked at the kerb, looked around him, opened the driver's door and settled in the seat. He pulled out from his parking spot and drove out into Dudley Road.

Ronnie tapped Bill on his shoulder and urged, "Wake up. I'm going to follow him."

Allison sat in his office with Mark. He was on the phone to Hurst. "Well, is it or…"

"It is," affirmed Hurst. The cuts match perfectly. They belong to our girl. Do you want me to take fingerprints?"

"Are you able to do that?"

"Of course. I'll scan them and email them across and you can check them against your data base. And one more thing."

"Yes?"

"Her vital organs have been removed."

"What?"

"Heart, lungs, kidneys and liver, pre-mortem."

"Why?"

"Obvious answer is someone killed her to harvest her organs."

Allison breathed in sharply. This was something he was not expecting and again he felt the taste of bile in his throat.

"Thanks, Johnny." Allison replaced the phone in its cradle and looked ahead thoughtfully. "Mark what do we have on Martyn Kelland? And can you pull up all known associates and financials? And while you're about it, see if you can learn anything about the black market selling of body organs. It seems our girl had them removed prior to death."

Mark nodded and left Allison to get to his PC.

Allison picked up his pen and began to doodle some notes on a pad. Who was this AW? How was he linked to Jonas Rakowsky? How was Clement Pugh involved? And why was a Big Issue seller so frightened she would not come forward and just left anonymous messages? Allison scratched his head and frowned. More puzzling was the illegal trade of body organs. Was this a one off for a specific person or something even more sinister?

His phone rang.

"Yes?"

"Sir, we have been following Ajeet out of Birmingham and it looks like he's heading for the M1. What do you want us to do?" asked Ronnie.

"Sounds like he's off to join Pasha in Bradford. Stick with him. If he turns off onto the M62. You'll have your answer. I'll ring West Yorkshire Police. They are watching Gurdip's grandparents' house, but if this Ajeet is on his way there it seems likely he's meeting up with Pasha and an attack will be imminent. Stay with him and keep me informed. I'll get you some backup if required. With a bit of luck, we might get the bastard very soon."

"Sir." Ronnie ended the call.

Allison replaced the receiver and reached in his drawer. He needed his chocolate fix and opened his middle drawer where he kept his stash. He counted the bars staring temptingly at him. Could he manage to limit himself to just three a day? He would have to try. He needed to trim up for the wedding or get a new suit. The one in his wardrobe was now far too tight. He sighed and grabbed one of the Mars Bars and slammed the drawer shut. Mary had suggested hiring a suit and Allison thought it might just come to that especially if Cally and her fiancé decided that morning dress was to be the order of the day for the principals officiating at the wedding.

Allison peeled back the paper on his bar and sunk his teeth into the yielding sweetness and a look of pure pleasure crossed his rugged features. His tongue whipped out to catch a strand of caramel that had stretched from his lips and he sighed contentedly as he munched, putting all thoughts of a diet out of his head.

11

AJEET WAS BLISSFULLY UNAWARE THAT an unmarked police car was tailing him as he was following his Sat Nav instructions, which told him that he would arrive at his destination in two hours and nineteen minutes. He would have travelled one hundred and ninety-nine miles. Ajeet popped a piece of gum in his mouth and chewed. The minty taste refreshed his mouth and calmed him somewhat. But he couldn't still the fluttering beat of his heart as he reasoned with himself.

Pasha was his cousin and the rest of his family had since returned home. Pasha was reliant on Ajeet carrying out his wishes but Ajeet was only helping Pasha because of his own fear of the man. He didn't like violence and he was increasingly unhappy at being involved in the persecution of Gurdip's family. He felt shame and guilt over the death of Balbir, Gurdip's father. He was also frightened at the decisions Pasha was making and his ruthless plan to attack his own cousin, Kalbant. But to walk away or refuse to aid him would only bring Pasha's wrath down on him and possibly even kill him. Ajeet hated to admit it but he was frightened for himself and his own family.

Ajeet looked at his fuel gauge, the needle of which had dropped dramatically towards empty, and decided to refuel at the next service station. He drove into Hartshead Moor between Junction 25 and 26 and pulled in at the pumps to fill up.

There was a queue.

Ronnie and Bill had been following Ajeet quite safely and they took the opportunity to swap drivers as Ajeet stopped. They hung back and waited to see if Ajeet was going to take a comfort break or grab a coffee and bite to eat, in which case they would do the same. They watched and waited while Ajeet filled up and disappeared into the service station to pay. Bill's tummy rumbled, "Cor, could do with a sarnie or something."

"You'll have to wait. Let's see what he does. If he takes off, we've no choice but to follow."

"And if he doesn't?"

"You'll get your sandwich or whatever."

Bill crossed his fingers.

Ajeet emerged and climbed into his vehicle.

"Shit! He's taking the lane to the motorway," Bill grumbled.

"Can't be helped. Grub will have to wait. Come on, follow him."

They pulled out into the stream of traffic and joined the line of cars waiting to get back onto the motorway. Bill tapped the steering wheel impatiently. "Keep an eye out, Ronnie and watch him in case we get stuck behind this white van."

They managed to move forward and slip out reasonably easily into the oncoming traffic. Ronnie kept his eyes fixed on Ajeet's car.

"I hate driving when I don't know where we're going," moaned Bill.

"You don't need to know. Just follow."

"That's all very well," said Bill. "But what happens when we get off the motorway? It will be harder to remain unseen. Remember he's seen you before."

"But he hasn't seen you. As long as I keep my head down, we should be okay."

"Famous last words," complained Bill. "Look out, he's pulling out to overtake that lorry."

"And we will do the same," reassured Ronnie.

Bill watched his rear-view mirror for a suitable slot to slip out after Ajeet and kept his indicator on. A blue mini was coming up and flashed to let him in. Bill drove out and put his indicators on, first one side and then the other as a thank you. Bill followed Ajeet in the outside lane and pulled in, when Ajeet moved in. He was careful to keep two cars behind his quarry.

It was fairly smooth going until they approached junction 29 to enter the M62. They were two very busy roads and today they both seemed flooded with traffic. Bill was worried as he had now ended up directly behind Ajeet. Ronnie had ducked down in his seat and pulled his cap forward to hide his face in case Ajeet glanced in his rear-view mirror but he needn't have worried, Ajeet was keeping his eyes firmly fixed ahead. Bill waited until Ajeet had made it into the stream of traffic and followed carefully, slowing just enough to allow two cars to overtake. He breathed a sigh of relief as he was now back in his favoured position of two cars between them.

They proceeded in this fashion until they reached junction 26 called the Bradford Spur motorway where the M606 left the M62 near Cleckheaton and headed into Bradford to join the A6177 Bradford ring road. Now Bill was kept on his toes, his eyes everywhere trying to keep on Ajeet's tail but not being obvious about it. He complained to Ronnie, "This ain't easy, mate. First chance we get we can swap over."

"No, you're all right," said Ronnie, grinning, "I'm in no hurry to take over."

"I bet!"

Ronnie was reminded of some old cartoons he'd seen of a reboot of Wacky Races in 2017 with Dick Dastardly hunched over the steering wheel and Muttley with his huffing chuckle. "Anyone ever told you, you drive like in Wacky Races?"

"Oh yeah? Who am I supposed to be, then? Penelope Pitstop?"

"More like Dick Dastardly."

"In that case you must be Muttley," said Bill with a grin.

"I can take that," said Ronnie with a Muttley type laugh. "Hang on, Bill. Less of the banter. Our man is turning off."

Bill shook himself and focused. He followed Ajeet off the ring road and travelled into busy Bradford. Ajeet signalled and turned into the car park of the Midland Hotel. Bill Rennie yelled in a panic, "What do I do? What do I do?"

"Follow him in," instructed Ronnie. I'll duck right down. Get a parking space but not on top of him. Go!" Bill pulled at his shirt collar that was chafing his neck. He had begun to sweat. Ronnie looked across at him concerned, "Breathe, Bill. Deep breaths. Come on, calm down."

Bill tried to do as Ronnie asked and gulped hard before turning across the traffic to enter the hotel car park. Ronnie shielded his eyes as Bill turned narrowly missing an approaching BMW that screeched and skidded to a halt and blared its horn at him. The other car had missed them by a whisker.

Ronnie had grabbed hold of the sides of his seat and become rigid. He dipped his head as they entered the car park and saw where Ajeet had stopped. Bill meandered slowly into a vacant place and manoeuvred their car into the spot and waited. They watched Ajeet. As he took a bag from his back seat and strode away.

"What now?" asked Bill, still recovering from his close encounter.

"We wait."

"We could be here all night," complained Bill. "And let's swap over. If there's any more chasing, you can do it."

Ronnie rolled his eyes and got out of the vehicle and they swapped seats.

"We'll give him fifteen minutes, if he's not out, we'll go inside and find out which room he has checked into. You never know, he may be meeting Pasha, in which case we'll follow them."

Bill snuggled down in his seat, "In that case, you don't mind if I take a nap. You can have first watch."

Ronnie laughed, "We're only going to be waiting… like… fifteen minutes…" But Bill had tipped his seat back and closed his eyes. Ronnie looked bemused. He fiddled with the car radio and found Radio 2. He turned the volume down so he could just hear it and settled down to watch.

Minutes passed. Ronnie looked at his watch. They had been sitting there thirteen minutes. He was just about to nudge Bill when he saw the door swing open and Ajeet walked out and marched to his car, which chirruped as he unlocked it. Ajeet didn't give any other car a second glance. He reversed out of his place and travelled up the ramp to the exit.

Ronnie started their motor and slipped out from his bay to follow Ajeet.

The sound of the engine and Ronnie's urgent voice roused Bill from his dozing. "Wake up! We're on the move."

Bill snorted as he came to and hurriedly raised his seat as Ronnie watched which way Ajeet had gone and managed to filter out into the traffic a few cars back from Ajeet.

Ajeet drove from the city centre towards Shipley on the A6037 where the houses appeared more affluent. They continued on towards the Hollins Hotel, Golf and Country Club. There was an impressive drive leading up through the golf course to an elegant stone building with a conservatory at one end and a newer extension at the other. Ronnie hung back as Ajeet drove on towards the car park. He paused in the driveway, switched off the radio and wound down his window until he heard a car door slam. Assuming it was Ajeet he slowly processed up the sweeping drive and parked away from Ajeet's car. They just caught sight of him disappearing through the glass doors.

"Surely, he's not come here to play golf?" muttered Bill.

"Well, it looks like he's checked into that hotel in town, maybe Pasha is staying here. Let's wait and see, and not jump to any conclusions."

Bill groaned, "We'll never get back at this rate."

"Why? What you got on? A hot date?"

"No," said Bill petulantly. "I'm supposed to be taking the missus out tonight. She doesn't even know where I am."

"Best ring her then and apologise," said Ronnie. "We could be stuck in Bradford overnight, you never know."

"Bugger that!" exclaimed Bill. "Wait…" Bill pointed towards the glass doors, "That looks like Ajeet now. He's with someone else and he's carrying a very large bag. Is that him? This Pasha?"

Ronnie screwed up his eyes in an attempt to study the man's features. "Looks like it. Get ready, Bill. Appears they're going off again."

They watched as Pasha and Ajeet, stowed the bag in the boot and set off back down the sweeping drive. Ronnie started the car and began to follow, carefully.

Ajeet's vehicle joined the A650 and proceeded through busy traffic towards Usher Street off Wakefield Road. They turned off and passed an imposing red brick building with a white pillar frontage. The sign read, Gurdwara Guru Nanak Dev Ji where their car slowed and then continued along to a crossroads and turned right into Hall Lane. A little further on they turned right again into Walton Street. Outside one of the houses a police car was parked. They passed this car and went onto Prospect Street where Ajeet stopped.

Ronnie and Bill went around the block and parked along the road from the police car. "That must be Gurdip's grandparents' house," said Ronnie. "The West Yorkshire police are watching it."

"Surely Pasha won't strike with a cop car outside? That's madness," said Bill.

"I wouldn't be too sure. It didn't stop them torching my house. They know I'm a copper."

"Yes, but they can't risk being seen. They wouldn't be so stupid."

"Never underestimate someone hell bent on revenge."

"So, what do we do?"

"I guess we wait."

Mark had picked up a Chinese take-away and as Beth prepared the table he stuck the trays in the oven to keep warm while he opened a bottle of wine for them both when his mobile phone rang. He frowned as it was a withheld number. "Hello?"

"Mark? Mark Stringer?"

There was something familiar about the voice. "Who is this?"

"Dammit, man. You asked me to call you…"

Mark suddenly realised who he was talking to… "Alex?"

"What do you want?"

"Not here. Can we meet?"

There was a pause and then finally, "Okay. But it's against my better judgement. Where?"

Mark thought for a moment, "Nowhere we're known… What about the Garden House Hotel, Hagley Road?"

"Good choice. I've had many assignations there… when and what time?"

Mark looked at his watch and the table laid ready for their meal, "I'm just about to eat. Either later tonight or tomorrow?"

"Let's make it tomorrow at midday. Is that okay?"

"Yes, that's fine. What if something crops up? How can I contact you?"

There was another pause, "You can't."

"But…"

"Look, I'll ring you again tomorrow before I leave. About 11:30. Okay?"

"It'll have to be."

Alex ended the call.

Mark wondered if he was doing the right thing and looked up thoughtfully to see Beth watching him from the doorway. "What is it?" he asked.

"Nothing, except you have that look on your face and I find that worrying."

"What look?"

"The one that tells me you're speaking to someone you shouldn't and you have doubts about it."

"Very perceptive. Look, forget all that let's sit down and eat. I'm starving."

Mark was at his desk in Lloyd House going through the evidence and information they had so far on the bodies' murders. His mobile rang. "Stringer."

"Are you still able to meet?"

Mark sat up straight as he recognised Alex's voice. "Sure."

"Right. See you soon." He hung up.

Mark jumped up from his seat, grabbed his coat and dashed from the squad room. He called back to Pooley and Taylor, "If the chief asks for me, tell him… tell him, I'm following a lead." Mark hurried out.

Mark took his car and drove to the Garden House Hotel. He parked and wandered inside, his eyes scanning the different rooms. He couldn't see Alex. He walked to the first bar and ordered a cappuccino and sat himself in the corner on a window seat. He picked up a menu and perused it while he waited.

Alex Wallace sauntered in and looked around the bar. There were very few customers as the lunch rush hadn't yet started. He spotted Mark in the corner and strode across and sat.

"We meet again. Do you want a drink? I've got a coffee coming."

"I'll have the same."

"A Cappuccino?"

"Flat white, please."

Mark went up to the bar to collect his coffee and ordered another, indicating where they were sitting. The waitress acknowledged him and took payment. Mark returned to his seat. "Won't be long. The waitress will deliver it. Now, I think we need to talk."

"What about?"

"Kelly's Wine Bar. You didn't look like you were there to dance or drink champagne."

"That's very perceptive of you." Alex stopped as the waitress with a name badge that said 'Maisie' crossed to them with Alex's flat white.

They waited until she had moved away before resuming their conversation.

"It looked like you were watching three guys in the Bistro."

"Was I?"

"Come on, Alex. You were with Roy Chapman. I recognised him. I feel sure that he belongs to some special force and I suspect you do, too. The MRF. We're on the same side. You helped us out in Bradford at the shopping centre. You saved my life twice and for that I am eternally grateful."

Alex paused and scrutinised Mark's face. "How many people know about this?"

"At the moment, just me. And Josh, of course. He was with me at Kelly's. Your secret is safe with both of us."

Alex frowned. "You should forget you ever saw me, forget that you know me."

It was Mark's turn to pause. He looked Alex directly in his eyes. "So, we're at an impasse… I have a proposal."

Alex's expression was difficult to read. "What?"

Mark took a deep breath before he started to explain. "We have an interest in Martyn Kelland. Something is going on there. His partner Jonas Rakowsky was murdered, brutally, I might add, and chopped to pieces. We had a job to identify him. We need to find out who killed him and why. We have learned that he was in touch with an agent referred to only as AW. That's you, isn't it?" Alex said nothing. "What I'm proposing is a sharing of information. No one else need know about it. I will tell you what I know and you can tell me your interest in the man."

"That's a hard ask."

Mark rolled his eyes. "Wait, don't judge me yet. We could be useful to each other."

"How?"

"Help us take him down. We have another body disposed of the same way as Rakowsky. This time an unidentifiable woman. What's going on?"

"Supposing you're right. I am interested in Kelland. Can you guarantee keeping me and my name out of it?"

"I have done so far. No one knows about Bradford."

"What about your friend, Josh?"

"He's safe. I can promise you that."

Alex sucked his breath in between his teeth making a whistling sound. "Get us another coffee. I have a call to make and then we'll see."

Mark rose and walked to the counter while Alex slipped out to the car park and spoke to someone on the phone. Mark could see him through the window pacing around. He appeared to be remonstrating with someone before he finally flipped his phone shut and strode back inside as Mark returned to the table with two more coffees.

Alex sat, and even though the day was cold he was sweating. His mouth was set in a grim line, his expression hard to read. "Okay, tell me what you have. How did you discover Jonas' identity?"

Mark responded by offering his hand, "Do we have a deal?"

Alex took it and they shook hands. "A gentlemen's agreement."

Mark began to detail what they had discovered thanks to the pacemaker. He described his visit to West End Products Ltd and Alex listened closely.

When Mark had finished Alex asked, "You didn't find the tracker?"

Mark shook his head puzzled, "Tracker? No."

"Inside his arm?"

"The autopsy noted an incision on the inside of one arm. The pathologist couldn't work out what the injury was, which was apparently done Post Mortem."

"We inserted a tracker, with his permission, in an attempt to keep him safe. So, we would know where he was at all times. Someone obviously sussed that and had it removed and destroyed it after death"

"I didn't know there was the technology to do that."

"Believe you me, the people I work for have all types of gadgets for surveillance including this. It's not on the market yet. We believe it's also something Kelland and his gang have access to. We were just being cautious. But you say, nothing was found at the PM?"

"No, nothing. Why would you need to do that?"

"Jonas knew that he was involved in something very dangerous. It was to guarantee him safety."

"It didn't work, then, did it?"

Alex said slowly, "No. Sadly. Jonas discovered that Kelland was using the business to bring in girls from abroad. He was trying to help us get information and evidence about Kelland's activities."

"Sex trafficking? Like Takagi."

"Something like that, but that's not all of it. Yes, Martyn Kelland and his henchmen are unscrupulous, greedy fiends. They are as bad as, if not worse than Takagi and his gang."

Mark nodded, remembering the abduction of his fiancée Beth and other girls including Chapman's granddaughter, Cathy. Alex had been instrumental in getting them out and breaking up the ring, causing Takagi's death in the process.

"Cut off the head of the hydra and another one grows to replace it," said Alex. "Nasty business and this one is much worse."

"Why?"

"We learned that girls who didn't make the grade were disposable. Used for black market transplants, providing another service, if you can call it that.

Where someone desperate for a heart, liver or kidneys can approach them. It's a disturbing and abhorrent practice. It must be stopped, as must the trafficking of young girls to become sex slaves."

Mark's eyes widened as he listened. "That explains it."

"What?"

"The second body we found that had been dismembered was a young woman, and all her internal organs had been removed. Now we know why."

"So, how can we bring Kelland down?"

"That my friend, is where we work together."

Bill's stomach growled like an angry teddy bear. "How much longer?" he complained. "I'm starving."

"Nothing we can do about it, yet," said Ronnie. "I'm sure they will make a move soon but they won't want to be seen."

"Can't we warn the grandparents? Get them out from their house?"

"That's not a bad idea. If it can be done discreetly."

"How do we do that?"

"We'll call it in. Bradford police have been made aware that we are in pursuit of Pasha. In fact, I'll do that now and you better ring your missus, tell her your meal out is off."

Bill grimaced, "She's not going to like it."

"It can't be helped. Tell her you'll take her tomorrow."

Bill mumbled something else and wriggled around in his seat to retrieve his phone from his back pocket. He got out from the car and made the call while Ronnie was making contact with the local police. As he talked, he explained what he had discovered.

Night had fallen, shielding Pasha from view as the billowing clouds clustered around the moon dressing it in darkness. The street lamps in the road produced an orange muddy hue, at least, the ones that were working did. There were parts of the road reliant on the light from the moon to illuminate the street where Pasha and Ajeet waited. But the enveloping blackness gave Pasha an arrogant confidence. They exited their vehicle and Ajeet went to the boot of his car and opened it revealing some rags, glass bottles and a full petrol can. There was also a handgun, which Pasha shoved into his trouser waistband.

The men dispensed the fuel into two empty wine bottles and plugged each of the necks with a soft rag. Ajeet took out his Bic lighter in readiness while Pasha played with his Zippo lighter. "Are we gonna do it now?" asked Ajeet nervously. "What about the cops?"

"What about them?"

"They're parked outside watching."

"They won't be for long."

Ajeet looked at his cousin, "Why? What do you have in mind?"

"A little distraction, Ajeet. To get them away from the front door. Let's fill another bottle."

"I don't understand."

"You will. Once I have made another of these beauties. Follow me."

Ajeet frowned. He knew he wouldn't like what was going to happen but what could he do?

Ronnie was on edge as he sat upright fully alert. His eyes scoured the dark for any movement in the menacing shadows but Bill not so much, he was relaxing back in his seat trying to control his tummy rumbles when there was an explosion behind them at a house further down the street followed by some gunfire.

The noise with glass exploding made Bill jerk awake. He clasped his heart. "Bloody hell. What was that? Frightened me to death."

"I think that is a distraction arranged by Pasha and Ajeet. Look the cops are moving away from the house to investigate. We, however, will make our way to Gurdip's grandparents' house."

"You sure?"

"Never more certain."

"What do we do? Have you got a plan?"

"Come on. I'll explain as we're walking."

Ajeet had heard the explosion from Pasha tossing his homemade bomb in the open door of a garage further up the street and firing his gun three times into the air, sending roosting birds fluttering up from the trees. Ajeet had been ordered to move in on Gurdip's grandparents' house as soon as the cop car had moved out to investigate what had happened.

Ajeet could see that people had come out of their houses and he believed the emergency services were bound to have been called. Pasha must have doubled back to the car by now to wait for him. But Ajeet was nervous and sweating profusely. He knew that all he had to do was smash a window and toss the Molotov cocktail in through the broken pane but he didn't want to do it. He was afraid. These poor people were innocent of any wrongdoings. He didn't know how he could get out of this or what he would say to Pasha if he didn't follow through. He was scared, very scared. Pasha was unpredictable, cruel and violent. Could he risk not following through?

His hand was shaking so much he couldn't click his lighter. Ajeet dithered indecisively and gulped back a sob, when he felt a hand on his shoulder and he froze.

"You don't want to do that!" said Bill Rennie as he removed the lighter from Ajeet's trembling hand. "You're nicked."

Ajeet broke down sobbing and dropped the bottle, which smashed on the ground spilling its contents all over the path. He dropped to his knees and put his hands over his face, "I didn't want to do it… I didn't…" His voice was jerky coming out in juddering gasps. Suddenly, he screamed as the petrol ignited around him and flames leapt up and licked his limbs. Bill was stunned. He grabbed Ajeet and pulled him away from the fire, took off his coat and wrapped it around Ajeet's legs and frantically patted out the spreading flames, creeping up his trousers, which had started to melt onto his skin.

Ajeet's eyes were wild with fear and pain. He yelled and gurgled in fright. Once Bill was sure the fire had been extinguished he got onto his phone to call for an ambulance and sirens were soon heard in the distance. One of the coppers came running back to the house. Bill flashed his warrant card, "Stay with him. I'll be back."

Meanwhile, Ronnie had skirted back to Prospect Street. Ajeet's car was empty. He punctured the front tyres before standing back in the shadows to watch from the other side of the road. He saw Pasha hurrying around the corner and making his way towards the vehicle. Pasha fumbled with his keys, which he dropped in the road. As he bent down to retrieve them he noticed the tyres and rose up quickly and reached for the gun lodged in his trouser waistband.

Ronnie stepped out and crossed to the Sikh. He grabbed Pasha's arm, "Not so fast. You're under arrest."

Pasha was filled with fury and manoeuvred his body away from Ronnie, which allowed him to take out his gun, which he levelled at Ronnie.

"You don't want to do that."

"Why not? Who's going to stop me?" sneered Pasha.

A voice came out from the darkness, "I am."

Pasha spun around in the lamplight to see Bill striding towards him. He hesitated not knowing where to point his revolver. This gave Ronnie enough time to tackle Pasha who let off a shot that went wide of Bill. Pasha dropped his firearm and Ronnie managed to bring Pasha to the ground. He yanked his hands behind his back and cuffed him, before dragging him to his feet. "Pasha Chand, I am arresting you on suspicion of murder, attempted murder and arson You do not have to say anything, but it may harm your defence if you do not mention when questioned something, which you later rely on in court. Anything you do say may be given in evidence." Ronnie and Bill dragged Pasha to his feet. Flanked on either side, he was marched around the corner to the police at the end of the road, who placed him in custody and locked him in the riot van while Ajeet was being attended to by paramedics. It appeared that Pasha had ignited the petrol that had engulfed Ajeet, who they believed, was now only too willing to talk.

Ronnie asked, "And the grandparents?"

The copper jerked his head towards the prisoner, "Safe. We were expecting him. The Singhs are in a local B & B. They will be able to return home now."

Ronnie nodded, "You'll take it from here?"

"We will. Thanks for your help."

Bill turned to Ronnie, "And now can we please get something to eat?"

12

RONNIE WAS ON THE PHONE to the estate agent who had helped him escape Pasha's attention. "So, is the flat I viewed still available for rent?"

"It is. You're in luck. Someone else snapped it up after you had to pull out but unfortunately the person's credit references were not up to scratch and the owner refused the contract. It came back on the market this morning."

"Terrific! Can you put us forward? I'll come and fill out all the forms."

"Perfect. I'll be in the office until five. Hope to see you before. I can only hold it for so long, you do understand don't you?"

"Of course. Thank you." Ronnie curtailed the call and immediately rang Gurdip, who was delighted. He said he would call Siri and tell her the good news.

"You better hang fire until it's all confirmed," advised Ronnie. They have to check our references but I don't think anyone will question the chief's word, do you?" Ronnie terminated the call. He was feeling great. Things seemed to be looking up and he would soon see Siri again. Life seemed to be getting back on track he thought.

His line rang again. "Soper."

"DC Soper, West Yorkshire police here. DC Marriott speaking. Thought you'd like to know that Ajeet Singh is singing like a bird. He's only too ready to put the blame on Pasha Chand. I must say it's one of the most awful cases we have come across. And I've seen a few in my time."

"When you've finished with them, they have charges to answer here."

"Aye, lad. Our super will be talking to yours. They'll have to work something out between them. Any road thanks for your help."

"Pleasure." Ronnie felt better than he had in a long time. It also meant that Gurdip would be back at work now that Pasha had been caught. He couldn't stop himself from smiling.

Mark had fully digested all he had learned from Alex. He knew, now, that Jonas had been flagged up by Interpol and Europol for his own good as a smoke screen regarding Kelland's men and when the teams in Russia and Bulgaria used their sources to check out Jonas' background it would look as if he was a criminal like them, just one that hadn't been caught. He had been working undercover with Alex and his agency but someone had found this out and thus he had been eliminated.

Mark knew Allison was keen to confirm the identity of the woman and he wanted to visit Kelland again. Mark had to be careful how he proceeded with the explanations of his theories. He was hoping the chief wouldn't discover his deception. It would be tough. Allison was more than shrewd as he had a nose for uncovering the truth. Like a pig seeking a truffle he would root it out.

Mark was online, flagging up missing person cases in the area specifically looking at teenage girls and young women. There were several. He also checked the police data base for those that had been circulated from other police forces. He studied the faces of each girl within the age range but so far had found no one that matched the features of the girl whose head was found in Clement Pugh's freezer. He yawned noisily, "Oh excuse me," he apologised to no one in particular as he stretched up his arms and tightened his muscles. He was just about to take a break and grab a coffee but then he looked at the bottom of his screen and thought he'd look at one more. He gasped as the next photo popped up. He picked up the artist's impression of how she would look alive and compared it with their victim. He snapped his fingers. It had to be her. He was sure of it.

He called over Bill Rennie and passed him the artist's likeness to compare against the missing person. "What do you think, Bill? Is it her?"

“Certainly looks like it. Yes. I’d say it was her.”

“Excellent!” He printed off the photo and file and marched to Allison’s office and knocked before entering.

“Chief! Think we’ve found her.”

Allison looked up and gestured Mark across and took the printouts. He nodded agreeably, “Looks like you’ve struck gold. What have you learned?”

“Her name’s Sally Marchant. She ran away from home after a family row. She’s been missing for two years. No record. Looks like she may have fallen victim to a sex trafficker or worse.”

“What could be worse?”

“Someone harvesting organs for transplant. At least, after looking at the body that’s what it seems like.”

Allison grunted, “You could be right. We shall have to check HOLMES for anything similar. See what comes up. Can I leave that to you?”

“Yes, sir. I’ll get onto it right away.”

“And we need to pay Kelland another visit and look further into these Big Issue sellers.”

“Sir.”

“I’m expecting a call from Bradford CID. I also want to talk to Holly again. See if she’s picked up anything else.”

Mark nodded and left the chief to it. *So far so good*, he thought.

Holly watched as Paul created a winter scene on canvas. He was an excellent architect, which paid the bills, but his heart lay in his painting and conceiving works of art he felt passionate about. She wished they could afford to take a leap of faith and just trust in his talent.

Holly sighed. She stared at the table of items in their plastic bags that had come from the police that sat on a work bench and crossed to them.

“That was a world-weary sigh,” noted Paul.

“Yes, I’m hoping I might get something from these to help the chief.”

“And aren’t you?”

“I haven’t really tried, yet. I just have this funny feeling circling in my tummy. It’s weird.”

"How weird?"

"It's hard to explain, a kind of emptiness, like something's been taken."

"Maybe it has."

Holly grabbed a high stool and sat before the bench and Paul stopped painting. "You keep on with your work," said Holly quickly. "I can't work with you staring at me like that." Paul shrugged, picked up his paintbrush and continued but cast furtive looks at Holly every now and again.

Holly picked up the bag with the paper knife inside and stared at it. She closed her eyes as if in meditation, but underneath her lids her eyes moved rapidly as if surveying some scene. She thrust the bag down and opened her eyes.

"Problem?" asked Paul.

"I thought I could do it through the plastic bag but it's not ideal. I'll have to take it out."

"What are you worried about?"

"Contamination."

"Greg wouldn't have given it to you unless they had taken all they wanted from it. Take it out and do your… you know."

"Psychometry. It's called psychometry." She sighed again, "Of course, you're right. I don't know why I'm reluctant to hold it. Stupid."

Holly opened up the zip lock bag and took out the paper knife. She began with the same process again, holding the knife close to her chest, closing her eyes and focusing. She appeared to drift away into REM sleep as her eyes moved rapidly under her lids as if surveying the countryside going past from a train window. Suddenly, she jerked herself awake and ran to the sink in the studio where she vomited.

Paul was immediately concerned, "What the hell did you see, Holly?"

Holly mopped her lips and chin then ran the cold tap. She scooped up a handful of water and swished it around her mouth to clear the taste, before grabbing a mug and filling it with cold water to drink. "Ugh!" she grimaced.

"What?"

"That was sick, disgusting and sick."

"Tell me."

"There was this man, who attacked the victim from behind and just sliced through his throat. There was blood everywhere. The place looked like a slaughter house. In some kind of warehouse. A big floor with stands and shelving filled up with boxes and all sorts of paraphernalia. There were two men. I couldn't see their faces… the pain was horrific. Blood fountained out like a burst water main. It just kept on spurting… hideous. One man wearing a hood, took his arm and gouged a slice out of the victim's arm, inside below the elbow and cut something out, which he crushed underfoot. They stripped off his clothes and the other man had a saw, an electric saw." Holly stopped as she gagged again. "He sawed off his head. Oh, Paul… I saw his eyes blink. They chopped off his head when he was still alive…" she shuddered.

Paul took her in his arms as she was shaking and he tried to still her trembling body by hugging her to him. He sat her down carefully on the stool, "Are you sure you want to go on with this?"

"I have to. Yes. Just give me a moment. I'll be okay, honestly."

"I think you've seen enough for one day, don't you?"

"I have to try again. I might be able to stop it happening to someone else."

Paul held her tighter, he knew that when Holly made up her mind about something there was no deterring her. He waited until her shivering had subsided. "Have it your way, but just have a break, please. Let me get you a drink."

"I'll be fine, I promise but a drink wouldn't go amiss."

"Coffee with a tot of brandy?"

Holly nodded, "I don't know what I'd do without you."

Today, the sun was shining down benevolently and there was hardly a trace of any type of cloud in the sky except for the short, detached, hair-like cirrus clouds, which can be seen at high altitudes. Their delicate wispy strands with a silky sheen, looked like tufts of angel hair and wings, and were whiter than any other cloud in the sky.

Ronnie beamed at his friend Gurdip. The weather was perfect. Perfect for collecting Siri and Ayesha. The day promised a new beginning for all of them. They had secured the furnished flat in Poplar Avenue. Ronnie had smartened himself up and was looking quite handsome in his new clothes. His entire wardrobe had gone up in smoke and he had to force himself to go shopping. Both he and Gurdip had gone to a Gents' outfitters in town and bought a number of items.

Ronnie's mum was staying on with her sister until she could find somewhere new and the insurance money had come through. Ronnie had a real spring in his step that could be described as jaunty, and he had bought a Baker boy cap that he had set at a rakish angle.

"This is it, then," said Ronnie with a grin. He turned to Gurdip, "Have you got the keys?"

Gurdip nodded and flashed a bunch of keys with ones that he had had cut especially. "All set," he said with a smile. He had not yet regained his confidence after everything that had happened but Ronnie's bouncing positivity was rubbing off on him.

"Right, let's go."

"First things first," said Gurdip. "We have to call in at George Dixon Primary School and drop off Ayesha's enrolment papers."

"That won't take long."

"No, but once the girls are safe with you, here, I have to go to see the Gurdwara Committee, they can help, especially now that Pasha has been caught. We might then also have to file for divorce in your court of law, but let us hope the elders agree. It will save us so much time."

Ronnie nodded, "Well okay, let's get this show on the road. Come on bro."

Gurdip nodded and for the first time in a long time, Ronnie saw the return of his friend's confidence and his beatific smile.

Allison looked out of his office window, the day was much brighter than before and he believed with a bit of luck that they just might get some constant sunshine. At least that is what he hoped. He moved back to his desk and picked up the report from Interpol on Jonas Rakowsky and began to study it. It seemed that his company was mixed up in some murky dealings as suspected and the initials AW appeared again.

Allison leaned forward in his chair and opened the drawer that held his stash of Mars Bars and he pulled one out, ripped off the paper and sunk his teeth into it. He demolished his sweet treat in just three bites.

There was a knock at his door. Maddie entered with a cup of tea, "I thought you could do with one. You looked somewhat distracted when you arrived."

"Yes. Thank you, Maddie. I am just mulling over some things. Has anyone left any messages?"

Maddie shook her head, "Sorry, Chief. No."

"Hmm. I had hoped we might have heard from that young girl again. I really need to talk to her. She must know more than she's saying." He paused, "When Mark arrives, send him in."

"Sir."

Allison rubbed his bristly chin as he perused the papers on his desk. He sighed heavily and ran his fingers through his hair and picked up the phone. He hesitated and replaced it in its cradle before picking up his directory of numbers and searched through them. He found one and dialled. "Hello, Simon? Allison here. I need to know… What can you tell me about the MRF?"

Katy was spending her first night in her new studio apartment in Gillott Road. She stretched, enjoying her own space. It might have been small but it was hers and it felt good to have somewhere of her own to call home. Katy walked to the window to draw the curtains and looked outside. She gasped as she saw the same black BMW X5 parked opposite and she stepped back quickly. Why was it there? Was it a coincidence? Katy didn't believe in coincidences.

Katy peeped cautiously outside once more. A man wearing a hoodie got out of the driver's side and looked up. Katy was sure it was the same man that she had seen before helping to bundle the Big Issue seller into the vehicle. Her previous euphoria at waking up in her own place dissolved and she became very afraid. She stepped back and flopped in the beanbag chair by the window as her mind began to race.

Perhaps she could alert Big Den? He wouldn't have left yet and he usually walked with her to catch the number 9 bus to town. But, what if this man wasn't alone? As if to answer her question she stole another look out of the window. The passenger door opened and the well-built man with the long grey ponytail stepped out of the passenger door. He joined the other man on the pavement and they both looked up at her window. They seemed to be having some sort of disagreement, when one of them removed his mobile phone from his pocket and answered a call. The conversation was short and both men got back in the car and the vehicle pulled out from its parking place and turned around in the road. It sped off towards the direction of the Hagley Road.

Katy didn't know what to think. They clearly knew she lived there. Her newly found sanctuary was short-lived. She needed to find somewhere else to live. Katy decided there and then that she would ring the police again but this time she would speak to someone. But now her biggest problem would be getting out of the flat and finding somewhere else to stay at short notice. The squat was no good and she couldn't sleep on Big Den's floor. But where could she go? And what about her deposit? Blow the deposit. She had to escape.

Katy hurriedly washed and dressed. She needed to get out. She packed her few meagre belongings in her bag and looked back at her little bits of shopping she had bought for meals and decided, Den could have those. She hurriedly scrawled a note to Big Den and scurried down the stairs. She pushed the note under his door with her key and fled.

Big Den had just woken up. He lumbered into the sitting room, the key and the paper on the floor caught his eye. He picked them up and groaned as he read the note. There was clearly nothing he could do now. He just hoped he could talk some sense into Katy when she came to collect her papers at the distribution centre that is, if she hadn't decided to leave town and go somewhere else. He didn't worry about the studio flat. He would try and get her to return but if not there were some other sellers he knew who would be glad of a more permanent address.

He screwed up the paper and dropped it into his kitchen bin.

Katy was sitting upstairs on the bus and she looked anxiously out of the window. The sun was streaming through the trees and the effects through the branches was like that of a flashing strobe light. Katy blinked and delved in her bag for a pair of sunglasses. Her head was buzzing, her heart was pounding and she couldn't quell the trembling that had manifested in her hands or the fluttering in her tummy. For the first time in her life she was finding it tough to make a decision. Normally, she was decisive and even if she'd made up her mind and chosen the wrong thing to do she could make up her mind to a suitable course of action but this time she was dithering.

When her mother's boyfriend had attacked her in a drunken stupor, after a row, and then come on to her and had made up tales that she had attempted to seduce him she knew exactly what to do. She left. She didn't argue. She didn't defend her actions; she had dug her nails in his face and scratched him badly. She knew she had left her mother feeling confused but she also knew she couldn't go back not unless he had gone. Katy hadn't contacted her mother to find out. Perhaps she should? Perhaps now was the right time? Katy's dilemma was growing as she argued with herself inside her head, over a number of things. Katy felt she should go to the police but what then? How safe would she be?

Katy's panic was growing but it made up her mind. She alighted from the bus at Lloyd House. She would go to the police station first. Her mum could wait until later. Her mouth had gone dry and she licked her lips and swallowed, trying to generate some saliva to prevent her teeth from sticking to her lips. She walked towards the thirteen-storey building with its impressive entrance. It was paved with tiles to the entrance with its semi-circular canopy reminding Katy of a protractor she'd used in a school geometry lesson. The glass awning was supported by white pipe-like metal powder coated struts that fanned out like rays of the sun. She stood by the huge steel letters announcing, West Midlands Police Headquarters and gazed towards the entrance doors with its flash reception desk and braced herself. Was she really going to do this? She decided she was. Katy took a deep breath and marched to the sliding doors and entered.

Big Den was out on the street outside his flat. He began his walk to the number 9 bus stop. His eyes narrowed as a black BMW X5 cruised past him. He stopped and looked back watching the vehicle park in a vacant space opposite his flat. No one alighted. Den turned on his heel and strode towards the four by four. He stopped by the driver's door and tapped on the glass.

The electric window slid down gracefully. A thin faced man, wearing a hoodie, peered out at him. Big Den asked pointedly, "Can I help you?"

"I don't expect so, mate," came the gruff response.

"I noticed you parking here a couple of times as if you were looking out for someone."

"What's it to you?"

"I live here. I might be able to help."

"I doubt it."

"Try me."

Big Den's bulk filled the window as the man assessed him. "Look, we don't want no trouble. We're on surveillance."

"What kind of surveillance?"

The man hesitated before he spoke, "We had a report of a runaway. Her mother's worried. Came to see if we could persuade her to go back home. I told you. Nothing to do with you."

The stocky man in the seat next to him answered his phone, which had begun to ring, "Yeah?" He appeared to listen before nudging his companion, "Bernie, gotta move. Boss wants us."

The pinched face man cut off anything else Den might say as the window rolled up. He started the vehicle and they pulled away leaving Den looking after them. Marcus turned to Bernie and muttered, "Silly sod. He'll have to go. We'll deal with him later."

"Won't be easy. Have you seen the size of him?"

"Don't worry, I have a plan."

Katy stood at the desk of Lloyd House Reception trying to reason with the man asking her questions. "I've already told you; I'm not speaking to anyone else. I want to talk to the bloke in charge of the bodies in the suitcase murders."

"Miss, you can explain it to me and then I can decide who's best for you to be referred to."

"Bugger that!" Katy turned away and began to walk away as DCI Allison came lumbering into the entrance hall. She called back over her shoulder, "Try to do the right thing and that's all the thanks I get."

Allison raised his eyebrows and instinctively moved after Katy. He stopped her, "Excuse me, miss. Can I be of help?"

Katy shrugged then stopped. She studied the chief and a flicker of recognition crossed her eyes. "I know you. I saw you in the paper. You're the one in charge of that case. Yes… you can… You're the one I need to talk to."

The security man behind the desk who had started to come after Katy was waved back by Allison, "It's okay, Sam. I'll take it from here." Sam returned to his spot and Allison turned to Katy. "Follow me." Katy had to speed up her steps to keep pace with him. Allison marched on with Katy hurrying after him. Finally, he arrived in the squad room at his outer office and walked into his own. Maddie glanced up a look of surprise on her face.

"Two teas please, Maddie." He looked at Katy, "You do drink tea?"

She nodded, "Milk no sugar. Thank you."

They entered Allison's office and he gestured her to sit. Katy scrambled into the indicated chair looking uncomfortable.

"Now, miss… I didn't catch your name."

"I didn't give it," she said tartly.

Allison raised one eyebrow and studied her critically. "I have to call you something."

"It's Katy."

"Katy…?"

"Just Katy."

"Very well, Katy. What was so pressing that you had to speak to me?"

13

KATY SAT WIDE-EYED, STARING AROUND Allison's office with its big glass windows. Allison fixed her with his gaze as he assessed her. Maddie broke the silence as she entered with the tea and biscuits and left discreetly. Allison pushed a mug towards her, "Help yourself," he gestured to the plate of biscuits.

Katy studied him as she reached for a chocolate digestive. She hesitated fractionally, and muttered, "I shouldn't have come. I should have just moved cities and become lost somewhere else." She took a bite and crisp biscuit crumbs speckled the front of her coat, which she brushed off. "Sorry." She indicated the smattering of crumbs that had tumbled to the floor.

Allison leaned back in his chair but said nothing. She took the mug of tea and cradled it to her as if it had some calming magical properties. Allison waited for her to speak. She didn't.

Katy took a sip of her tea and this time Allison spoke. "You said you needed to speak to me… that you had important information?"

His words hung in the air. Eventually, Katy spoke, "Yes. It's the right thing to do."

"Can you please tell me your name?"

"Katy."

"Katy…?"

"As I said before… just Katy."

"So, what is it you wanted to tell me?"

"You are the man? In charge of the case?"

"Which case?" Allison was ensuring she would respond.

"The bodies in the suitcase."

"That's me."

Katy bit her lip and then blurted out, "I saw them and not just once. The men with the suitcase."

"Why don't you start from the beginning and tell me everything."

Hesitantly but gradually growing in confidence Katy began to relay exactly what she had seen at the station and where else she had seen the man with the grey ponytail. Allison didn't interrupt he made notes as he let her words flow. He leaned forward as she described the abduction of the young Big Issue seller and frowned.

Katy was all talked out and she flopped back in her seat. "I have another problem." Allison raised his busy eyebrows questioningly. "These men… they know where I live. I have to leave."

"Whoa!…Wait… wait a moment. Where are you going?"

"Home. I should have done it before. These men are dangerous and they know I saw them abduct that girl."

Allison rubbed his emery chin, "Where is home?"

"Devon."

"What if we can keep you safe?"

Katy shook her head, "Uh, uh. I don't think so."

"Why did you run away?"

Katy sighed heavily, "My stepdad. He's a rat. No, worse… He's a paedo bastard."

"And you feel it's wise to go back?"

"What else can I do? I don't have the money to get anywhere at home. Priced out of the market and these men know who I am. They will be looking for me. I shouldn't have come." Katy stood up to leave.

"No, stop. Please." Katy halted. "At least call your mother. You can ring from here. What if you go back and this man is still there?"

Katy faltered and turned back. "Then what?"

“At least, you’ll know.” Allison picked up the phone, “What’s the number?”

Katy hesitated, closed her eyes and said firmly, “… 01271 333294”

Allison dialled, “It’s ringing… hello? Mrs?” he looked at Katy.

“Vicary.”

“Mrs Vicary?... This is the West Midlands Police.” There was a quavering wail that came down the phone that even Katy could hear. Allison put the phone on speaker and Katy returned to her seat.

“You’ve found her haven’t you?” Katy could hear the sob in her mother’s voice. “My poor, poor baby. What’s happened?” she sniffed loudly.

“Mrs Vicary, your daughter is safe and well.”

“She’s alive?” the relief in her voice was apparent. “Oh my God that is the best news I’ve heard. Has she done something wrong?” A note of anxiety crept into her tone.

“No… in fact she is helping us. Do you want to speak to her?” He nodded at Katy.

“… Mum?”

“Katy!” Mrs Vicary dissolved into tears. “Oh, Katy love. Please come home.”

Katy steeled herself, “Is *he* still there?”

“No, love. No. He’s gone. Don’s gone. After you left, I challenged him and he made up some story about you coming onto him. Said you’d attacked him because he’d turned you down. I didn’t believe him. I know you wouldn’t do that. I… I told him to go. Later on, I heard he’d been caught hanging around the school gates in Pilton.” She stifled a sob. “Come home, please love. I miss you so much.”

Allison cut in, “Mrs Vicary. Katy is a witness to some very serious incidents. I just need to talk to her some more and then she will call you right back. Is that all right?”

“Yes, yes, please. I’ll be here and waiting.” Allison ended the call.

“Well, okay, Miss Vicary. Your home is safe to return to. But we may need to call you as a witness if we can track these people down. Will you do that?”

Katy's eyes were glistening as she nodded.

"Have you got the money to get home?"

Katy mumbled, "Some. Not enough for the train. I could manage a coach."

"Hmm! I expect they will be looking for you to run. They will be keeping an eye out at train and coach stations."

"I could hitchhike."

"That's not a good idea."

"Then what do I do?"

"Let me make some phone calls. I'll get Maddie to take you to the canteen. We can ring your mother again afterwards." Allison buzzed his intercom. "Maddie, take Miss Vicary to the canteen and let her have some lunch. Take the money from petty cash, then bring her back." He turned his piercing eyes back on Katy, "I also think you ought to report this Don fellow to the police when you get home." Katy just nodded.

Maddie popped her head around the door, smiled and signalled to Katy, "If you'd like to come with me." Katy rose and followed Maddie who chattered cheerily trying to put Katy at ease.

Allison waited until they had gone and picked up the phone.

Ronnie had been shopping, he'd packed everything away and set the table in their new partially furnished flat. The West Midlands police benevolent fund had helped Ronnie and Gurdip furnish their flat with a grant as they were in need and suffering hardship. They had bought the basics but were still in need of many items. Most of the force had chipped in to help with something. Mary Allison had donated bedding and curtains. She had come around to help set them up.

Ronnie had cooked a simple meal with spices, mixed peppers, onions, mushrooms, sweetcorn and halloumi. He had chopped up some Richmond meat free vegetarian sausages, too. Baby new potatoes were chopped and baked with garlic and rosemary and a couple of Uncle Ben's golden vegetable rice were on hand for good measure. He was feeling excited. He would see Siri and he began to sing along with the radio that was playing a Robbie Williams' hit, Angels, but Ronnie was not quite reaching the high notes.

Ronnie set his wok onto simmer and covered it after sloshing in a generous helping of Riesling to add to the liquid. He poured a glass for himself and went to the front room and peered out of the window.

Allison put the phone down to Mrs Vicary and smiled. This was good. A runaway returning home. Excellent. "Well then, that's settled," he said to himself. He picked up the phone again and called his wife Mary and explained everything to her. She was more than happy to be able to help.

"So, if you can come in now and pick Katy up that would be grand."

"I'll come in right away. Where will she be? In your office?"

"Yes. Park and come straight up."

Allison replaced the receiver and glanced up as his office door opened. Katy stepped inside ushered forward by Maddie.

"Thanks, Maddie. Mrs Allison will be along in a short while just send her straight in. And you, young lady, you sit back down and I'll explain exactly what is going to happen."

Katy looked none too sure but sat anyway and as Allison unfolded his idea a smile began to manifest on her face, "Are you sure? I mean… you don't know me."

"I know enough. You will stay with me overnight. You'll be safe. My wife Mary is coming to pick you up from here. Tomorrow, Mary will drive you to the station and put you on a train to go home and your mother will meet you."

"But I don't have enough for my ticket," Katy protested.

"Don't worry about that. We will sort it out. In the meantime, did you have a bite to eat in the canteen?"

"Yes, thank you."

"Good. Now all you have to do is sit and wait. Soon you'll be home."

The dwindling light had finally faded to dark. Marauding clouds had ambushed the moon, which struggled against its captors to shine in the gloomy dark. A massive European truck was parked outside the large roller doors of West End Products clearly waiting to be met and admitted to the warehouse.

A tall, lean Bulgarian man, Bogdan, who looked typically Slavic with thick, dark hair, nut brown eyes and sallow skin, hopped down from the vehicle and took out his mobile phone, which was ringing. "…Yes? … We're here… As far as I know… The consignment should be intact. We'll know more when we unload. How long?... Very well." Bogdan ended the call. He climbed back up to the cab and rapped on the window. "Prigotovi se. Tryabva da se raztovarim." He was telling them to get ready and unload. A couple of men jumped down from the lorry.

A little while later a BMW X5 appeared at the canal side by the roller door. Marcus Paulson and Bernie Carter stepped out. Carter unlocked the building and went inside. Moments passed and then the large electric steel door wound up slowly and one of the Bulgarians climbed into the cab. He started the engine and manoeuvred the vehicle around and drove into the warehouse. The door rolled down again shielding everything from view.

Inside West End Products, Bogdan instructed one of the Bulgarians to open the back of the lorry. "Otvori go."

A stout pudgy faced Slav with a closely cropped beard unlocked the back and opened the door. All that could be seen were stacked boxes that rose to the ceiling looking as if they filled the truck. The men began to remove them. Eventually, they reached the back. Twenty young girls crouched or squatted silently. None of them spoke. They huddled together and were shaking in fear.

Bogdan yelled, at them to move it. "Premesti go. Bŭrzo!"

The Bulgarian language was so close to Russian that the Russian girls there understood. One by one the girls moved to the open doors and jumped out. They were hustled into one of the rooms off the warehouse and ordered to strip. The girls looked on in horror as Bogdan wheeled in a rail of clothes and instructed them to change into something more alluring. "Preoblichane"

One of the girls, a pretty redhead dared to speak, "Zashto?"

Bogdan smacked her face. "Tikho." He indicated the rail of clothes.

Another girl a petite blonde dared to speak in English, "Why do you want us to change?"

Bogdan moved up to her and eyed her up and down, "You are here for a new life, are you not?" The girl nodded. "You need to change, look attractive. How can you become a bride in those shabby clothes you have travelled in?"

The girl moved tentatively to the rail. She selected an off the shoulder red dress, with a black diamante diamond in the centre. She turned to the other girls, who still looked fearful, and explained. The girls all shuffled to the rail and began looking at the clothes. As they changed, Bogdan's men stood by and ogled them.

"You," Bogdan indicated the blonde. "What is your name?"

"Ivanka Georgiev."

"Ivanka, you speak English?" She nodded. "That is a bonus." He turned to the other girls, "Anyone else speak English?" Four others raised their hands tentatively. "Good, good. It is good. When you have dressed, come and stand on this side." He addressed the others, "Vie, drugite, zastanete tam." The other girls were ordered to stand on the opposite side.

Bogdan ordered his men, "Keep the non-speakers here." He looked at Ivanka, "You five come with me." He took them into another room with a white screen where a camera was set up. They were each made to tidy up their looks with make-up that was provided although some girls had their own cosmetics in their handbags. They were each ordered in turn to sit on a stool in front of the screen and pose for photos, announcing their name and age. "First names only," insisted Bogdan. He looked at their feet in distaste, "You will have to make do with your shoes until we get to the house where we have a range of footwear more suited to your attire."

He then demanded their passports, snapping his fingers, claiming that it was for safety purposes and that they would be returned. He whisked them away and secreted them in a large leather satchel. He then ordered them back out onto the warehouse floor. His men were told to return to the lorry after they had fully unloaded the few remaining boxes. The electric door was lifted up and the truck manoeuvred out of the warehouse space and went on its way. The warehouse doors came down again and sealed them inside.

The English-speaking girls were hustled into a side room. "You will wait here. A minibus will be arriving shortly to take you to your accommodation. I will need your mobile phones for security." The girls shook their heads not wanting to give them up, but Bogdan was menacing as well as persuasive. Reluctantly they gave them up to Bogdan who declared they would all be returned when they reached the safe house. That is all except Ivanka. She felt around in her bag and produced one, which was immediately snatched away to put with the others. Bogdan didn't see that she had another smaller one zipped into a side pocket in her purse. One girl claimed that she didn't have one and was immediately searched and her handbag emptied out. Her phone tumbled out, and that too, was grabbed and put with the others.

Ivanka narrowed her eyes. Something was wrong. She was sure of it. Things just didn't seem right but she sat quietly and waited. The other girls were hushed and clearly feeling all was not as it should be.

Some one and a half hours later, all of the girls were dressed and had been photographed. They were given coats to cover their clothes and were paired into twos. One other girl who spoke broken English joined Ivanka's group.

Three minibuses arrived and the girls were ushered out and driven away. Bogdan climbed in with the driver of the minibus transporting the English speakers. They headed off through the city, around the ring road through to the jewellery quarter and arrived at a large house with electric gates. Bogdan punched numbers in the outside keypad and the gates slowly began to open. He jumped back in the van and drove through as the gates shut behind him.

He drove up the winding path to a large house where the girls alighted and they were admitted into an impressive hallway. The girls looked around in awe at their surroundings, clearly they had never seen anything like it. They were moved down a corridor to a kitchen where a man stood waiting in a white coat. The man, a doctor, with his receding hairline, wire framed glasses, and fine moustache, was a cross between Heinrich Himmler and Dr Hawley Crippen. This man, too, had the whiff of evil about him.

Bogdan reassured the girls, "There is nothing to be frightened of. The good Doctor Charles will check you over after your long journey. He will take your blood pressure and some blood for your group type. He also has to perform a minor surgical procedure. This all to keep you safe, healthy and well. Do not be worried." He repeated all this in Russian and the girls exchanged anxious glances. "You will go one at a time into the next room with Dr Charles then you can all return to the kitchen and have a decent meal. I expect you are all ravenous." He put his fingers to his mouth and mimed eating, saying, "Yesti." Then he explained the whole thing again in Bulgarian for the few Bulgarians with the Russians.

Marcus Paulson entered the kitchen and insisted on looking the girls over. He made them stand in a line and eyed them up one by one and whistled appreciatively. "You have surpassed yourself this time, Bogdan." He pulled out Ivanka, "You go first," and gestured that she follow the doctor.

Ivanka clutched her bag to her and went into the room off the kitchen and the door closed behind her.

Ivanka was told to sit in a chair next to a table laid out with medical instruments. She looked alarmed and hesitated, "What is this?"

"Nothing for you to worry about," said the Crippen, Himmler looking, Dr Charles. "Now, sit." Ivanka sat, albeit reluctantly, her eyes still on the medical equipment. "Now, firstly I have to check you over, make sure you are okay after your long journey." He sounded reassuring but his voice had an oily quality that made Ivanka shudder.

He rested her left arm on a pillow placed the blood pressure cuff around her upper arm. Now just relax, don't talk and don't move." He waited a couple of minutes and then the cuff began to tighten. Ivanka felt her arm would burst. He studied the reading. "Hmm, a little high, but not a problem. Understandable in these circumstances." He removed the cuff. "Now, for some blood. The veins should be more prominent after that. Now hold still. You will feel a sharp prick." He inserted the hypodermic and drew a phial full of blood, removed it and labelled it. "You are Ivanka, yes?" She nodded. "Now, just one more procedure. This is to keep you safe, while you are here."

"What is it?"

"Nothing to worry about. It is a tiny device, a microchip and means if you get into any trouble we will be able to find you and bring you back safely."

"Why would I get into trouble?"

"You're in a new country. Anything might happen. We don't want anyone to take advantage of you. It is purely a precaution. Also, we want to dispense a contraceptive implant."

"Why would you do that?" said Ivanka suspiciously.

"Just in case you become involved with the wrong person and decide you don't want to marry him. You can have it removed at any time quite easily and the Nexplanon implant lasts for three years. It's very safe."

Ivanka studied the doctor's face, "What if I don't want either of them? What then?"

"You will be returned to Russia. It's up to you. But think of what you'll be missing."

Ivanka was becoming more alarmed. She watched as Dr Charles prepared a syringe. "What's that?"

"Just a local anaesthetic. You won't feel a thing."

Ivanka stood up and faced the doctor. "No. I don't want it. Any of it. I'd rather go back home." She placed her hand on the table and removed one of the chips from the dish and held onto it, whilst holding the doctor's gaze.

The doctor eyed her coldly through his steel wire framed specs. "Very well. You can wait in there." He pointed to a door leading off from the small utility room. Ivanka began to stride towards it. She opened the door and was struck from behind. She felt a sharp pain in her neck, fell forward half in and half out of the cupboard and blacked out freeing the chip, which slid unnoticed under the shelf of cookery books and cooking utensils.

Dr Charles pulled her back, closed the door and set to work fitting her up with a tracker inside her arm and the Nexplanon implant in her upper arm. He opened another door to a walk-in larder and dragged Ivanka's body inside. "There. That should keep you quiet for a while."

The doctor closed the larder door. He then opened the kitchen door. "Next!"

Paulson raised his eyebrows, "Where is Ivanka?"

"She just needed a breath of fresh air, so she has gone for a little walk outside. She'll be back soon."

Paulson pursed his lips and nodded slowly in understanding. "Right, next one, please. Svetlana."

Svetlana, a curvaceous petite blonde entered the kitchen and the door closed. Firmly.

14

THE BELL RANG AND RONNIE'S heart beat faster as he opened the door wide and saw Siri standing outside with Ayesha. She lifted up her huge dark eyes fringed with the longest lashes Ronnie thought he had ever seen.

The cab driver walked up the path with two bags and placed them on the step. "There you go." Ronnie thanked him and ushered the two inside. Ronnie placed the bag at the bottom of the stairs and urged them, "This way, this way. Gurdip is in the kitchen and has he prepared a feast!

Gurdip came out from the small kitchen and his eyes filled with tears as he saw his sisters. Siri ran to him and he hugged her fiercely while Ayesha stood uncertainly, wondering what to do. Ronnie took the little girl's hand, "Would you like to see your room?" Ayesha nodded and Ronnie led her to the foot of the stairs. He let go of her hand and picked up the bags, "This way. Follow me."

Ronnie climbed the staircase. He pointed out the bathroom and the different bedrooms. "That's where Gurdip sleeps. This one here is mine and this one is yours and Siri's."

He placed the bags inside and studied the little girl's face, which puckered into a grin. "Mine?"

"All yours and Siri's."

There were two single beds in there. "Which one is mine?"

"Which one would you like?"

"The one by the window."

"They're both by the window." Ayesha looked at both and then firmly plonked herself on the right-hand side. "Very well. I'm sure Siri will agree." Ronnie picked up her bag and placed it next to her on the bed. "There you go. After dinner you will be able to unpack your things and put them where you want. Now, let's get downstairs and get something to eat." Ayesha nodded happily and skipped out of the room. Ronnie sighed; things would be markedly different but they would be good. He was sure of that and he followed Ayesha down the stairs.

Gurdip and Siri were already in the dining room and chattering happily. The table was laid with all manner of treats, vegetable and meat samosas, a variety of pakoras and bhajis. There was a bowl of cucumber raita, another of lime pickle and one of mango chutney. A large dish of hot steaming vegetable rice was centre sitting on a hotplate and another of a creamy chicken korma, naans and flatbreads also graced the table alongside a bowl of hotter, mixed meat curry.

Siri looked up expectantly as Ronnie and Ayesha sat. Ayesha licked her lips, "This looks yummy, Gurdip. I have missed Bebe's cooking so much," and her eyes filled with tears.

Siri lightly scolded her, "This is not a time to be sad. This is a time for celebration for family and friends to meet as one and share in this feast." She turned to her brother, "You have surpassed yourself, brother. I am so proud of you."

Gurdip laughed, "You had better taste it all first. It won't be like Bebe's. Mother was a wonderful cook."

"Maybe not, but it looks and smells delicious," said Siri and picked up her plate to begin serving herself. "This is our new home, now. Gurdip and I will share the cooking between us."

"What about me?" asked Ronnie.

"You'll get a turn. But we don't want pizzas and burgers every night."

"No, only on take-away nights," said Ronnie with a grin. "After all, we must have a night off!"

The meal continued with lively chatter and every now and then, Gurdip caught his sister smiling shyly at Ronnie, but this time he didn't bristle or allow any prejudices to surface. He glanced at his friend, smiling back at his sister with great love and respect in his eyes and he was satisfied.

"Tomorrow, I will go around to the Gurdwara Committee. It's time we sorted out your divorce, Siri. And now let's eat, laugh and enjoy your welcome home evening."

Allison woke Katy gently holding a cup of tea, "I have to leave for work now. When you're ready go downstairs and Mary will give you breakfast. You have a big day ahead of you."

Katy sat up in bed and rubbed her eyes. She gratefully accepted the tea and smiled at Allison, "I can't thank you enough. You have been so kind. I don't think I shall ever look at the police in the same way again."

"You just make sure that when you get home, you sort out what you want to do and go for it. Remember the only failures are those who give up and I believe that for you, failure is not an option."

"Isn't that what they say at NASA about their astronauts and space exploration?"

"Possibly. I know I have heard it before somewhere. But I have to say. I agree. Well, goodbye, Miss Vicary and good luck. If we need to contact you, I know now where to find you."

"What about Big Den?"

"I'll get someone along there to explain to him that you're safe. Will that suffice?"

Katy nodded slowly, "Yes, thank you."

"Well then, this is it. I wish you well." Allison smiled and nodded before he disappeared out of her room and closed the door. He had a merry twinkle in his eyes and he felt good, almost as if he had already had a Mars Bar.

Katy sat up in the bed, a proper bed and drank her tea. She was feeling positive, happy and safe. For the first time, in a long time, she was looking forward to the future.

Allison arrived in the building and appeared very cheerful as he stepped into his office. It was rare for him to be so genial first thing in the morning. "Tea please, Maddie."

He said this with a smile and Maddie looked up in surprise, "Well, hello. Someone's in a good mood."

"Yes, for once I feel as if I have done something to improve someone's life."

"The young girl who was here yesterday?"

"Yes, Katy Vicary, a runaway who should be now…" he glanced at his watch, "on the way to the station and her home." He took off his coat and hung it up, rubbed his hands and smiled again, "Now, how about that tea?"

"Coming up," said Maddie and moved to the kettle and mugs in the office.

"Oh, and tell Mark I want to see him when he gets in."

"Sir."

Allison settled himself at his desk and perused his files. They needed to visit West End Products again and he promised Katy he'd speak to Big Den. They could cross those off the list first when Mark arrived and they paid both places a visit. In the mean-while he'd review the final reports on Bannen Sadler to close the file and that of Pasha Chand.

Big Den had got up late that morning his alarm had not gone off and without Katy to remind him, he had just forgotten to set it. It was never a problem when she stayed there, as she would always knock on his door if he hadn't emerged by half past seven. He stepped into his bathroom intending to strip wash and shave.

He would shave first. He was trying to conserve energy and water. His utility bills were set to sky rocket and he only budgeted for so much a month, but he felt he needed a proper shower. He wouldn't linger and it used less water and he would feel cleaner.

Outside the flat in Gillott Road a black BMW X5 was parked. The sun was just beginning to rise and the promise of lighter mornings ahead must have set the birds singing. They were trilling chirpily in the trees at the dawning of a new day, which promised to be good according to the weather forecast; otherwise the street was quiet.

Marcus Paulson checked all around him before he stepped out of the vehicle and signalled to Bernie Carter who also alighted. They crossed the road to the house converted into flats and stepped inside the gate behind the high hedge and large beech tree that sat in the front. They were hidden from view from the road.

Bernie pulled out a pack of cigarettes and lit one. He took a long drag. "So, what's the plan?"

"As discussed, try not to be seen. There's no cameras so that's an advantage. We know the drill for this house. Flat one and four always seem to come out first. Our man is in flat six. If we can gain access after they have left we should be able to surprise him."

"In the meantime, we keep shtum."

"Correct."

Bernie continued to draw on his cigarette, while Marcus played on his phone. He suddenly became alert as he heard footsteps coming down the stairs and along the corridor towards the front door. He put his fingers to his lips and both men stepped between the tree and hedge. They were now hidden from view.

A scruffy student type whistled as he walked past with music blasting into his earphones while his eyes were glued to his phone. He was followed by a smartly dressed woman carrying a briefcase, swinging her car keys. She looked neither to the left nor the right. If she had, she would have seen the two men slip out from behind the tree and move swiftly to the front door to prevent it from closing. Safely inside, they sneaked up the stairs to the second floor and paused outside flat six and listened.

Sounds from people in the house waking up and preparing to go to work were apparent. "We'd better be quick," hissed Marcus. "We daren't be seen." Bernie nodded at Marcus before studying the door and lock. There was no spy hole for anyone to see who was outside and no letterbox to peer through. They listened at the door but couldn't hear anything. Bernie took a tool from a small roll of utensils he carried in his pocket and fiddled with the Yale lock until it clicked and opened. They both entered just as a female came from the floor above but she only caught the tail end of the men disappearing inside Big Den's flat and to begin with she thought nothing of it. All she saw was the back of a man and a wisp of a grey ponytail.

Paulson and Carter tiptoed quietly into the flat and could hear the water running from a shower. Big Den was warbling a version of Daniel Merryweather's song, Red. Marcus Paulson moved into the sitting area and sat in a chair facing the small hallway where the bathroom and bedroom were situated. Bernie Carter secreted himself behind the partition wall leading from the front door. They remained there quietly.

Eventually, they heard the shower switch off and an electric toothbrush whirred into life. Marcus signalled to Bernie to get ready. Big Den pink and freshly showered emerged from the bathroom wrapped in a towel and crossed into the bedroom opposite without a glance to the sitting room where Paulson sat.

Paulson could hear Big Den shuffling around his room, presumably getting dressed. He signalled to Carter, rose and moved out of view of the small corridor and waited. The tension began to show in his body. The veins in his neck began to pulse and stood out like cords. He removed a Glock 17 from behind his back and fitted a silencer taken from his inside jacket pocket. He was poised like a predator ready to spring.

Big Den emerged from his bedroom, whistling. He stopped momentarily, patted his pockets and returned to his bedroom and re-emerged with his wallet in his hand and muttered, "Won't get very far without that." He strode into the living room unaware at what was waiting for him.

Carter leapt out behind him and jumped on his back. Big Den swung around trying to shake off his assailant. It was then he saw Paulson circling into view and levelling his gun on him. In a sudden surge of strength, Big Den bent forward and threw Carter off him, overturning a chair in the process.

Carter smashed onto the coffee table and the glass cracked. Roaring like a deranged bull, Big Den charged at Paulson and the gun went off with a strange pfft sound. Groaning, Carter struggled to his feet and limped towards the two men locked in a clinch, who slowly slid to the floor. Paulson arose shakily and saw the blood pulsing from Big Den's chest. Carter hissed, "Leave him. He'll die anyway. Let's get out of here."

Paulson nodded, "I'll just make sure" and he raised the weapon and pointed it at Big Den's head when there was a knock on the door.

"Den? Den are you all right?" came a woman's voice. Paulson put his fingers to his lips to hush Carter. "I heard some banging… Den?"

Eventually footsteps could be heard moving away and down the stairs. Carter grabbed Paulson's arm. "Leave it. Come on." Paulson reluctantly lowered his gun and replaced it in his trouser waistband and they crept to the door tentatively opening it and slipped back down the stairs.

Flat four, underneath Big Den's, opened a crack and a woman peeped out and just caught the back of the man with a long grey ponytail. She went to the stairwell and heard the front door close before returning inside and rushing to the window to see Paulson and Carter getting into a black BMW X5. She strained to see the number plate but her heart was racing away and she couldn't grasp much.

Lily Golden, twenty-five years of age was a petite, strawberry blonde with red highlights. She frowned remembering the shouts and crash from upstairs. Now the men had gone she left her flat again and mounted the stairs two at a time to Big Den's. The door had not quite shut and locked so, she pushed it with her fingertip. As soon as she entered she saw the mound of a man next to a broken coffee table and overturned chair and she ran to Big Den's side.

She saw the blood pulsing from his chest now frothy and red. She grabbed the throw from the settee and bundled it up and pressed it against the gunshot wound trying to keep pressure on it with one hand, while fiddling in her pocket for her phone.

Big Den's eyes flickered and she urged him, "Stay with me, Den. Stay with me, please." With only one hand she nimbly dialled 999 with her thumb and waited.

Allison and Stringer were on the way to Gillott Road unaware of what was unfolding. An ambulance screamed past them, lights flashing and sirens blazing and turned off the Hagley Road into Gillott Road, closely followed by Allison and Stringer.

Mark turned to Allison and questioned, "You don't think…?"

"I don't know," said Allison drawing his bushy brows together. "Put the siren on and let's find out."

They crossed Portland Road and continued up Gillott Road into the three hundreds and pulled up behind the ambulance. Two paramedics jumped out and opened up the back to get a gurney. Allison and Stringer exchanged a look and entered the property. They bounded up the stairs and saw flat six's door had been propped open.

They dashed inside to see Lily sitting at the side of the mountain of a man that was Big Den. She had tears streaming down her face and was covered in blood. She sobbed aloud as Allison announced them both.

"I think you're too late," she whimpered, but she still kept a firm grip on the throw against his wound. The paramedics hurried inside and moved Lily away to check Big Den's vitals.

"He's lost a lot of blood. But there is a faint heartbeat. Quickly, let's move him out."

Allison looked across at Lily, "We will need you to come to the station and make a statement. Did you see what happened?"

Lily shook her head slowly, "No. But I heard it. And I caught a glimpse of the two men who did this, but just from the back. One of them had a long grey ponytail."

Mark and Allison exchanged a look, "Anything else?"

"They drove off in a black BMW four by four. I'm not very good on cars."

"Licence plate?"

"I'm not sure. I caught a quick glimpse, but it was too quick and I was upset."

The paramedics had managed with a struggle to load Big Den onto the stretcher and were manoeuvring their way out of the flat and down the stairs.

Lily sniffed, "Do you need me to come now?"

Allison gently replied, "If you could."

"Can I get changed first?" she asked.

"Of course. We'll wait here."

Allison instructed Mark, "Get a team of SOCOS here pronto. Don't touch anything."

Gurdip walked to the bus stop that would take him into Smethwick and the Gurdwara Nanaksar. He was feeling nervous. Occasion for divorce in Sikhism was so very rare he could only hope one of the women on the committee would be sympathetic and pass judgement in Siri's favour. He was armed with photographic evidence and hospital reports of the violence perpetrated against his sister and the police reports of the deaths of family members and more.

Ronnie and Siri had taken Ayesha to George Dixon Primary School for her first day in school. They were meeting with Miss Lupton the infants' reception class teacher. Siri was then going back to Birmingham University to try and re-enrol on her nursing course. Gurdip prayed that she would be successful. But now, he had to focus on how he was to present his case. He would then go with Siri to the Law Courts in Birmingham and officially put in place her divorce papers, so there would be no doubt that Siri would be a free woman.

But, now… now he had to get to Waterloo Road in Smethwick. Gurdip set off with determination in his stride.

The Russian and Bulgarian girls were now in another wing of the house, two to a room and the doors locked. Ivanka lay on one of the beds and began to come around as Svetlana paced the room. She moved to Ivanka's side as she began to groan.

Svetlana shook Ivanka and urged her, "Znaesh li bulgarski ezik?"

Ivanka murmured, "Net… no… I can't speak Bulgarian." She turned over and tried to sleep again.

Svetlana whispered more urgently, "Very well, we speak English."

Ivanka just muttered something unintelligible.

Svetlana shook her again. "Wake up! Please wake up."

Ivanka sat up groggily and shook her head as if trying to clear it. "What? What's happened?"

"I don't know what's happened to you. Been drugged, I think. This isn't what it's supposed to be."

Ivanka nodded, beginning to think a little more clearly, "I believe you. I think we're prisoners here."

"Well, the door is locked. They've taken our passports and phones." She indicated her arm, "We've been doctored with something…."

"It's a tracker and a contraceptive implant," said Ivanka coming to her full senses.

"Then what do we do? We're trapped."

"Firstly, keep calm. We have to figure a way out of here."

"I've looked. The door is locked. So, are the windows. We are on the first floor."

Ivanka rose from the bed and stumbled to the door and rattled the door knob. Then she crossed back to the window and peered out. Part of the grounds outside would light up at any sort of movement, but not immediately outside their window. Ivanka took this as a good sign. The grounds appeared to be patrolled by two guards with dogs. Ivanka tried to open the window. She couldn't.

"I told you it's locked."

"It's not. There is no lock. It's painted shut. See."

Svetlana examined the window and nodded, "If we can get something to work at the seals and break the paint we can open the window."

"With what? We need a knife or something sharp."

"Is there anything in the room or in there?" Svetlana gestured to the en suite. Ivanka hurried in and began to search the bathroom cupboards as Svetlana examined the drawers in the dressing table and bedside tables.

Ivanka came out shaking her head, "Nothing that I can see."

Svetlana seemed to have drawn a blank, too. She opened the wardrobe, which housed some clothes and pulled out a thin wire coat hanger, "We have this."

Ivanka nodded, "It's worth a try."

Svetlana opened the slim wire up and twisted it, bending it back and forth to try and break it in to two.

"Here, let me. I have an idea." Svetlana passed the hanger to Ivanka who worked at the weakened spot and then took it to the door of the en suite. She pushed the wire by the door catch and succeeded in closing the door. She repeated this action until the wire looked ready to snap.

"Careful," warned Svetlana. The paint on the door is crumbling. It looks like we've done something."

Ivanka stopped. She could see the wood was splintering. She dashed to the bed, "Where's my bag?"

"In the nightstand. They shoved it in there when they brought you in here."

Ivanka opened the cupboard door and pulled the bag out. She breathed a sigh of relief as she felt in the pocket and the phone was still in there but she didn't disclose that information, yet. She rummaged further and pulled out a pot of clear nail varnish and attempted to repair the damage to the door. "There. It doesn't look so bad now. Maybe they won't notice."

"Maybe," said Svetlana uncertainly.

There was something of a ruckus outside in the corridor and both girls looked in alarm. Svetlana put her ear to the door to listen as Ivanka secreted the weakened wire under the mattress of her bed and shoved her bag back in the bedside cupboard. She lay on her bed and feigned sleep. Svetlana stepped back from the door and hurried to the other bed where she lay staring up at the ceiling as the door opened.

Bogdan entered and perused the room. He pointed at Svetlana, "You. Come with me."

Svetlana cringed on the bed but was dragged up roughly by Bogdan as one of the other Bulgarian men stood filling the doorway. Ivanka dared not speak. She heard Svetlana struggling against Bogdan and asking, "Why are you doing this to us? Zashto ni prichinyavish tova? Zashto? Why?"

The door slammed and locked. Ivanka sat up and stared about her wildly. She had to get out. She had to get out… now.

Gurdip had spread all of the shocking photographs of Siri's abuse onto the table in front of the five Gurdwara Committee members. There was also a copy of the hospital report cataloguing her injuries. Finally, the police reports of Pasha's misdeeds, the murder of his parents, the arson attacks and attacks in both the Punjab as well as in Handsworth and Bradford. He made an impassioned plea for his sister's release from her marriage to Pasha.

The four men studied the pictures distastefully and the one female member, Harpal Kaur stifled an exclamation of disgust. Gurdip could see in her eyes that she was horrified at the brutality his sister had suffered.

Harjinder Singh Badungar whose benign countenance belied his heart of steel, peered over his rimless glasses and scrutinised Gurdip's face. He made his first statement. "You will leave these items with us to peruse. I need not tell you that divorce is a very serious matter. It is not something that we take lightly unlike our Western brothers. In fact, in my time on the committee we have never had to deal with a case like this. Divorce is never considered if mediation can take place. Pasha and Siri are one soul in two bodies and it goes against everything we believe about marriage. However, these are serious accusations and no family should have their lives put at risk in a case such as this. Please leave us and we will discuss together the way forward and our judgement. You may return on this day and time next week, which will give us time to consider the matter and to converse with Pasha in prison. He must be allowed to speak in his defence." With that he dismissed Gurdip, who left offering his thanks. The committee watched as he walked away regally from the meeting.

Svetlana kicked and attempted to bite and scratch as two Bulgarian men tried to drag her down the passage and back to the kitchen, where she faced Dr Charles again, who was standing next to Bogdan. The doctor stared at her through his rimless glasses with his fish-like eyes. "I think you need a little something to calm you down. Make you more compliant. Bogdan here wants to try you out. He doesn't want a spitting hell cat. Hold her. Tightly."

"Wait! There must be an easier way," said Svetlana as she glanced at the medical instruments on the table.

"Well, that's better. Come. Sit here." The men pushed Svetlana towards the chair by the table of instruments. Svetlana appeared to stumble and lose her balance as they released her. She fell onto the table and surreptitiously secreted one of the scalpels in her hand and placed it in her pocket.

"I think you had better hold her," said the doctor. We don't want any accidents." Bogdan's two henchmen caught her by the shoulders securing her on the seat.

Dr Charles took a syringe and filled it with a clear liquid from a phial. He crossed to the squirming girl, leaned over her and pulled up her sleeve. With all the force she could muster, Svetlana spat in his face. Dr Charles calmly wiped away the spittle and prepared the syringe. His voice was icy and filled with menace, "You will regret that, Svetlana. And if you do not pass this test, you will pay with your life. A healthy young girl like you can save many lives with your organ donations." He plunged the needle into her arm and Svetlana became disorientated and slumped. "Take her where you will, she will be obedient."

Dr Charles nodded at the men who lifted the dead weight ready to half carry and half drag the subdued girl. Bogdan looked at the semi-conscious young woman. "This one will be worth a lot. I hope you don't have to carry out your threat."

"We shall have to see," replied the doctor coldly. "Take her away."

The men did as asked and removed her, dragging her along the passage to another room. Bogdan followed. Svetlana was thrown on the bed and Bogdan ordered the men to leave. He announced in Bulgarian. "You will get your turn."

The men guffawed and left the room, which Bogdan locked after them. He eyed the girl spread-eagled on the bed lasciviously and walked towards her slowly undoing his trousers.

15

ALLISON AND MARK WERE AT the hospital. They weren't saying much but waited for the doctor who had been attending to Big Den to report back. They were relieved to see the physician striding along the corridor towards them. Allison and Mark rose from their seats and looked at the doctor questioningly.

The doctor looked at them. "I won't deny he's critical. He has lost a lot of blood but he is a big man with great strength and is a fighter. The bullet has been removed. He is in recovery now."

"Will he live?" asked Allison. "When can we talk to him?"

"I don't know, to both answers. He will be monitored closely. We will keep you informed. He was lucky that young woman found him when she did. Another ten minutes and he would have been dead."

"What about the bullet?"

"We have that bagged for you."

Allison nodded, "We'll take it away and I will get a guard posted at his door. Where will he go after recovery?"

"Into CCU."

"Thank you, Doctor…?"

"Johnson."

"Dr Johnson… Let me know as soon as he's awake, please. You have my number." Allison passed the doctor his card. "Ring anytime. Day or night."

The doctor nodded, "I'll get the bullet." He strode off, quickly followed by Mark and Allison.

Ivanka continued to try and prise open the widow using the coat hanger wire. It was proving to be more difficult than she thought. The wire just wasn't sharp enough. Ivanka, ever alert, heard a noise in the corridor and hurried back to her bed. She hid the wire under her mattress once more and lay back feigning sleep.

She could hear the sound of her door unlocking and waited hardly daring to breathe. Her muscles tensed involuntarily and she forced herself to relax as the door opened. Two men dragged Svetlana into the room while a third stood at the door. They threw the girl on the bed.

"What about her?" said one in Bulgarian.

"Nah! She's still out of it. We'll come back for her later." The men laughed and exited the room. Ivanka heard them locking the door after them.

Ivanka opened her eyes and glanced across at Svetlana who was curled into a foetal ball. Her eyes were glassy and staring. Ivanka jumped off the bed and shook her gently, "Svetlana, Svetlana… wake up please."

Svetlana turned her head and tears streamed from her eyes. She studied Ivanka's face and said, "You were right. Something is very wrong. We have been tricked. That man, Bogdan… he raped me." Svetlana curled up even tighter and her face creased in anguish.

"I'm sorry, so sorry but we can't let our guard down. We have to get out. Come on. Go to the bathroom, freshen yourself up."

Svetlana sat up and rasped, "I'll never get the stink off my body from that rat."

"No…" Ivanka's voice was measured, "but we will find a way. A way to make him pay. Make them all pay."

Svetlana got off the bed and limped towards the bathroom and turned. "We will get out. I have something to help us." She ferreted in her pocket and removed the scalpel. "Look!"

Ivanka gasped, "But how?"

"I will tell you later. You get to work while I try and get clean." She passed the tool to Ivanka who hurried to the window and began probing at the paintwork around the catch and along the sill. In the background of running water she heard Svetlana retching into the toilet bowl and shuddered.

Svetlana and Ivanka had managed to cut through the hard paint that sealed the window and gouged it out from around the catch, which was now working albeit with difficulty. Ivanka tried the window latch. It moved. They had unsealed the bottom of the window and now were working on the sides of the sash and making progress.

Ivanka put her fingers to her lips, "Hush. I can hear someone outside." Svetlana secreted the scalpel and curled up on the bed. Ivanka, hid the wire and still pretended to be comatose as the lock was heard opening from outside. Two men marched in. They looked at Svetlana still curled up and snorted in derision. Muttering in Bulgarian how she had better shape up and get used to it.

They crossed to Ivanka and tried to haul her up. She flopped back and groaned letting her eyes roll back in her head and dribbled. The men looked at her as if she was faking it and one took a knife from his waist and pressed it into Ivanka's arm. She didn't move even though it had cut and was beginning to bleed. "Leave her," said one.

"Give her another hour and then she'll be properly awake to enjoy what we have on offer." They both guffawed cruelly and left, locking the door behind them.

As soon as they heard them go, Ivanka sat up. She climbed off the bed and studied her cut arm. It had taken all her strength not to wince or jump when they cut her. She grabbed a chair and forced it under the door handle then she whispered, "Svetlana, help me." Svetlana turned and saw that Ivanka was standing by the chest of drawers and wanted help to move it. Together they carried it to the door, removed the chair and effectively barricaded the door to prevent it opening.

Ivanka hunted through the wardrobe with Svetlana. Unfortunately, their own clothes were nowhere to be seen. They had to stick with the evening dresses. "Good job we still have our own shoes," said Ivanka looking at her feet.

"Now what?" asked Svetlana.

"We get out," said Ivanka with a grin. "Get your coat and bag. And be quiet."

"What about our phones and passports?"

"We have to leave them for now. First we need to escape and get these trackers taken out of our arms. Otherwise, we will never be free and always be on the run."

"Easier said than done."

"Never mind that. Let's go."

Ivanka slowly undid the catch, which moved with a squeak. They stopped and listened in case the sound had carried. All seeming well and with their hearts thudding loudly in their chests, Ivanka finished working the sides of the window sash. "How long?" she whispered to Svetlana.

"We've been fifteen minutes."

"Nearly there…"

Ivanka gouged the final piece of paint from the wood and tentatively caught the handles at the bottom and it began to lift, but made a terrible noise.

"What now?"

"Look in the bathroom, see if there's any oil-based cosmetics or something to lubricate the sides."

Svetlana dashed to the bathroom and pulled out a bottle of shampoo. "Will this do?"

"Perfect," murmured Ivanka.

Ivanka took the bottle and liberally poured the silky liquid down both sides of the sash. "Now, you grab one handle. I'll take the other and when I say 'go' lift with all your might. Ready?" Svetlana nodded. "Okay, after three. One, two, three, go!"

The young women tugged with all their strength and finally the window began to grind its way up. "That's far enough," said Ivanka. "Take the scalpel. Got your bag? Coat?" Svetlana put on hers, and slung her bag from her shoulder across her body, leaving her hands free. "Okay, now let's go, urged Ivanka."

"But where?"

"I'll be right behind you. We'll figure it out."

"It's quite a drop and there are dogs."

"What's the worst that can happen?"

"We'll get caught…"

"Not if I can help it. Quickly now. Hurry"

Svetlana dropped the eight feet from the sill into the flower bed below, bending her knees and rolling over. It had knocked the wind out of her but she was unhurt. Her heart was racing as she waited for Ivanka.

Ivanka had placed the pillows in their beds and covered them over with blankets to make it look as if they were sleeping. It just might give them a minute or two of extra time. She hurried back to the window, closed the curtains, threw down her bag and clambered out. She clung to the sill while struggling to close the window. It finally shut with a loud squeak. After manoeuvring herself to sit on the sill she took a deep breath and dropped as relaxed as she could be and landed softly in the flower bed.

Now, now they had to get out and that was not going to be easy. Ivanka looked at her watch. In just over fifteen minutes, they would be back at her room to take her down to Bogdan or one of the other men. They had not got long. They had to cross the garden without going on the main path, which swept from the gates to the front of the house. They needed to find a place to safely climb over the wall without attracting the dogs and guards. Nor did they want one of the many sensors to light them up and reveal their position.

Then, there were the trackers. Ivanka didn't know if they were constantly monitored or if they had some time before they would be pursued. Svetlana pointed to a large oak that had evenly spread strong looking branches and one branch dipped low to the ground. It was right by the high wall.

Ivanka nodded, slung her bag across her body, like Svetlana had done, and they ran quickly towards it. Ivanka scrambled onto the first low branch and walked up it, snagging her red evening dress as she did. In annoyance she caught hold of it and ripped the hem off shortening the skirt some inches and then tucked the rest of the material inside her knickers.

Svetlana hitched up her dress and tucked it up as well and scooted up behind Ivanka just as the sensor lights at the corner of the house flooded on and a guard walked around with a large Doberman on a strong leash.

The young women remained quiet and immobile, scarcely breathing and waited for the man to pass along the path. The sensor light went out and the girls resumed their climb. The tree would have been heaven to a child who liked to climb. They managed to scale the tree until they were level with the top of the wall. They had just inched their way across when all hell broke loose in the house. Lights blazed on the first floor, there were raised voices. The guards were alerted and they released their dogs.

Ivanka got onto the top of the wall and looked down at the street below. No soft flower bed to land in there, but fear and adrenalin spurred her on and she dropped, falling on her knees and grazing them. She scrambled up and hissed at Svetlana, "Now… Jump!" But Svetlana was frozen. "I can't… you go."

"You must! Do you want to be raped again? Or worse, beaten?"

Something registered in Svetlana's eyes, which she closed tightly and jumped. Ivanka half caught her and they struggled up and began to run down the street, hobbling slightly on their bruised legs.

In the house, the men were trying to force their way into the barricaded room. Eventually, with five of them they managed to push open the door enough to see inside. One lean man squeezed through the gap and was able to shift the chest of drawers away from the door and the men piled in. They ripped off the bed covers to see the pillows and searched the room and bathroom looking for the girls' hiding place. Bogdan moved swiftly to the window and threw back the drapes. He saw the splintered wood and yanked up the sash window swearing loudly when he realised that this was their route of escape. He yelled instructions to his men and shouted at the guards outside before racing from the room and dashing down to a chamber on the ground floor filled with technical equipment. He ordered one man to pull up the tracker programme to be told that it hadn't yet been loaded and activated and he slapped the man hard across the face and urged him to do it now.

The men were commanded to search the house and grounds, while he waited for the tracker programme to be set up. The techie argued that they usually waited until the women were in their placements but Bogdan screamed that it wasn't quick enough and the techie went back to work.

Svetlana and Ivanka limped along the road, they had only a little money, and had no idea where they were. Ivanka urged her new friend, "We need to find the city, bright lights and people and then we can get help."

"But I don't have much money."

"No, nor do I but I do have a credit card and a phone."

"But I thought you handed it in?" Svetlana gasped.

"I did… one of them. But I have two. I was just being prepared, in case of what I don't know but it seems my gut instinct was right."

"Well, let's use it."

"I don't have the charger. I want to conserve the battery. I will switch it on when we're safe."

The young women hurried along Woodbourne Road as the road sign said. They could hear the sound of noisy traffic and turned towards it into Westfield Road. They hurried along and came to the very busy Hagley Road. On the opposite side they could see a hotel, a Quality Inn, which Ivanka pointed out but first they had to get across to the other side. Their eyes searched left and right and as soon as there was a gap in the cars they raced across the road and hurried towards the hotel's main entrance.

They burst in through the doors into the polished tiled floor foyer and scuttled to the big wooden reception desk and waited. There was a partially open door behind reception and a woman was sitting inside working on a computer. Ivanka coughed loudly. The woman turned and came to the front. She smiled and asked, "How can I help?"

"Do you have a room available, please? A double room?"

"Of course, let me see." She tip-tapped away on her computer. "Yes, do you want twin or a double bed?"

"It doesn't matter."

The woman continued to type and then looked up. "Can I have your names please?"

Ivanka hesitated and then said, "Ella Purdom and Nancy Brodie."

The woman typed the names into the online hotel register, "Address?"

Ivanka thought quickly dredging some long-lost memories of London from her mind, "5, Parkhill Road, London NE 3."

"NE 3…?"

"I'm not sure of the rest. We've only just moved there."

"No matter, I can look it up," said the receptionist with a smile.

"How would you like to pay?"

Ivanka rummaged in her bag and fished out her credit card and passed it across the wi-fi symbol on the keypad. It was accepted. The woman proceeded to process two key cards whilst giving them the spiel about breakfast times and where to go. Ivanka nodded politely and took the keys.

"Room 12, floor one. The lift is just there."

Ivanka thanked her and the two women hurried to the lift to take them to the safety of their room. In the elevator, Svetlana asked, "Where on earth did you think up those names and the address?"

Ivanka, tapped her nose with her finger, "I had a penfriend, when I was in school. That was her name and address"

"And the other name?"

"I just made it up. Ella was my penfriend and I have always liked the name Nancy, Brodie was a character in a TV series I liked." Svetlana laughed at her friend's ingenuity. The lift doors opened and they hurried along the corridor to room 12.

Once inside, Ivanka drew the curtains and studied the room. She noticed the tea and coffee making facilities and suggested Svetlana make them both a drink, before searching around the room and en suite for anything that could help them. She dug at the micro-chip in her arm. "We have to get rid of these, cut them out."

"What?" squealed Svetlana in horror. "How?" She stopped and turned from her tea making.

"Do you still have that scalpel?"

"Somewhere."

"Find it, we'll need it."

Svetlana grimaced, "I'm not sure about this."

"Neither am I, but if we want to escape we have to do it."

"There's a phone here. Let's just ring the police, if they can be trusted."

"Oh, we'll ring them. But only once we're safe."

"How did you manage to keep your credit card? They went through my bag when Bogdan was… you know."

"They couldn't search us all before. It would have been too suspicious. I suspect as soon as we were one on one with them they would do that."

"But they drugged you. Why not search you then?"

"I don't know. Besides, I kept my card in my bra. That is until we left. Good job, too. Now, let's have a hot drink. It will give us courage to remove these things." She looked distastefully at the small lump under her skin on the inside of her arm, where the tracker had been implanted.

All hell continued to break loose in the house where the girls had been taken. Bogdan screamed at his men in Bulgarian ordering them to search the house and grounds thoroughly, again. All the other girls were checked on and accounted for. It was clear that Ivanka and Svetlana were the only two missing.

Bogdan ran down to the basement and dragged one of the men from his game of cards where he was playing with two others, into a room filled with hi-tech equipment and shoved him in front of an array of screens, where CCTV covered the grounds of the house to check on any movement. There was nothing. He then yelled at the other man, attempting to load and activate the tracking software on the computer, instructing him to hurry up and get the application that tracked the girls' movements going.

The techie stumbled up and fumbled with his glasses as he attempted to access the programme but then encountered a glitch, which did nothing to improve Bogdan's temper. Bogdan paced around the floor waiting for the man to connect with the app. He took out his mobile phone and dialled a number. A muscle in his cheek pulsed in agitation as he waited for someone to answer.

"Marcus? We have a problem." He relayed what had happened and concluded, "We have to bring everything forward. If we can't get to these girls we cannot risk anyone coming here and finding the others… We're working on that now … Yes, I'll keep you posted … How fast can you move?… Good." He ended the call and turned to the man, "Any joy?"

"It's loading now," said one man peering over the techie's shoulder.

Bogdan grunted, pocketed his phone and went to continue watching the screen that covered the grounds.

"Hold still," said Svetlana. "My hands are shaking enough as it is."

"It's no good," murmured Ivanka. "Give it to me." She retrieved the scalpel and went into the bathroom, grabbed a towel off the rail and turned on the taps in the sink. "Help me. Hold my arm."

Svetlana looked concerned, "Are you sure?"

"Yes, it's got to be done. Hold my arm, tightly, please."

Svetlana bit her lip, turned on the cold tap in the wash basin and braced herself. She held onto Ivanka's arm as Ivanka steeled herself to cut. Fortunately, the microchip was just under the skin and Ivanka told herself that she wouldn't have to cut too deep. She took a deep breath, held it and then, breathed out slowly before taking another breath in and setting the scalpel onto her skin. The adrenaline rush helped to focus her mind and control her fear. She squealed as she inserted the blade in the area that was already sore and she cut, stifling the need to scream and flinch at the action.

The blood flowed freely and Ivanka delved deeper until she could lift the foreign body from her arm. She dropped the scalpel in the sink and held her arm under the cold tap letting it run before wrapping the towel around her wound. She looked at the offending intruder before throwing the chip on the floor and grinding it with her heel. Just to be certain she thrust the battered chip into the loo and flushed it away.

"Your turn now, Svetlana. We have to get rid of them."

Svetlana turned pale and whispered, "I can't. Don't make me, please. I can't."

"You have to, or they will find us and take us back, please," she begged.

"I'll take my chances. Please don't make me," and she started to cry.

Bogdan watched the screens running the CCTV footage and caught a slight movement, "Spri se… Stop! Stop there, spri tam. Can we get a better picture? Mozhem li da poluchem podobra kartina?"

The techie tried to enlarge and improve the resolution but without much luck. Bogdan slammed his fist into his hand in frustration. "We must get cameras into our blind spots outside. They obviously used one to their advantage," he growled in Bulgarian. He crossed to another of his men, who was English, a Kevin Bartholomew, known as Bart who was working on the tracking software. "Any luck?" Bogdan asked.

"It's just all loaded."

"And?"

"I'm just inputting all the tracking numbers, now."

"Forget the others, for now. Concentrate on Ivanka and Svetlana."

"They're all done."

"Well, where are they?"

"No sign of Ivanka."

"Why?"

"There's nothing, no signal."

"How come?" The man shrugged. "What's the range on these?"

"Same as a dog tracker, several miles."

"Well, she can't have got that far. What about Svetlana?"

The techie highlighted Svetlana's tracker and it could clearly be seen pulsating a few roads away.

"Either they've split up, and Ivanka's taken a bus or taxi or it's just malfunctioned. It doesn't look like Svetlana is moving. Where is that place?"

The techie dib-dabbed on his keyboard so a more detailed map came up on screen, "Norfolk Hotel, Quality Inn on the Hagley Road."

"That's not far. How did she get in there? She hasn't any cash…"

"Either she did have or someone has helped her."

"Keep watching… all of them. I am going to the hotel." He pointed to another man, "Penka, you come with me."

Penka was short and stocky but well-muscled. He grabbed his jacket and followed Bogdan swiftly and popped a piece of gum in his mouth, which he began to chew vigorously.

Ivanka was desperately trying to persuade Svetlana to let her remove the implanted chip. "They may have already discovered where we are. This is our only chance. Please." The desperation in Ivanka's voice was hard to dismiss.

Svetlana nodded with tears streaming down her face, "Okay, okay. Do it now before I change my mind. Quickly."

"Hold still; this will hurt."

Svetlana averted her eyes and gripped the rim of the wash basin with her free hand. She closed her eyes as Ivanka urged, "Ready?" Svetlana nodded and gritted her teeth as Ivanka cut.

Svetlana struggled not to cry out but whimpered like a beaten puppy and forced out an expletive and swore. Ivanka was quick and as the implant was just under the skin she didn't have to dig too far into the flesh. Svetlana suffered the burning sting of the blade and bit her lip almost drawing blood, but it was done. Ivanka grabbed the chip and flushed it down the toilet as she had with hers and then thrust Svetlana's arm under the cold tap to cleanse the wound before wrapping another towel around it. "Keep the pressure on it. It should stop. Tomorrow we will get something to cover our wounds. Are you all right?"

Svetlana stifled a sob but nodded again, "I'll be okay. What happens now?"

"We try and get a good night's sleep. After breakfast, I'll find out where the local police are. They will know what to do. They can't all be corrupt like ours."

"What if those men have already tracked us?"

"Don't think about that now. We'll cross that bridge when we come to it."

Bogdan and Penka were headed for the Hagley Road when Bogdan's phone went off. He answered and put it to his ear. The English man tracking Svetlana spoke quickly. "She's on the go and moving fast."

"Where?"

"Possibly in a vehicle, she's hurtling down the Hagley Road towards Five Ways. You'll need a car."

Bogdan swore. He turned to Penka, “Change of plan. We’ll head back and get a car. Bart can direct us on the phone. The two men turned swiftly and retraced their steps.

Mark paused on his way to Lloyd House. His mobile phone vibrated in his pocket. He took it out but it was a strange unknown number, “Hello?”

“Mark.”

“Alex?”

“Yes. Thought you should know, a consignment of women arrived at West End Products last night. We estimate there are about twenty girls. More alarmingly, a doctor was seen entering their premises.”

“A doctor?”

“Yes. We believe it’s someone who has been struck off and now earns his living with this gang. God knows what that means.” Mark felt chills down his arms and spine as he said that.

“We plan on visiting the warehouse again today with follow up enquiries.”

“Be careful and keep an eye out for anything unusual, anything at all.”

“Like what?”

“I’m not sure. Use your initiative. Any help in discovering where they’ve taken them will help.”

“Don’t you know?”

“If we did, they’d be in custody.”

“How did you miss them?”

“A truck parked inside the roller doors. They must have unloaded them inside. Our men followed the truck when it came out. It was stopped and searched but revealed nothing so it went on its way back to the docks, Bristol I think. The guy we left on surveillance lost the minibuses that took the girls away. We don’t have a clue where they were headed.”

Mark swore softly, “Did your guy, at least get a registration number of the vans? How many were there?”

“Three. And to answer the first question, no.” Alex sighed. “There should have been two operatives but there wasn’t. All our guy can remember is the last vehicle had the starting letters and numbers, WF 66… Sorry.”

"That will help, what colour and make?"

"From his description they are seven-seater vehicles, Ford Tourneo Custom in a metallic bronze colour."

"That narrows the search down. I'll get onto it. Now, how do you know the man was a doctor? Do we have a description?"

"Directional audio, parabolic microphone picked up Bogdan calling him doctor. And he was carrying a medical style bag. As for what he looked like… we don't have much. He was Caucasian, of medium height around five foot nine or ten, slim build. He wore a hat that hid his hair, which appeared to be cropped short. No discernible hair colour but he did wear glasses. What type he couldn't say, but he saw his hand come up to his face with his index finger and push something back in place. He thought it was spectacles that had slipped down his nose."

"Hmm, that will be useful. Anything else?"

"Not at the moment. Let us know the minute you've got something."

"You have my word." The call ended.

Allison lumbered into his office, grunted his good morning and requested tea. Maddie immediately obliged. He muttered, "As soon as you see Mark tell him I want to see him."

Moments later, Mark strolled in and Maddie signalled to him, "Mark? Chief wants you."

Mark nodded and crossed to Allison's door. En route to Lloyd House he had worked out exactly what he was going to say. He straightened himself up, took a deep breath, knocked politely and entered Allison's office. "You wanted to see me, Chief?"

"Yes. I want to visit West End Products again. Sniff around and see what else we can learn."

"I was going to talk to you about that." Allison raised an eyebrow. "I've done a bit of digging and some covert surveillance."

"Yes?" said Allison a little too sharply.

"All off the books. I couldn't stop thinking about what this Bogdan was supposed to have said after his name was heard in the club regarding a consignment of girls, I went down to the canal basin to watch. I saw a huge truck drive up and the door came up and they drove inside."

"So, you didn't see any girls? Or anything else?"

"Not exactly, but three vans drove up. I was too far away to hear anything or see too much. But it looked like each van was loaded with young women, which drove away."

"Did you follow?"

"No, I was on foot." Allison's eyebrow shot up again. "I came from the club. Beth and I went into Kelly's for a drink and she caught up with the girls. I just went outside for a breath of fresh air and a bit of a walk. I found myself by the canal basin. I did see the vans were all the same, a metallic bronze colour. One licence plate was WF 66 something. I didn't catch the others or see any more. They looked like Ford Tourneo Custom Vans, which each have around seven seats."

Allison whistled through his teeth, "Lucky you were there at the right time…?"

"It was just a fluke."

"Never mind how you got the information. It's worth checking it out." Allison gazed at him steadily.

Mark felt his face flush with colour. He was never very good at lying. The chief hadn't exactly called him out but Mark knew he was suspicious that he wasn't being entirely truthful. "Oh, and one more thing…"

"Yes?"

A man arrived shortly after the truck and was admitted. I think he was some sort of doctor."

"Doctor?"

"It looked like he was carrying a medical bag. A man with a long grey ponytail admitted him, the same one I saw at the club, with Martyn Kelland, I think. And this doctor chap… I believe he wore glasses. I saw him push something up onto the bridge of his nose. I thought it must be specs and I caught the word doctor but nothing else. I was hoping to see what I could find out this morning…" Mark trailed off.

"I see." Allison's voice was measured. "Okay see what you can learn and then we'll pay West End Products a visit. Who knows, you may remember something else."

"Sir." Mark turned to leave when the telephone rang and Allison signalled to him to stay.

"Allison … Yes? ... We'll be right there." Allison rose from his seat and grabbed his coat. "Come on. We're going to the hospital. Big Den has regained consciousness."

16

SVETLANA WOKE UP FEELING GROGGY, her arm was stinging. Ivanka was already using the tea and coffee making facilities to make them a drink. She had washed the towels in cold water to rinse out all the blood and had them draped over the radiator to dry. She was freshly showered and although still in a ripped red evening dress, she looked alert and well.

Svetlana sat up and winced as she rested on her injured arm, "What's the time?"

"I'm not sure. I'll put the TV on. It may give us the time." She gestured to the window where the drapes had been drawn with only the gauze net curtains shielding them from the outside world. "But the birds are singing, the sun is shining and traffic is flowing freely outside." She fiddled with the remote control and found the BBC Breakfast News, which displayed a clock at the bottom of the screen. It was 8:45 a.m. "Once you're up and dressed, we'll head down for breakfast. Don't want to miss that."

Svetlana swung her long limbs out of the bed and wandered into the bathroom. Ivanka heard the shower switch on. She listened to the local news and tried to understand what was said but found some of the narrative was spoken too quickly for her to fully understand. There seemed to have been some kind of hit and run in a place called Erdington and a house in Balsall Heath had been searched by police resulting in two people being arrested suspected of terrorism offences.

Ivanka sighed and returned to get her cup of coffee, as she did so she glanced out of the window now the drapes were fully drawn and saw through a gap in the nets. She gulped in horror as she observed Bogdan with another man getting out of a vehicle they had parked in the car park at the front of the hotel. They were striding towards the front door and reception.

She hurried to the bathroom, “Svetlana, you have to hurry. That man, Bogdan. He’s here.”

She heard Svetlana gasp and switch off the shower. She emerged quickly, “What do we do?”

“Nothing at the moment. Firstly, you get dry and dress.”

Ivanka looked out of the window again. She couldn’t see the men. She hoped the receptionist would not divulge anything about them. Surely, guest information was confidential? She also wondered if there was a back way out of the hotel. There had to be another form of escape, say if there was a fire in the foyer or something. She crossed to the door and studied the framed map on the inside of the door. There was!

“What are we going to do?” asked Svetlana looking anxious.

“Firstly, keep calm. We wait. See if they leave.”

Svetlana had begun shaking uncontrollably, “I can’t go back there, not to those men. This is all my fault. If I had been braver I would have had that thing cut out of me before and they wouldn’t have found us.”

“We don’t know that. Look settle down, try taking some deep breaths.”

“What if they come up here? What then?” said Svetlana beginning to cry.

“We just have to sit tight. Be patient. Be cool…”

Ivanka went back to the window and saw the two men coming out from the hotel. They returned to their car and got in. Ivanka watched and waited. After a few minutes the car started up and left the hotel car park and went down the Hagley Road in the direction of the town. Ivanka heaved a sigh of relief, “They’ve gone… not for long, I’ll bet. Dry your hair, quickly and we’ll grab some breakfast. I have an idea.”

Allison and Mark waited in the relatives’ room for the doctor attending Big Den. Finally, the surgeon that had operated on him strode to the room where they sat. He was a charming Indian doctor, Dr Yash Mondal, so his name tag said.

"We understand, Dennis Crighton is awake?"

"Yes. That's right."

"Is it possible for us to see him? We need to ask him some questions."

"But of course, but not for too long. He is still very weak. He lost a lot of blood and needs to rest. I can let you have a few minutes. Follow me."

Dr Mondal led them from the room along the ward to a private room. Big Den was lying back against some pillows, down which he had slid. He was surrounded by a profusion of tubes and medical equipment that bleeped constantly. His eyes flickered open as they entered his room. He groaned and tried to pull himself up into a sitting position and lean against the bank of pillows behind him.

"Steady on," said Dr Mondal and he helped Big Den back into a more comfortable spot. Once he was settled, Dr Mondal continued, "These gentlemen are from the police. They wish to ask you some questions. Are you okay with that?" Big Den grunted and nodded his head. "Very well, I will leave you to it. I will be back in five minutes." He turned to Allison, "Don't tire him out. We don't want his condition to worsen." He left the room.

Big Den huffed as he attempted to sit comfortably and he focused his eyes on DCI Allison, "What do you want to know?" His voice was strained and low as if he had been punched in his windpipe.

Allison spoke gently, "In your own time, can you tell me what happened?"

Big Den cleared his throat, "I'd just come out of the shower, and when I'd dressed and walked to the sitting room, some bozo came at me from behind. I managed to shake him off and this other fella had a gun pointed at me. We got into a struggle and the thing went off, shooting me. I remember thinking I was a gonner as he levelled the gun at me, to finish me off, I think, when someone knocked at the door. I heard someone call my name, which is when I blacked out and they must have scarpered."

"Did you get a good look at these men?"

"It's a bit hazy, it happened so fast, but yes. I think I would know them again."

"Could you work with an artist to draw up a likeness?"

"I expect so," he grimaced as he moved into another position. I can tell you one of them had grey hair tied back in a ponytail." Allison and Mark exchanged a look. "He was a thickset man. Worked out, I reckon."

"And the other man?"

"Taller and leaner, still well-muscled. He wore a hoodie. Can't recall much about his face except for his eyes."

"What about them?"

"There was something odd about them."

"In what way, odd?"

"Dunno. I think they may be a different colour. And I've seen both guys before."

"Where?"

"They were parked outside the flat. I spoke to them."

"What were they driving?"

"A BMW X5"

Allison and Stringer swapped looks again just as Dr Mondal returned. "I think that's enough for today."

"Thank you, Doctor. We will have someone stop by tomorrow, a police artist." He turned to Big Den, "That's if you feel up to it?"

Big Den nodded, "I'm sure I'll feel better tomorrow. But now, I just want to sleep."

"One more thing," said Allison. "We don't want word getting out that you're alive. At least not yet. We will run a story in the press about your attack and subsequent death."

"Fake news, eh?"

"It's just to keep you safe. We don't want anyone coming back to finish the job," said Allison.

"That may be a problem," chipped in Dr Mondal. Allison looked questioningly at him. "We have had several phone calls asking after him. And although we haven't given too much away, we have said that he is in a stable condition."

"Very well. The story will run that after rallying he took a turn for the worse, his condition became critical and then he died. It will give us some breathing space"

"Hope none of this is prophetic," mumbled Big Den.

"Do we know who called?"

The doctor shook his head, "I'm sorry. No."

"Any more calls for him, please instruct the staff firstly, to check who's calling, get their names and to say he has relapsed and is back in a critical condition. Our stories must be the same. I'll let you know when you can say he's succumbed to his injuries. Okay?"

"I'll do what I can," said the doctor. "I'll call a meeting and have this relayed."

"Staff must be made to understand that this mustn't get out."

Big Den turned over with a sigh and snuggled down, "And I am going to sleep. Good day to you all."

Ivanka and Svetlana made their way downstairs and grabbed some breakfast. Ivanka noticed that the person on reception was not the same as the one who had checked them in. She took this as a good sign. They finished their coffee, juice and toast. Ivanka made Svetlana wait in the restaurant while she went to the desk.

A foreign looking man looked up from the desk, "Yes? Can I help you?"

"We are just checking out and wish to give you our key card."

"Pop it in the box at the end of the counter. Is there anything else?"

"Yes… I wondered if there had been any messages for us."

"Sorry, you are?"

"Oh, we were in room 12."

The clerk perused his screen, "Ella Purdom and Nancy Brodie."

"That's us," said Ivanka a bit too brightly.

"How was your stay? To your satisfaction?"

"Yes, thank you," gushed Ivanka. "We will be back."

"Are you on holiday?"

"We were here for a business meeting, we return today."

The receptionist raised an eyebrow but was non-committal. "No, no messages…"

"That's fine. See you again, maybe."

The receptionist smiled and watched Ivanka hurry to the restaurant to collect Svetlana. "Hurry, come on. I don't think I trust that guy."

The man watched the girls as they walked quickly across the foyer and back out onto the leafy Hagley Road. There was a bus stop practically outside. He picked up the phone, "Those two girls you were looking for. I think they were staying here, after all… They've just left." He listened a moment… "They're outside now walking towards the bus stop." He put the phone down a satisfied look on his face.

At the bus stop, Svetlana was panicking, "Where to now?"

"We get to town and find a policeman. Come on."

They waved down the first bus that came and hopped on.

Ivanka asked the driver where the nearest police station was and paid their fares using her card as a contactless payment.

The driver was a cheery man with a ruddy complexion. He smiled amiably and said, "Well, ducks. We pass Lloyd House. Is that good enough?"

"What's Lloyd House?"

"It's the main cop shop in town. I'll give you a shout when we're there."

The girls thanked him and sat near the front of the bus. They watched the traffic out of the window just in case they saw the vehicle Bogdan was driving.

The bus halted at each stop down the dusty tree lined street. They came to an underpass where there was a large roundabout and zipped through. Moments later the driver called out, "Lloyd House." The girls scrambled up and waited by the driver to alight. He pointed to a building. "Over there. You can't miss it." The girls thanked him and got off.

Ivanka took a deep breath and grabbed Svetlana's arm; she winced, "Sorry, forgot about your bad arm. Come on. Let's get moving. Bogdan could be anywhere."

The young women hurried towards the big building that was the headquarters of the West Midlands Police Force. Steeling themselves, and looking braver than they felt they marched inside.

Allison and Mark left the hospital and collected their car. "Where to now, Chief?"

"West End Products. Too many coincidences. Let's pay them another visit." Mark nodded and headed for Brindley Place and Broad Street.

En route Allison's phone went off. Allison wriggled his considerable frame in his seat to try and retrieve his phone. As he pulled it out, it stopped ringing. Allison frowned as he studied the number. It was withheld. "If it's important, they'll ring again."

"Could be the hospital, your bank, something like that. They never divulge their numbers."

"Hmm," grunted Allison who disapproved of the practice. The phone rang again as he was returning it to his pocket and he answered grumpily. It was almost a growl, "Yes? Allison here." He listened carefully. "On our way." He pocketed his phone and instructed Mark, "Change of plan. Back to Lloyd House, now."

Mark swerved back into the inside lane to approach the roundabout and turn off to Lee Bank. He looked at the chief questioningly, "What's up?"

"Two girls have turned up at the station having escaped from Bogdan's clutches. Think that takes precedence, don't you?"

"Absolutely." Mark's heart began to race. He would need to share this with Alex and wondered what information these girls would have.

Gurdip had just dropped Ayesha off at school and was walking back along City Road towards Sandon Road. He was feeling positive about the future and much better in himself. However, every now and then a wave of pain and sadness would envelop him, when he thought of his family. There was nothing more he could do. He couldn't bring them back. He had to protect his sisters. He was now the elder in the family. Their future was in his hands. That thought filled him with trepidation. He continued to walk on but couldn't shake off a feeling of uneasiness. He didn't know why. Pasha was in Winson

Green prison on remand. Ajeet was in hospital, so what was bugging him? He looked around him and spotted another Sikh who looked more than familiar, getting into a hire car.

To his horror he recognised, one of Pasha's brothers, Kamapal. He was supposed to have gone back to India but must have returned. That was the only explanation. Gurdip felt the first fluttering of panic.

Ivanka and Svetlana sat at the station gazing nervously around them. Svetlana whispered, "Are you sure we should be here?"

Ivanka nodded, "Definitely. We both know what is going to happen to the other girls. Bogdan must be stopped. We have to be brave."

Allison and Mark strode into the waiting area and beckoned the two girls to follow them. They marched through the various spaces and squad room to Allison's office, where they were invited to sit.

Allison's manner was gentle as he quizzed the girls and Mark took notes. Ivanka took the lead and gave a detailed report of the house from which they had escaped. They gave a reasonable account of the people who had transported them, the warehouse and people working there, which included a beefy man with a long grey ponytail. Allison and Mark exchanged a look. Then Ivanka went on to describe Doctor Charles and what he had done. The girls showed the inside of their arms where they had cut out the trackers themselves. Svetlana added details of the type of goods in the warehouse, of the photographs, racks of female clothes they had been told to select from and wear.

Svetlana suddenly broke down and was unable to speak as she tried to document what Bogdan had done to her. Ivanka came to her aid and said in frustration, "She was raped in the most horrible manner and I was drugged. What more do you need?"

Allison nodded, "Mark, we have enough to get a warrant. See to it."

Mark rose and left the room, leaving the young women with Allison, who turned to them and spoke softly, "We will find the other girls and these men. Now, we need to get you somewhere safe. Have you eaten?"

"Not much on the journey, nothing last night and not much since we fled the hotel after seeing those men."

Allison rubbed his bristly chin, "I'll send someone down to see the receptionist and see what he can tell us. Can you describe him, too?"

Ivanka made an effort to give him a picture of the woman who checked them in and the man on the desk in the morning. Allison took notes. He went into the squad room and called Ronnie and Bill across, "Get over to the Norfolk Hotel pronto. Interview the guy on reception. Find out what he said to the two men who came to his desk early this morning." He looked back at the girls and their clothes and called in Maddie.

"Maddie, can you accompany these two to the canteen and get them something to eat? Let them wait there. They will be safe enough and go into town to the charity shops and find them something decent to wear. You can gauge their sizes, I expect. Here." Allison removed two twenty-pound notes from his wallet. "I can claim this back. Go now." The girls stood up and without hesitation followed Maddie out.

Allison was just about to return to his office and enjoy a Mars Bar from his stash when Gurdip arrived in a terrible state. Allison looked at him, "Whatever's the matter? What's happened?"

"It's Pasha!"

"What do you mean?"

"I've just seen his brother, Kamapal. He must have come back from India and he saw me. I came straight here. I am worried for Siri. If Kamapal sees Pasha, he's bound to guess that Siri will have tried to resume her studies and he will have an idea where Ronnie and I are living now. I don't know what to do."

Gurdip slumped down into a seat and put his head in his hands. All the recent confidence he had gained seemed to evaporate and he looked broken. Allison attempted to chivvy him up. "Now's not the time to give up, Gurdip. Tell me what this Kamapal looks like and we can bring him in."

"What for? We have nothing on him."

"On suspicion of being involved with Pasha in his crimes. I will call the governor of the prison and ask him to make a note of all Pasha's visitors and maybe we can nip this in the bud."

"Is Ronnie about?"

“He’s gone with Bill to interview someone connected with another case. Why don’t you just take a moment here? They shouldn’t be too long.”

Gurdip said nothing but just sat there looking defeated.

17

PASHA SAT IN HIS CELL. There was a rap on the door, "Pasha Chand, visitor." He rose and stepped forward wondering who it might be. The door unlocked and he was led down a corridor to the room where his visitor waited. He stared in surprise, "Kamapal! Whatever are you doing here?"

Kamapal bowed his head and spoke quietly, "I came as soon as I heard. Our father is worried. He thinks you have brought disgrace on our family."

Pasha snorted in derision, "He encouraged me. It is nothing he wouldn't have done himself."

"Yes, but it should have been Siri to pay, not the entire family."

"That is a matter of opinion," Pasha growled.

"I know. And I am with you, brother." Pasha merely scowled in response. "I think I might have a way of getting you out."

"I don't think so. It's impossible. Can't be done."

"It may be…" Kamapal looked around him and lowered his voice still further. "If we can make you seem sick enough to go to hospital…"

"And how do we do that?"

"Leave it with me and trust me. I will be back again shortly. I will try and get some ipecac syrup. I can get it online."

"What is it?"

"It's an emetic and makes you vomit. It was used in cases of poisoning. Not available over the counter now."

"How will you get it to me?"

"When I visit. I can pass it to you."

Pasha looked about him, "How?"

"Let's say, I will arrange a little distraction. Do you have anywhere to hide it on your person? And in your cell?"

"I have pockets in my kurta. I can hide it in my mattress."

"Good. Is anyone else visiting you?"

"I have heard a member of the Gurdwara Committee will be coming to see me this week. I am allowed three visits a week, while I am on remand."

"Good. It is good."

"What is this stuff you speak of?"

"It is foul tasting. You will have to stomach it. It will make you ill. Hide the evidence and they should remove you to a hospital."

"Why not the infirmary?"

"You will have to exaggerate and play up all the other symptoms, then it should work."

"And if it doesn't?"

"It will."

"But, if it doesn't?"

"Then we will find something else."

"We don't have long. Ajeet is testifying against me. He is singing like a bird."

"Let me worry about Ajeet. Who else visits you in here?"

"No one, yet. Just my lawyer."

"Cousin Kalbant?

"No, he refused to help me. It was only Ajeet."

"And now he has turned against you?"

"So, it seems."

"Worry not, brother. You will soon be free." With that Kamapal stood up and walked to the exit.

Alex sat with his cat Snooks on his lap. He gazed out of the window at the river and sighed. It was a glorious day. There was scarcely a cloud in the cerulean sky and hardly a whisper of a breeze. He took a deep breath and the edge of a smile played on his lips as he rubbed Snooks behind her ears and she let off a rumbling throaty purr. He scrutinised his cat carefully, "I know you're not going to like it, but I'll never get going at this rate. I have work to do. Just be patient. I'll be back before you know it and I promise you I'll make it up to you." Snooks gazed up into her master's face as if she didn't believe him. She jumped off his lap and sauntered to her drinking bowl and lapped some water before proceeding to wash herself and made a point of ignoring him as if she had heard it all before.

Just then his work mobile phone rang. Alex picked it up, "Yes?"

"It's Mark."

"Yes?"

"Got some important info for you."

"Shoot."

Mark relayed all he had learnt from the two young women and the events.

"Where are they now?"

"Safe."

"I'll need to speak to them."

"I'm afraid that's not possible."

"Then make it happen."

"They're in a safe house."

"Then it shouldn't be a problem. Just tell me where. I'll do the rest."

"I can't do that."

"We had a deal."

"Yes. But it's harder than you think."

"What then?"

"Let me tell the chief."

"No. This stays between us."

"Come on, Alex. The chief's aware of the MRF. How hard can it be? Trust me."

"I'll get back to you." Alex terminated the call just as his girlfriend, Jane, breezed into the house.

"Morning, Snooks," she said brightly and stooped to stroke the cat who stood on hind legs to enjoy the petting putting her nose up to Jane's in greeting.

"I see," said Alex. "You just want me for my cat."

"Of course, didn't you know that? Snooks puts the sparkle in my eyes," Jane said teasingly. "She makes my smile shine," she added with a grin.

"Now you sound like a tin of Mr Sheen," said Alex with a laugh. He rose and put his arms around her. "Listen hon, I have to dash."

"Not writing today?"

"'Fraid not. I have to earn a living too, to pay the bills."

"Time for a coffee?"

"Just had one. I shouldn't be late."

"Where are you going?" she caught Alex's expression, "I know… Don't ask… Just wish you did something a little less secretive for a living. It's like living with James Bond."

"If only… just imagine the excitement, the women…"

"All right, all right. I won't press you to break the Official Secrets Act. Just let me know later what time to expect you."

Alex kissed her on the lips. "Okay, promise. And now I really must go. Look after Snooks for me."

"Don't I always?"

Snooks turned her head at the mention of her name and blinked inscrutably before taking herself off to her basket and settling down with her paws tucked under her. Her green eyes followed her master as he disappeared out of the door.

He strode to his car, taking out his phone as he marched. He unlocked it and sat in the driver's seat, tapping his fingers on the steering wheel until it was answered, "Roy? More information on Bogdan and his consignment. Where can we meet?"

Allison thanked Hilda and Jessica profusely over a cup of tea together with Svetlana and Ivanka who listened carefully. "We really appreciate all you have done for Siri and Ayesha and now Svetlana and Ivanka."

"Not at all. We have enjoyed having them here. I just hope you catch these beasts who have trafficked these poor girls."

"I'm coming onto that. I need one or both of the girls to come with me to show us where they were being held. I can then get a warrant to search the place." He turned to the girls, "You'll recognise it?"

Ivanka nodded, "Yes, I think so. I can show you the room where we were imprisoned. They won't have had time to correct the damage we did getting out. Will that help?"

"It will. Anything else?"

"The tree in the garden, the one we climbed to get over the wall."

"Good. It doesn't need both of you. Ivanka if you agree to come with me, Svetlana can remain here in safety."

Ivanka smiled and said, "Anything to get those ublyudki. Zveri. This shouldn't happen to anyone else."

"Thank you." Allison rose and beckoned Ivanka. "I will bring her back safely, I promise."

Martyn Kelland swore at Carter and Paulson. He continued, "This has made it impossible. Where is Bogdan now?"

"Returned home with his men. He left once he knew the girls were missing."

"Great. So, the problem sits squarely with us." Carter nodded. "Where are the other girls now?"

"Split up. English speakers have gone to the house in Portland Road."

"And the others?"

"On their way to your country retreat."

"What?" roared Kelland.

"There was nowhere else we could put them that was big enough and secure."

"Dammit, Marcus. What were you thinking?"

"We had to do something and do it quickly. There was no choice."

Kelland grunted, "We have to move them. My wife and family are headed there this weekend. I don't care what you do – get them out of there. Take them to their placements. Anywhere…"

"But, they're not ready."

"Then make them ready. Your mess. You fix it!"

Kamapal opened his hand baggage in his hotel room and removed a small bottle of ipecac syrup and another tiny phial the size of a perfume sample given away in department stores. He carefully dropped the contents of the miniature ampoule into the syrup and shook it. He secreted the bottle in his pocket and rummaged through his case and pulled out his passport and paperwork to check his return flight to Amritsar airport, which was later the following day.

Kamapal smiled to himself and tucked the E-Pass ticket back into its wallet. He took out his phone and dialled. The smile was apparent in his voice when he spoke, "Yes. I have it ready. By tomorrow it will all be over. There will be no come back."

Allison armed with two search warrants gathered his team together. "Mark you lead one on the warehouse, take Pooley and Taylor and the designated uniform officers. The rest are with me on the house in Westbourne Road. Ivanka will be with us. They won't expect us to hit both places the same day. Right. Let's go."

The officers gathered themselves together and left the squad room. Allison spoke softly to Ivanka, "Are you sure you are all right to do this?"

She nodded, "Yes, these men must be stopped. They're peddling dreams to innocent girls in search of a better life."

Allison acknowledged her and she followed him out. It was then he wished he had a Mars Bar. He needed one right now.

While the officers were assembling, Mark covertly called Alex and gave him the latest information. He was brief and to the point curtailing the call before he joined Pooley, Taylor and uniform. They left the building in two vehicles and headed for West End Products.

In Westbourne Road, Ivanka pointed out the house and the large tree, which helped them escape. They buzzed on the electric gates but no one responded.

Allison signalled to his tech expert who attacked the key pad allowing entry and began work. The gates opened and the police vans and occupants drove up the drive to the main entrance.

Uniformed police clearly announced their presence but there was no response and Allison indicated they gain entry by using the enforcer. Two men rushed at the door with the red battering ram and pounded on the door, which finally gave way. Officers piled into the house and were instructed to search the place.

Ivanka led Allison to the room that she had escaped from and showed him the damage to the bathroom door frame where she had tried to break the wire coat hanger, which she retrieved from under her mattress. She showed him the window from which she and Svetlana had chipped away the paint to get out. The wire hanger was placed in an evidence bag.

Ivanka then led him downstairs to the kitchen where Dr Charles had implanted the trackers and contraceptive devices and then revealed the cupboard where she had been drugged. Allison's eagle eyes scoured the shelves and the floor. He caught a glint of something under the bottom shelf by the wall that was almost hidden. He put on a pair of surgical gloves and puffed as he bent down to retrieve it. It was a microchip. That went into another bag.

Allison meticulously searched the jars, packets and bottles in front of him. There was nothing of any consequence. He then went to the fridge and at the back of the salad crisper drawer he discovered a small tray of ampoules, which were whisked away. In the refuse bin under vegetable peelings he found one syringe. Allison smiled grimly. The evidence was stacking up.

Mark and his team marched into the warehouse and announced themselves, but Martyn Kelland was unavailable nor were any of his henchmen. The only person Mark could find was the willowy tawny-haired beauty with the glorious tresses. It seemed Mr Kelland and associates were away at a business meeting, but she couldn't say where. A systematic search of the premises began. Mark began with Kelland's office. Computers and desk diaries were removed and taken away for forensic examination. Mark rifled through the desk drawers, the waste paper bins, filing cabinets and shelves. He picked up the Rolodex that, too, went into a large bag. The files were collected, memo pads and all other papers that would be sifted through for any red flags to do with Jonas Rakowsky, Bogdan or the girls. There was a shout from Taylor downstairs. Mark dashed down.

David Taylor pointed out a patch of what looked like blood on the warehouse floor close to the rack of women's clothes. It was found underneath a large cardboard box that Taylor had lifted out of the way. Mark removed a Kastle–Meyer test kit from his pack and took a sample of the blood before moistening the tip of the swab with a phenolphthalein reagent. He waited a few moments and then added a couple of drops of hydrogen peroxide. The swab rapidly turned pink. It was definitely blood. The serological analysis would need a larger sample as would DNA analysis. Mark left Taylor to continue with that.

There was another yell from Pooley who was searching a cupboard off the main warehouse floor and had come across a locked metal strongbox. Mark instructed him to open it. Pooley struggled with a screwdriver and managed to force the lock and prise the container open. Inside were a number of passports and mobile phones. Mark grinned; this was looking good. Still wearing his surgical gloves, he flicked through the passports and found ones belonging to Ivanka and Svetlana. He closed the chest and passed it to Pooley, "Bag this and take it away."

A black dustbin bag revealed a number of clothing items and some shoes. These too were taken away. All the time the tall beauty watched biting her lip. She retreated into the office and dialled a number.

"Martyn? The police are here. They are taking everything… I couldn't stop them. They had a warrant."

Expletives could be heard on the other end of the line, before Martyn ordered, "Get yourself out of there. Quickly as you can."

"But where do I go?"

"Leave everything. Check in at the Midland Hotel. Text me the room number. One of the boys will get you out. Don't speak to anyone. Understood?"

“Yes, Martyn.”

“Now go.”

The woman grabbed her coat and bag and began to leave the office. Mark stopped her as he arrived back at Kelland’s office, “Where are you going?”

“I am not staying here. I don’t know what’s going on but I have no wish to be involved. Mr Kelland can deal with it. I am out of here.”

“Where can we contact you? If necessary?”

The woman paused, “You’ll find me here.” She passed Mark a card, with her name, job description, phone number and address.

Mark accepted the card and studied it, “Thank you, Kira… Miss Petrov.”

The woman nodded with a toss of her head and exited. She darted down the stairs her high heels clattering as she went while Mark looked after her thoughtfully. He nabbed Pooley, “Follow her. See where she goes but be discreet.”

18

PASHA CHAND SAT WAITING FOR the representative of the Gurdwara Committee that was coming to interview him. A tall Sikh with an imposing air, entered the visitors' room and strode up to the table. He sat facing Pasha. "You are Pasha Chand?" Pasha nodded. "Your brother-in-law, Gurdip Singh has been to see us, asking that his sister be considered for a divorce."

Pasha scowled, "It is not our way. No divorce. Marriage is for life, two souls in one body."

"This is true but we have video and photographic evidence of the cruelty and harm done to Siri. This too is against our tradition and beliefs. Man and woman are equal and such violence is not acceptable."

"It is an exaggeration."

"Then you do not accept that harm came to her by your hands?"

Pasha sighed and shrugged, "Just a little friendly discipline. She was going to leave me. That would bring disgrace on me and our family."

The elder studied Pasha's face and his manner, "What have you to say in regard to the deaths of her family? Her father and mother, her little brother and other family members? You are in here for those crimes and more." Pasha remained surly and silent. "I came here to hear your side of the story to take back to the committee. I am strongly against divorce but you are giving me no option."

Pasha lifted his eyes up defiantly and stared at the man, "What can I say to make you change your mind?"

"It is not what you say. But what you have done and with no explanation, no reason, no semblance of defence. There should be a point of mediation."

"She was wilful, disobedient and refused to return with me to India. She wished to pursue her career in defiance of me. I could not allow it."

The committee member rose, "I have heard enough. I shall take back what you have said to the Gurdwara."

"Take back, too, that she wanted to be with another man."

The Sikh sat back down and with some sympathy in his voice said, "Tell me everything."

Pasha's eyes gleamed and sensing an advantage proceeded to talk, lacing his lies with poisonous venom.

Pooley had followed Kira Petrov at a safe distance and travelled behind her. He watched as she parked her car outside a large house in Montague Road and he pulled in further up the road and waited.

The sky had turned a dusky grey and the bubbling clouds massed together to launch an attack of rain. Raindrops the size of two pence pieces began to fall and soon the dusty street was awash with water that travelled in haste down the drains.

The woman appeared to be waiting for the rain to ease and as soon as the sudden downpour dissipated into a lighter shower, she emerged from her car and hurried up the drive of the big house.

Pooley got out of his car and turned up his collar and proceeded to the very large detached Victorian house and slipped a tracker on the underside of Ms Petrov's car before moving onwards to the house that had an immense front garden and a wrought iron gate leading to the back. He stepped back into the shrubbery by the wall and observed Ms Petrov disappearing inside the heavy wooden door. Moments later she reappeared looking extremely worried. She hesitated on the doorstep as if to go back inside, shook her head and began to hurry down the long brick paved drive. Pooley remained out of sight when the door opened again. Marcus Paulson and Bernie Carter emerged. Pooley saw

Paulson tucking a gun into his trouser waistband. He stiffened unable to do anything as he was alone. They rushed up to Ms Petrov and manhandled her back up the drive. Paulson pulled the gun from his trouser band and shoved it in her back. The two men forced the young woman back to the house and roughly dragged her inside.

Moments later, Carter emerged and sprinted down the drive. He ran out to the road and unlocked Ms Petrov's car. He started it up and drove into the grounds of the house taking the vehicle around to the back and out of view.

Pooley observed all the movements. He knew he had to get help, but how was uncertain. He needed to get back to his car and radio the station. He came out from the shrubbery while his mind was racing when to his horror he felt a gun press against his spine and a chilling voice said, "Don't turn around. Put your hands on your head. Slowly now." The man patted him down and removed his mobile phone. "Turn towards the house and walk up the drive. Move it."

Pooley was shoved from behind and propelled up the path going towards the mansion. He didn't know what to do. No one knew where he was. He was aware that he wouldn't be missed for some time and groaned inwardly.

Pasha sat in his cell brooding. He was angry that the Gurdwara Committee had been consulted about his marriage and that Siri had requested a divorce. He believed the man who had come to see him was reluctant to agree to divorce especially now he had filled the man's head with lies about Siri's fidelity. He felt he may just have a chance of convincing them that divorce was not an option and that he had done what needed to be done. It would at least explain his actions. He waited to be called by the guard that his brother would be visiting. He knew Kamapal had made an excuse that he needed to see him before he flew back to the Punjab.

Pasha waited.

The key turned in the lock and a guard beckoned him to rise and he was marched to the visitors' room where Kamapal sat waiting. Kamapal grinned broadly as he rose and stretched out his hand to welcome his brother. As Kamapal's hand connected with Pasha's he shook it warmly and clasped his other hand around Pasha's who could feel the small bottle as he moved his hands around and secreted it firmly into Pasha's grasp. As they released with a warning look and shout from the guard the switch was made and Pasha was able to insert the bottle into the pocket of his kurta. So far, so good or so Pasha thought. They sat and began to talk in hushed tones as Kamapal outlined his plan.

Pasha returned to his cell feeling a bit more optimistic about his future. Although he didn't relish the thought of drinking the syrup, which he had been warned was vile tasting and would make him vomit, he realised that if it would get him into hospital then Kamapal had assured him there would be a way of getting him out and away from the authorities. He was arranging a new passport to fly him home. Pasha sighed and almost managed a smile.

He removed the small bottle of ipecac from his pocket and studied it. Could it really work? Might it make him ill enough to be taken to hospital? Could Kamapal help him escape this unfair, so-called British justice? He had taken some convincing and now he believed it was possible. He would deal with Siri and Gurdip some other way. As for Ayesha she would be all alone in the world and that would be punishment enough.

Pasha unscrewed the small bottle. It looked innocuous enough. The liquid was clear and had a mild odour with something else impinging on the smell that he couldn't quite place. He had been instructed to take the whole bottle and then to hide the evidence. Pasha had removed some stitching on his mattress, which would allow him to insert the empty bottle inside and thus hide it away.

He steeled himself, pinched his nose with his thumb and forefinger on one hand and downed the bitter liquid, gagging on the acrid taste. He quickly shoved the bottle deep into the mattress, before his throat constricted and he grabbed at his chest. His lips began to turn blue and he fell to the floor with a gurgling scream.

Alex Wallace aka The Chameleon, now MRF agent surveyed the scene at the house in Montague Road. He had witnessed the altercation between Ms

Petrov and Carter and spotted Pooley observing the house and his subsequent demise, recognising Sergeant Pooley as one of the detectives who worked with Mark Stringer. There was one thing he needed to do, now; phone Mark.

Alex slipped back into his vehicle and rang Mark. "Mark? Alex. One of your men is in trouble." He quickly explained what he had seen. "What do you want me to do?... How long?... I don't think we have that much time…I'm going in."

Mark's protestations came down the line as Alex ended the call. He called Chapman, "Roy? We have a situation…"

Alex grabbed his Glock from the glove box. He donned his body armour hiding it under his coat. He inserted his earpiece, and placed his favoured antique military fighting knife in its sheath. He grabbed a smoke bomb and grenade and prepared to move. He moved into the entrance and skirted the outside wall around the house. At least there were no gates on this property, which made Alex believe they had moved there in a rush and so must be on the defensive. He saw Ms Petrov's vehicle and sidestepped towards it. He ducked quickly at the side of it when he heard voices. A window on the ground floor was partially open and angry raised voices filtered through to him.

"You fucking twat! What the hell do you think you're doing bringing a copper in here?"

"Someone had to do something. Stop him prowling around."

"You've certainly done that all right."

"We can't let him go."

"No, not now, you pillock."

"What then?"

"We'll have to get rid of him."

"And the girl?"

"She has to go, too. She knows too much."

"Martyn won't like it."

"Damn Martyn. He's not here."

Alex's phone began to vibrate and he hurriedly answered, in a whisper, "Yes?... I need backup… Then, I'll have to go in alone … I don't think we have much time. They're talking about getting rid of them." He curtailed the call and slid down the car and rolled under it, while he worked out a plan. He needed to survey the whole house and assess how much firepower the occupants had, and how many men there were.

Paulson and Carter stood remonstrating with a greasy haired subordinate, while Pooley was being restrained by another fit-looking man. Ms Kira Petrov sat on a leather sofa looking concerned.

"I should go," said Kira.

"I think you had better stay," said Paulson icily.

"But why? What are you not telling me? Martyn will be furious when he finds out."

"Martyn is not going to know… yet."

Kira folded her arms tightly as if to protect herself and stuck her chin out defiantly. "Why? What are you going to do?"

"Don't worry your pretty little head about that," he said demeaningly.

Kira bristled, "I'm calling Martyn."

"Oh no, you're not." Paulson grabbed her roughly by the arm.

"Let go. You're hurting me!" He yanked her to her feet.

Paulson nodded at Carter who came across and snatched Kira's handbag. He rifled through it ignoring her protestations and fished out her mobile phone and tossed it to Paulson who removed the sim card and ground it under his heel. He tossed her phone in the waste paper basket.

"What are you doing?" shouted Kira.

"Shut her up!" yelled Paulson.

Carter moved to the desk and removed a roll of duct tape. He cut off a length and bound Kira's hands behind her back and took another swatch and plastered it across her mouth. He bound Pooley's hands in the same way and silenced him, too. Carter removed Pooley's car keys.

"Take them for a little drive." He indicated the subordinate, "You go with them and deal with them both."

Outside, Alex had crept near enough to the window to listen and he had heard enough. There was nothing he could do alone. He sneaked back stealthily to his vehicle and climbed inside and tried again to call Roy leaving another urgent message for his boss. He relayed what he'd heard and that he didn't know how many men were in the house but two were leaving with prisoners. He was going to follow. He started his car as he waited for the men to emerge with Pooley and Kira.

He glanced at his phone and scrolled through his contacts to Mark and dialled. He didn't have long to wait. Once Alex had explained he moved off down the road keeping Carter's vehicle in sight. As he passed he saw the greasy haired bloke from earlier getting into Pooley's car and following Carter.

"Mark, I don't have backup. Roy is getting a group together but it may be too late. I couldn't go in alone. Any help would be gratefully received."

"Tell me where." Alex gave Mark his position and the road he was travelling. "What are you driving? What are the targets' cars?"

Alex gave Mark the information adding, "I'll keep the line open and tell you the route. Hurry."

Mark ran to his car and tossed his phone onto the seat and listened to Alex's voice as he travelled. He picked up the car radio and called Allison, "Sir, Pooley's in trouble."

"How? Where?"

Mark explained as best he could without using Alex's name.

"How do you know?" queried Allison.

"He was following Ms Petrov and I haven't heard from him since. He's not answering his phone."

"What aren't you telling me?"

Mark strained to keep his voice steady, "Tip off, sir. Sounds kosha."

"Get onto it. I'll get back up, where are you headed?"

Mark relayed as best he could where the car with the prisoners was travelling. He ended the call and spoke again, "Alex, did you get that?"

"I did. Thanks for keeping my name out of it. Heading towards Bromsgrove on the A38. Bugger!"

"What?"

"They've moved off towards Chaddesley Corbett on the A456. It will be more difficult to follow. I'm going to have to drop back. Both cars still in view. I know this area. We will be passing through Lower Clent, soon. How far away are you?"

"If the traffic stays calm I estimate around fifteen minutes."

"Right. I'll send more directions when I know they're stopping." Alex ended the call. He watched as the cars turned off down an unmarked lane. He drove on past it and into the pretty village of Chaddesley Corbett where he turned around and drove back to the turning. He moved forward cautiously and decided to park inside an open gateway in a field. From there he moved swiftly on foot taking care not to be seen.

Alex reached a steep bank and crawled up and from there viewed a large country house. The two cars were parked at the side. He called Mark and gave him his position. He watched as Carter manhandled Ms Petrov towards the front door. She struggled against him and was rewarded with a vicious smack across her face and head and then dragged to the entrance. The door opened and Dr Charles peered out and ushered them in.

Alex had no idea who the Dr Crippen look-a-like could be.

Carter soon returned and helped his subordinate haul Pooley out of his car. Pooley's body appeared limp as if he had been drugged. Between them they manoeuvred the sergeant to the front door. Carter hammered on it and it opened quickly. They shoved the policeman roughly inside and the door closed again firmly.

Alex knew time was of the essence and decided he needed to get closer. He slipped over the bank and onto the expanse of lawn, which led to the house, sneaking between the shrubs and trees for cover. He cursed under his breath and urged Mark to hurry. He didn't like where this was leading.

Inside, Kira Petrov was looking terrified. Her nose was bloody and her lip split. The duct tape had been ripped from her mouth and had removed the skin. A livid purple bruise was forming on her left cheek from the violent slap she had received. Carter's heavy gold and diamond signet ring had grazed her face with the smack.

She whimpered quietly before whispering, "What are you going to do with me?"

Carter rushed across and held her by the throat. He put his face up close to hers. "Shut up and listen. Martyn can't save you now. You're a loose end and have to be dealt with."

"But I won't say anything to anyone. I promise. I don't know anything to tell," she protested wildly.

"You've already spoken to the police," he yelled accusingly.

"But I didn't tell them anything. Please. You have to believe me."

"Sorry, sweetheart. Your silence can't be guaranteed," he said cruelly.

Kira began sobbing wildly. "It can, it can," she hiccupped.

He grinned malevolently, "Dr Charles needs to do a few tests." He nodded at his greasy haired subordinate, "Nesbitt, take her out to the back of the house."

"No, no, please. I beg of you." She screamed loudly as Nesbitt grabbed and yanked her to her feet.

"There's no one to hear you here, sweetheart, save your energy. You're going to need it. Gag her!" Carter ordered. Nesbitt nodded as he bundled her out through the door.

Carter turned to Pooley, "Now, copper, your sticky beak has got you into some serious shit and you will have to pay the price."

Pooley still gagged, glared around crazily. His eyes appeared to widen as he stared towards the window.

"Think you're going to distract me with a look, do you? Well, think again."

Carter began to remove his gun from the back of his trouser waistband, when the window behind him shattered, showering Carter with broken glass. The wood frame splintered and Alex smashed his way in and rolled onto the floor. Carter, his face bleeding with shards of glass, whipped around towards the masked, kitted up gunman and levelled his pistol at him.

Pooley jumped up from his seat, even though gagged and his hands tied, he jumped at Carter kicking him behind his knees and Carter went down and his shot went wild. Alex was on top of him. He clubbed him hard in the temple, knocking him out and handcuffed him and crossed quickly to Pooley, who was now scrambling up and he removed the tape from his mouth. Alex took his knife and sliced through his bonds. "Quickly, come with me. The other man will be back any minute after those shots."

Pooley didn't need telling twice, he followed Alex out through the window just as Nesbitt flung open the door and bounded into the room. He looked at Carter on the floor and tested his pulse before he dashed to the window and looked out but there was no sign of Pooley or the intruder.

Alex and Pooley had sprinted to the side of the house and leapt into the shrubbery. "There's a girl, a brunette. She's a prisoner, too."

Alex just nodded before hissing, "Stay low and out of sight. I'm going to find her."

This time Pooley nodded and crouched down, wondering who on earth was this ninja who had appeared so miraculously. He stayed quiet and hidden and saw Nesbitt appear at the broken window again and look out before disappearing once more.

Alex had crept around the back of the property and was peering in the kitchen window where he saw the tawny haired young woman slumped and tied to a chair. Dr Charles was bending over the female holding a syringe. The kitchen door was open and Nesbitt burst through. He yelled at the doctor, "Leave her. We need to get out now. Carter's out cold and handcuffed and the copper has gone. I don't aim to do time for this lot."

The doctor's usual icy demeanour began to evaporate and he began to look panicked. "But she can identify us…"

"So can the copper. Heaven knows where he is now. You do what you like. I'm going. I am not into murder."

Dr Charles' cold fish-like eyes gleamed. "I will just give her a little something. It will look like an overdose."

"Suit yourself," said Nesbitt and he bolted back through the door as Alex watched, his brain working overtime.

"Come on, Mark. Where are you?" he muttered under his breath. He peeped back in the window and saw the doctor taking a tourniquet and tying it around Ms Petrov's arm. He ungagged her and untied her stuffing the used tape into a ball, which he took with him to a downstairs convenience and secreted it in the cistern, before returning to the kitchen. He was filling his syringe with a clear liquid from a phial, when he heard police sirens approaching. Hurriedly, he packed up his medicine bag and then returned to the woman. He took her arm and was about to plunge the syringe into the crook of her elbow when a voice rang out, "I shouldn't do that, if I were you."

Dr Charles paused and flicked his eyes to the doorway to see Alex filling the space, masked and tooled up. He shuddered and shouted, "Thank God, I'm trying to save her. She has overdosed. Here help me." He straightened up as Alex approached and raised the syringe. Alex sent it spinning in the air with a well-timed kick. The doctor roared and charged but he was no match for Alex, who floored him with one punch. He tied the doctor's hands as Kira Petrov was coming round. Alex could see the reflection of blue lights in the window and made a decision. He raced from the kitchen and out of the back door and fled. He couldn't be seen and he couldn't be caught. He hurtled through the rough grass towards the boundary fence and slipped over it. Now all he had to do was get back to his car and he knew that wouldn't be easy.

Mark and the team that had followed piled out of their riot vans and cars, which had spewed gravel in the air as they roared to a stop. They attacked the front door battering it in with the red enforcer known as Rammit. Police began a systematic search of the house. They soon found Kira Petrov who was in floods of tears. She pointed a shaking finger at the doctor still out cold, "He was going to kill me," she murmured.

In the next room, lay the abducted Big Issue seller with braided hair, dressed in a hospital gown. She had been drugged, was unconscious and lay on a gurney in a makeshift operating theatre. Mark ordered a uniformed copper to carry her out to the waiting van and called for an ambulance. It looked as if they were preparing to harvest her organs. Refrigerated organ boxes were in position ready for transportation once the operation had been done.

Pooley had emerged from his cover and finally found Mark. "It was like something from a film," he gasped.

“Why? What happened?”

“A ninja, some sort of fighter, dressed all in black jumped through the window and got me out. Who the hell was he? If he hadn’t, I’d be dead,” and he shuddered.

Mark shrugged, “That was lucky. You’ll have to make a full report.”

There was a shout, “There’s another in here, the man’s unconscious and handcuffed.” Mark hurried towards the voice and saw Carter face down on the carpet and the broken glass and shattered window. He felt a flicker of pride knowing that Alex had saved his man, Pooley and that the young girl, Katy had seen abducted, had been found before they had operated..

Mark called into Allison once the search had been completed. “Pooley’s safe.”

“Thank Christ for that,” said Allison. “So, you got there in time.”

“Not exactly.”

“What do you mean?”

Mark launched into a potted explanation of what Pooley had told him.

“Convenient,” grunted Allison. “Who is this man?”

“I don’t know, sir, but without him the girl and Pooley would be dead.”

There was a long pause, “Do you think our friend Roy Chapman had anything to do with this?”

“But how could he have known anything about it?”

“I don’t know. Perhaps, you can tell me,” and he left the statement hanging in the air.

19

ALEX HAD MADE IT TO his car, he tore off his balaclava and removed his body armour and threw it in his boot. He placed his gun into his glove box and sat for a few minutes to recover his composure before retrieving his phone and calling Mark.

"You were cutting it fine," he accused.

"Couldn't get there any quicker."

"What now?"

"Thanks for saving Pooley."

"Is the girl all right?"

"Thanks to you. You also saved the life of another female about to be operated on. Thank you."

"Any other leads?"

"We know the property is owned by West End Products Ltd as well as the house in Westbourne Road. We have the doctor in custody and Carter. There's an arrest warrant out on Martyn Kelland and Marcus Paulson. It's just a matter of time."

"It goes deeper than that."

"What do you mean?"

"We've learned this is a much bigger organisation. Bigger than Takagi. This Midlands' lot is just one cog. The group is global. You can bet that this faction will be replaced by another. Look I've got to go. I'll be in touch."

Alex ended the call. He switched it off and tossed it onto the passenger seat. Alex started the motor and made his way back to the A456. He needed to get back to Ironbridge and his cat, Snooks. It would be good to see Jane, too. He'd call Roy once he was at a safe distance from the action.

A thorough search had been made of the property and the police had uncovered some interesting paperwork that had listings of various houses at different locations owned by West End Products including the one in Montague Road where Pooley had been abducted. Mark rubbed his chin thoughtfully. He would take this back to the chief but he knew there would be more difficult questions and some he would be unwilling to answer. Pooley had such a tale to tell, Allison was bound to suspect Mark was involved more heavily than he cared to admit. He shoved the relevant documents into the folder when something caught his eye. He removed the paperwork again and studied it. This time he looked at the different addresses more closely as he hadn't taken too much notice before. There was one address in Ironbridge that showed up a number of times. The estate agent was the same one for all properties.

Pasha's body lay on the mortuary slab where Hurst was completing his post mortem. He finished stitching up the Y cut and went to the stainless-steel sink, peeled off his gloves and washed his hands. He passed his Dictaphone to Heather. "Ask Susan to type it up and email it. Allison will want it pronto. I'll give him a potted version by phone. I'll leave you to finish up."

Johnny relocated to his office and picked up the phone. "Greg? … Johnny. As suspected it was ingested cyanide poisoning. In the investigation, a bitter almond odour emanated from the victim and the presence of pink lividity during post mortem examination indicated acute cyanide poisoning. The blood present was cherry red another factor of excess oxygen in the blood. Cyanide rapidly reacts with ferric ions of cytochrome oxidase, a mitochondrial enzyme responsible for oxidative phosphorylation in the final pathway of cellular respiration. Inhibition of oxygen utilization caused a sudden surge of anaerobic metabolism."

"English, please Johnny."

"Sorry… His respiratory organs failed and he couldn't breathe. Death would have been very quick."

"Anything else?"

"His stomach contents contained ipecac syrup."

"What's that?"

"Used to be used in cases of poisoning to make someone vomit."

"So, he knew he'd been poisoned?"

"No. I think it was in the syrup."

"Why ingest it?"

"I suspect it was given to him, somehow to make him sick."

"To look sick enough to possibly get him out from prison and into hospital?"

"Could be. You'll have the full report today."

"Thanks, Johnny. If this stuff wasn't given by the authorities then who did pass it to him?"

"That's for you to find out. I don't believe it was suicide. That stuff is absolutely vile. Cyanide alone would have been almost instant and enough to kill him, rather than forcing down that jollop."

"So, we're looking at murder?"

"I'd say, so. Yes."

Allison hung up and thumbed through his rolodex until he found the prison governor's number and dialled.

"Governor? … DCI Allison. Can you let me have a list of visitors to Pasha Chand during the last couple of weeks with dates? … Great. Yes, you can email them to me. Thank you."

Allison opened his drawer and grabbed a Mars Bar as he murmured, "So, Pasha Chand was murdered. Now, who else wanted him dead apart from Gurdip's remaining family?"

Allison knew he needed to notify Gurdip that Pasha was no longer a threat to him, Siri or Ayesha but first things first, his Mars Bar. He ripped off the paper and bit deeply into the chocolate treat and began to chew as he thought.

Ronnie laughed at something Siri said and his eyes lingered on her face, alive and sparkling. Gurdip looked across at his sister and best friend and his eyes filled with tears as he hastily turned away when the doorbell rang. He moved to the front door and opened it. Standing there was the representative from the Gurdwara Committee. Gurdip ushered him in. He led him into the sitting room and bade him sit. "I thought I was to come to you?"

"This is too important to wait," said the Sikh.

"Do you want to see Siri?"

The tall Sikh nodded, "Please."

Gurdip retreated back to the kitchen and explained. His sister followed him into the sitting room and sat. Then Gurdip took his leave and left them alone.

Some minutes later, he heard raised voices and Siri burst out from the sitting room in floods of tears. "What? What is it?" asked Gurdip.

"Pasha. He's lied and lied about me." She fell sobbing into Ronnie's arms.

Gurdip's face turned purple in anger and he strode back into the sitting room to face the committee member. "What is this? Why is my sister so upset?"

"I went to the prison to visit her estranged husband. He told me a very different story of her infidelity with a non-Sikh."

"But that simply isn't true, " said Gurdip in shock. "The man has lied. He beat my sister severely; you saw the evidence. She has the right to walk away and obtain her divorce."

The committee member's face creased into a frown. "That is what I believed initially until the visit."

"You have to realise Pasha Chand is manipulative, violent and deceitful. I don't suppose you are aware of another girl in India who rejected his advances and offer of marriage? She ended up dead!" Gurdip's face was grim. "As for infidelity. I know that is not the case. My sister behaved impeccably and she tried hard to be a model wife in spite of the beatings. He'd already forced her to give up her nursing studies. Please, you must believe us," he pleaded.

The telephone rang and Ronnie answered. He listened carefully, "Thanks,

Chief. I'll pass it on." Ronnie smiled at Siri. "Don't cry. You are free. I will give Gurdip the good news."

Siri studied his face in wide-eyed amazement. "But, how...?" She followed Ronnie into the sitting room where her brother stood with the Granthi of the sangat.

Ronnie excused himself, "I'm sorry to interrupt but there is something you should both know that has freed Siri." Gurdip looked puzzled as did the committee member. "Pasha Chand is dead. He either took his own life in prison or was murdered. He is no longer a threat to your family nor will he have a hold over your sister. She is free to live her life as she wishes."

Kamapal stood in the queue, preparing to board the flight to New Delhi. He had a smugly confident expression on his face. Two police detectives entered the departure lounge and marched to the desk. They spoke to the Emirates' ground staff and were given the flight manifest, which they studied. They waited by the desk as each passenger came forward. When Kamapal handed over his passport. One man stepped forward, "Kamapal Chand?"

Kamapal's usual arrogance appeared to dissipate as his passport was removed from him. "What is this? I have a flight to catch..."

"Kamapal Chand, you have to come with us."

The detective took him firmly by his arm, which the Sikh shook off. "You have no right to do this."

At this remark the detective took hold of Kamapal and handcuffed his hands behind his back. "Kamapal Chand, I am arresting you on suspicion of murder. You have the right to remain silent. You do not have to say anything, but it may harm your defence if you do not mention when questioned something which you later rely on in court. Anything you do say may be given in evidence."

Back at the police station Kira was talking, anxious to tell her side of the story. "I could have been one of those girls. I was brought over by Bogdan two years ago but Martyn Kelland picked me out. He gave me a job at West End Products and made me his mistress. I wanted for nothing. As long as I didn't ask questions. I was all right. I don't know what happened to the other girls. I was lucky until this week."

"Where is Martyn Kelland now?"

"I don't know. He went abroad to Estonia, I think. He said it was for business and he would call me when he got back. That was four days ago. I haven't heard from him since."

Greg Allison looked across at Mark, "Get all flight manifests from airlines travelling to Estonia from four days ago. See if Kelland was on any of those flights. Put a tap on his office phone."

Mark nodded and rose. He left the interview room to find the information.

Allison turned back to Kira Petrov, "Tell me about his men. Marcus Paulson and Bernie Carter and any others."

"They are just thugs who do Martyn's bidding. They like hurting people especially women."

"How do you know that?"

"I saw what they did to one of the girls that travelled with me."

"I thought you said you didn't know anything?"

"I don't. Not really but there was this one time at the warehouse I was coming out of the office and I saw Paulson dragging a girl by her hair out of a store room and across the warehouse floor. She was battered and bruised and her clothes were ripped. She was crying, pathetically. Then Nesbitt came out onto the mezzanine floor to see what I was staring at. He warned me. Said, if I wanted to live I would pretend I hadn't seen anything. That was all."

"Who is Nesbitt?"

"He's one of Martyn's men. He was at the house. He's rough but not a killer. He once tried to help me get away, but it was impossible with this in my arm." She raised her sleeve and indicated a bump under her skin just below the inside of her elbow. "You see…" Kira began weeping again.

"All right… Kira you are as much a victim as the others, that will go in your favour and the fact you have cooperated with us. Anything you can tell us will be extremely valuable. Would you be prepared to talk to one of our consultants?" Kira looked up questioningly. "It's a woman and she will help you to remember things you may not realise you know or have forgotten. You do want to help us find these girls, don't you?"

Kira dropped her head and nodded, "Yes… I knew there was a lot of bad things happening but I was powerless to help. I was told Bogdan would go after my family at home, so I did the easy thing. I played dumb and went along with everything I was asked."

"Do you know where the girls were taken?"

"I heard they had gone to Martyn's country retreat."

"Where is that?"

"It's a property in his wife's name in Shropshire. I heard they were taken there and being moved back to a house in Portland Road."

Allison's bushy brows shot up, "Where in Portland Road?" He thumbed through the list of assets he had acquired. "It's not on the list of West End Products' properties…"

"No, he put that house in my name. He was giving it to me as a gift when he'd finished doing his business there."

"I need the number and details, now."

Kira nodded tearfully, and scribbled the address on the memo pad in front of Allison, who tore it off. He turned to Taylor who was leaning against the door. "Get a squad to that house, now." He passed him the scrap of paper.

"Okay, Kira. I'll get you something to eat and drink. You will remain here until my consultant arrives. Is that understood?" Kira nodded again. "I'll have a female officer come and sit with you while you wait. If you think of anything else, tell her." Allison went to the door and called along the corridor to a young WPC in uniform who came scurrying to him. Allison explained what he wanted and the WPC went into the room and sat with the young woman.

Allison called across to Bill Rennie, "Any news on the unconscious girl?"

"Hospital's going to ring when she comes round."

"Good, stick with it!"

The Granthi of the sangat's mouth dropped open and Gurdip said fiercely, "My sister is now officially a widow so there is no need for you to bring us this unjust, immoral decision. I understand the sanctity of marriage as does my sister but the brutality she suffered was hard to behold. As for her fidelity. Siri has never been with a man until Pasha and even then he abused her horrifically in the marital bed ignoring all our sacred rules of law. Pasha has made up these venomous tales for his own end. I must admit I am shaken to the core by your decision when you had all the evidence in front of you, as well as knowledge of him murdering another innocent young woman in India who would not bow to his wishes and marry him and we have witnesses to that."

The Sikh went to speak but Gurdip held up his hand to silence him, "For the first time in my life I am ashamed of my own kind. Siri is now free and she will date and maybe even marry again and it will be someone of her own choosing. I love our sacred Guru Nanak and all he stands for but it will be sometime before I feel I can visit the Gurdwara again. And now I would like you to leave." Gurdip walked to the door to usher the man out.

The representative turned and put his hand on Gurdip's shoulder. "I apologise. This Pasha poisoned my mind with these defamatory tales. I see that now. Please, go in peace, all of you and Gurdip I really hope and pray you will return to us once you feel able. Siri… I wish you well." The elder turned back and walked down the drive. Gurdip paused a moment before running down the drive after him. They exchanged a few more words and shook hands and placed their palms together as if in prayer and bowed.

Siri's huge eyes watched and tears rolled down her cheek. Ronnie was at a loss for words and just squeezed her shoulder before she turned back into the house. Ronnie waited on the step for Gurdip and asked, "What did you say?"

"That I accepted his apology. He is not a bad man. He just listens to our teachings with his heart. Pasha is the one who corrupted the truth with his lies." Gurdip put his arm around Ronnie and went back into the house. He closed the front door behind him. "And now my friend, we must celebrate the evil that was Pasha Chand is gone forever. We can live in peace."

Holly sat in Interview Room 2 with Kira. She held onto her hands and listened as Allison probed her some more. Holly's breathing became deeper and her eyes travelled from side to side under her lids. It was as if she was watching a tennis match from the grandstand. Suddenly, she opened her eyes wide and gasped aloud. Kira stopped.

"What is it? What have I said?"

"Don't worry. This is quite usual. There is no need to be alarmed," advised Allison. But Kira clammed up tight and wouldn't say another word.

Holly shuddered and her eyes rolled back in her head. She slumped forward onto the table in a dead faint. Allison stood up concerned and ordered the WPC, "Take Ms Petrov to the canteen, get her a cup of tea. Kira rose immediately and went willingly with the police woman. Allison was more concerned with Holly, who seemed to be floppy like a rag doll and totally out of it. Allison picked up the phone and ordered, "Get a doctor in Interview Room 2, now!"

The next moment Allison was chilled to the bone as he thought he saw a dark shadow that seemed to attach to Holly's back and her eyes flickered again. He shook his head and blinked to see more clearly. There was no shadow now. But the air became ice cold and Allison felt his scalp crawl as if teeming with insects and a thin nasal heavily Brummy accented voice came from Holly, "For if we live, we live to the Lord, and if we die, we die to the Lord. So then, whether we live or whether we die, we are the Lord's. Romans 14 :8."

A deep sigh escaped Holly's lips and she flopped forward again. Allison's notes on the desk rippled as if a breeze had come in through a window to disturb the papers.

Allison was alone with Holly. There was no one to corroborate what he had seen or heard. No one would believe him anyway. He grabbed the glass of water next to him and drank it down. His hands were shaking. What had just happened?

20

AN ARREST WARRANT HAD BEEN issued for Alan Nesbitt. His likeness had been posted to all police stations throughout the country. Ports and airports had been alerted but the man seemed to have gone to ground. From Ms Petrov's statement he had been a recently new recruit and Mark had passed that information onto Alex. Of Kelland there was no sign and the police were keeping watch on his house and place of work. There was an arrest warrant out on him, through Interpol and Europol. Mark had been talking to the police in Estonia who confirmed that he had arrived in their country and then flown on to The Dominican Republic where there was no extradition treaty. Of Paulson there had been no sightings.

Allison was trying to link all the threads of the case together but it was proving difficult. Kira Petrov's property in Portland Road had been searched and evidence of the girls had been discovered. Where they were now was anyone's guess. Allison was not happy. Nor was he happy about Mark whom he felt was holding something back. There was just something he wasn't saying. He could feel it. But what concerned him even more was what he'd witnessed happening to Holly.

Shortly after the episode, Holly came around and said she had felt faint. The summoned doctor had checked her over and found nothing wrong. He suggested her blood pressure may have dropped dramatically and that had caused her to faint. Allison was debating whether to tell Holly's partner,

Paul or Holly herself but something prevented him from doing so. The only one he'd spoken to was his wife, Mary. She knew better than to ridicule what had occurred. A spiritual person herself, she believed him and her only suggestion was to get the Church involved, which Allison was deliberating about.

Dr Charles and Bernie Carter were due in court for a preliminary hearing. Neither man had spoken about their activities and seemed unlikely to talk. With the evidence stacked up against them they were probably going to go down for a long time.

Big Den was now out of hospital and back at his pitch selling the Big Issue. It seemed unlikely that anyone would come after him now even though Paulson hadn't been caught.

But where were the missing girls? All Allison had was more questions.

Gurdip worked happily in the kitchen preparing a meal for his family. He was pleased to be returning to work the following day and wanted to celebrate the fact with those closest to him. He was looking calmer and stronger. He and Ronnie had resumed their martial arts training. He was feeling positive about the future and happy.

Ronnie arrived home to the wonderful aroma of Indian cooking and the table was laid up perfectly. There were even a few bottles of Indian Cobra premium lager in the fridge for Ronnie, as well as a non-alcoholic bottle of Belle & Co from Iceland that he was told tasted like Prosecco. The popping of the champagne cork on it would make it a real celebration.

Ronnie was entertaining Ayesha in the sitting room. Colouring pens were strewn over the floor and a colouring book of fairies and pixies were in Ayesha's hands and she was colouring furiously, her tongue protruding from her mouth in concentration.

Ronnie watched her enjoying the moment. He patted her head and muttered, "Won't be a minute, just got to ask Gurdip something." Ayesha just nodded and continued, her concentration intense. The pictures were coming on remarkably well.

Ronnie strolled into the kitchen and watched his friend for a moment. His mood was serious as if he was gathering courage to do something, "Can I help? Anything you want me to do?"

"No, you're fine. Help yourself to a cold beer," he jerked his head towards the fridge. "There's some Cobra lager in there."

Ronnie crossed to the fridge and removed a bottle, "My! They look big. Can I get you anything?"

"I could do with something. I am a bit dry."

"What would you like?"

"A lovely ice-cold glass of lemon squash."

"Got it," said Ronnie. He took out his bottle, placed it on the counter, and ran the cold tap in the sink to ensure it was cold and made a pint pot of lemon squash in a straight glass for Gurdip before opening his beer and pouring it out. He tasted it, "Mmm. Not bad," he said appreciatively.

Gurdip stopped chopping the mint for the raita and looked quizzically at him. "Was there something else?"

"No… er yes…"

"Well, make up your mind. What is it?"

"Just wondering if you meant what you said."

"What did I say?" said Gurdip impishly.

"You know…"

"No, I don't. What?"

"Um… about Siri."

"What about her?" Gurdip was enjoying drawing the words out of Ronnie.

"Would it be okay with you if I asked Siri out on a date?"

Gurdip paused and stared straight ahead without a word as Ronnie hopped from foot to foot. "You want to date my sister?"

Ronnie turned beetroot red, "Yes. If I have your permission…"

"On one condition…"

"Anything, yes…"

"You look after her and treat her with respect. I don't want you messing with her and leaving her with a broken heart. She's had enough sadness in her life."

"Of course," said Ronnie eagerly. "Anything else?"

"I will have to accompany you on all your dates."

"W…What?"

Gurdip put down his knife and rested his hands on Ronnie's shoulders. "I'm joking. You have my blessing. But you look after her and treat her well or our friendship is over. Understand?"

Ronnie nodded vigorously. "You know I'll do that. I will guard her with my life. I promise you. Our friendship means too much to me."

"I know. Just setting a few ground rules, here."

"I promise you, Siri will be safe with me."

"Then it's okay with me. Has she said yes, yet?"

"I haven't asked her yet. I wanted to speak to you first."

Gurdip resumed chopping, "Better ask her then. What if she says no?"

"Then I will leave it at that."

"She's not worth fighting for?" said Gurdip seriously.

"Yes, of course. But I won't push myself on someone who doesn't want me."

"Then ask her tonight. I'm sure she'll agree."

"Ask who? Who'll agree?" asked Siri as she walked into the kitchen and plonked her university bag on the chair. She looked from one to the other. "Tell me."

"Go on then," said Gurdip mischievously. "Ask her."

Siri turned her huge eyes on Ronnie, "What do you want to ask me?"

Ronnie looked from one to the other, "I… just wondered if…"

"… If?"

"If you'd like to come out with me sometime, to see a film or go to a club or have dinner or anything…" he blurted this out while turning a deep crimson.

"Of course," said Siri. "I'd love to."

"You would?"

"Yes."

Ronnie gave a whoop of joy and danced around the kitchen. "Let's pop the cork on the Belle & co. I'll get the glasses."

Siri began to giggle and Gurdip laughed at his friend's antics.

Ayesha came running into the kitchen. "What's happening?"

"Nothing," said Gurdip. "Go put your pens and colouring books away and wash your hands. Dinner will not be long.

"Can I have some of that?" she asked pointing at the bottle.

Ronnie looked at Gurdip for permission, "I don't see why not. It's alcohol free. Yes, why not? We have much to celebrate."

Marcus Paulson had his long hair tucked inside a Baker boy's hat. He had grown a small beard and used fake tan that had altered his appearance somewhat. He was driving a large truck and queueing for the Channel Tunnel. The truck was sound-proofed and inside were the girls. They were all drugged and boxes of West End Products were stacked in front to hide them from view should the doors be opened.

Marcus was sweating and feeling nervous. He knew he had to calm down. He studied his passport in the name of Amos Cox. Marcus had several passports and identities. This one appeared the most suitable for his purpose. He was to meet with his French counterpart on the other side. He was alert and wary. His paperwork ready he slowly drove towards the first check point.

Alex sat with Snooks on his lap, deep in thought. He had a pen in his hand and was doodling on a notepad as he weighed up the facts about the case. He had not long come off the phone from Mark. It disturbed him that the purchase of all West End Products' properties had gone through the same estate agent in Ironbridge. Paperwork had revealed the same solicitor had been used for conveyancing who was also in Ironbridge. He needed to get this information to Roy. It may mean something or it may mean nothing. He knew that many people preferred to deal with the same agencies and officials with whom they already had a relationship. But why in Ironbridge? And why, when the properties owned were mainly in Birmingham? He had even discovered another notably grand house in Wales? That would need checking out.

He had decided to call Roy, when his phone rang.

"Yes?"

"Roy…"

"I was just going to call you."

"Oh?"

Alex quickly explained what he had learned. Roy absorbed the information, "Sounds like there might be another couple of players that we don't know about."

"Possibly. What do you want me to do?"

"For the moment, nothing. We have a more pressing matter."

"Which is?"

"Paulson."

"What about him?"

"Our new facial recognition software has come up trumps. He has been spotted driving a lorry into Folkestone to board the Channel Tunnel."

"What do we do?"

"Fly to Calais."

"Where?"

"Get yourself to Stourbridge, seven miles west of Wolverhampton. The airport is at Halfpenny Green. Bobbington. A private plane is waiting for you. I'll meet you there. We'll catch him as he comes off and release those girls. Paulson will be there in thirty-five minutes so hurry."

"Post code?"

"DY7 5DY."

"Got it." He scribbled it down. "On my way." Alex curtailed the call and jumped up depositing an unimpressed Snooks, who mewed plaintively, onto the settee.

Marcus Paulson's face was covered in a sheen of sweat. He didn't like the way the security officer had studied his face and passport. But it had been returned and he had boarded the train. He just hoped his contact in Calais would be on time, collect the cargo and then he would be off to join Kelland in The Dominican Republic. At least, that was his plan. Once loaded he had to leave his cab and travel in the Drivers' Club car for the journey. He was glad to stretch his legs but remained anxious about his cargo and prayed none of the girls would come round from their sedation. No one seemed to be watching him and he joined in the banter with some of the other drivers, which made him feel a little more secure now that they were almost there and it was soon time to return to his cab. He didn't suffer any qualms now the train had arrived in Calais. He made his way back to the cab and waited patiently in turn before he could drive off and into the port. The truck in front of him began to rumble out of the train and Paulson followed. As the trucks disembarked he began to whistle but stopped short when he saw a number of officials the other end speaking to each driver as they trundled into the port.

Paulson's eyes narrowed. He didn't like the look of this at all. He scoured the scene around him. Most trucks were being directed onto what was called the green itinerary for the A16 motorway and out from the port with no further checks, while a few were being side lined towards the orange itinerary where further customs checks were to be made, which Paulson did not want.

His heart began to race and beads of sweat began to form again on his forehead. He hurriedly looked around again. There were two trucks in front of him. He didn't intend to be sent down the orange line. He was not going to be arrested, nor did he intend going to prison for West End Products. Leaving his engine running, he slipped out from his cab and made his way purposefully across the concourse. There was a shout from someone on Security and Paulson began to run.

Alex and Roy, together with two other MRF agents had landed at St. Inglevert airfield and were now on their way to Calais Eurotunnel. Their French counterparts had been waiting and supplied them with a vehicle and French driver. The French agents followed the British contingent to the Eurotunnel Terminal. The journey was to take them just twelve minutes.

They arrived to chaos as Security and French police were busy searching the terminal for the fleeing lorry driver. The situation was quickly explained. Roy and Alex pushed their way through protesting lorry drivers who had been held up on their journeys. The air was thick with profanities, which Roy commented was enough to make a barracks blush.

They moved on to the suspect lorry, which was still idling in the queue of freight traffic. Roy jumped into the cab and turned off the engine. He leaped down and went to the back doors, which Alex had already opened.

Alex, confronted with piles of boxes, shouted inside, "Anyone there?" There was no answer. "I don't like this," he muttered. There was a faint, almost imperceptible sound coming from the back. He shouted again, "Hold on!" There was also a whiff of something unpleasant emanating from behind the cargo.

Roy turned to one of the French Security Officers, "Get a fork lift here now. We need to shift these boxes. Hurry."

Alex was already trying to remove one of the smaller boxes from the stack. He passed it down to Roy who opened it. It contained, a highly decorated, porcelain pot. Alex heard another feeble whimper and yelled, "Where's the damned forklift?"

As he spoke, an officer returned driving a yellow JCB Teletruk and approached the rear of the truck. He began to unload the boxes, stacking them away from the queue onto the side of the road. Alex instructed the driver to clear a pathway through to the cab end and he clambered over the last few boxes to where the girls were lying. Most were comatose, there were a couple of girls just coming around. These were the ones he'd heard.

Alex shouted back, "Need to get some water back here, an ambulance and a doctor, and quickly."

Finally, all the crates and cardboard boxes were removed revealing the pitiful plight of the girls that had been herded in like cattle and obviously drugged. Cable ties were around their wrists and ankles. One of the youngest of the girls was deathly still. She had been partially crushed against the other unconscious females and sadly, had not survived the journey. Her body was taken out first.

The two girls who were becoming awake struggled to move their stiff limbs where they had been wedged up against the side of the lorry and the crates. Their bonds were cut and they rubbed at their sore wrists where the ties had cut into their skin. They managed to limp towards the doors and blinked in discomfort as the bright sunshine dazzled their eyes. Roy manoeuvred them towards a waiting ambulance where paramedics were ready to check them over. Other ambulances soon arrived and the remaining girls were stretchered out, many of whom were now beginning to recover from their sedation.

Roy indicated that they would follow the ambulances to the hospital where they could talk to and question the girls. One of their agents was a translator. He spoke both Russian and Bulgarian.

Roy turned to Alex, "Thank God we got to them in time. Who knows where they would have ended up. At least now, they have a chance at a decent life."

"The only problem is," said Alex, "we don't have Paulson or Kelland. Even worse, we don't have the ring of men over here that were to collect them and take them heaven knows where."

Roy grunted, "Hmm, yes. But we'll get the bastards, I promise you; you mark my words."

Back in Lloyd House, Mark had taken a call from Alex. He was kept up to date with events in France but it rankled that Paulson was still on the loose and Kelland was nowhere to be found. He wandered to Allison's office wondering how he would relay the latest events to the chief. He wouldn't lie, he just wouldn't reveal everything about his relationship with Alex and the MRF. He knocked on the chief's door and entered.

Allison was on the phone and his face was serious. He waved Mark into a seat and continued, "I tell you, Colin, I've never seen anything like it. Should we be worried? … I see … Yes, okay… We'll make a point of getting together. Anything we can do to help, just shout."

He put down the phone, thoughtfully and looked up at Mark, "What's up?"

Mark took a deep breath and began.

Holly stared dreamily out of the window gazing at the countryside. Paul came in carrying two glasses of wine. "Here," he said passing her a glass.

She looked at it puzzled, "What's this?"

"A pre-dinner drink, your favourite and it's perfectly chilled, madam, just for you," and he gave a formal little bow as he passed her the glass.

She studied the glass and sniffed it before taking a sip, "Mmm, lovely."

She set down the glass and studied her husband as if seeing him with fresh eyes. “My, you are a handsome one.”

“Okay, what are you after?”

“Nothing, just your body…”

“I can live with that,” said Paul with a laugh.

The timbre of Holly’s voice changed a little and the Birmingham accent ever so slightly impinged on what she was saying as her eyes fluttered back in her head and she said, “Above all, love each other deeply, because love covers over a multitude of sins. One Peter chapter four verse eight.” Then she laughed, picked up her glass and drank a deep draught.

Paul hesitated and then asked, “Since when did you start spouting verses from the Bible?”

Holly looked at him cunningly, “Since now. There’s a lot more locked inside my head from my childhood. It just seemed appropriate, that’s all.” She untucked her legs from beneath her and walked seductively across to him. “Forget dinner for a while. Let me take you upstairs. I’ll cleanse you with my love.”

Author Thanks

Many thanks for reading the fifth of the *DCI Greg Allison Crime Thrillers*. If you have a little time, I would appreciate a review. I really value my readers' thoughts about a book. It often helps me craft future stories. They are vital for indie authors like me.

You are welcome to contact me at elizabeth@elizabethrevill.com or visit the website: www.elizabethrevill.com

****

I have free stories for you as well, all I'd like in exchange is your email address and you can unsubscribe at any time.

The first is called *Dead or Alive* just follow the link.

I'd like to keep in touch. Either via the newsletter, I'll send out once a month, or you can join my Facebook page: Elizabeth Revill. If you join either, there will be notifications of new stories, releases of covers and the occasional giveaway and special deals just for you. There will also be an opportunity to join my *Advanced Reader Team*.

Other titles by Elizabeth Revill

DCI Allison Thrillers:

Killing me Softly

Prayer for the Dying

God Only Knows

Would I Lie To You?

Windows For The Dead

Dead Eyes Opened

Llewellyn Family Saga:

Whispers on the Wind

Shadows on the Moon

Rainbows in the Clouds

Thunder in the Sun

Against the Tide

Turn of the Tide

The Electra Conspiracy Part 1

The Electra Conspiracy Part 2

Stand Alone Novels:

Sanjukta and the Box of Souls

The Forsaken And The Damned

Web of Fear

The Dreamtime of the Artful Dodger with Norman Eshley

Children's book

And an illustrated children's book *The Secret of Gidon*

Printed in Great Britain
by Amazon

15862935R00150